HIDDEN GRAVES

A Dek Elstrom Mystery

Jack Fredrickson

This first world edition published 2016
in Great Britain and 2017 in the USA by
SEVERN HOUSE PUBLISHERS LTD of
19 Cedar Road, Sutton, Surrey, England, SM2 5DA.
Trade paperback edition first published
in Great Britain and the USA 2017 by
SEVERN HOUSE PUBLISHERS LTD

British Library Cataloguing in Publication Data
A CIP catalogue record for this title is available from the British Library.

ISBN-13: 978-0-7278-8664-4 (cased)
ISBN-13: 978-1-84751-767-8 (trade paper)
ISBN-13: 978-1-78010-834-6 (e-book)

Typeset by Palimpsest Book Production Ltd.,
Falkirk, Stirlingshire, Scotland.

HIDDEN GRAVES

A Selection of Titles by Jack Fredrickson

SILENCE THE DEAD

The Dek Elstrom Mysteries

A SAFE PLACE FOR DYING
HONESTLY DEAREST, YOU'RE DEAD
HUNTING SWEETIE ROSE
THE DEAD CALLER OF CHICAGO
THE CONFESSORS' CLUB*
HIDDEN GRAVES*

* *available from Severn House*

For Pop

ACKNOWLEDGEMENTS

Thanks again to my exceptional friends at Severn House, to Kate Lyall Grant for her enthusiasm, and to my always (patiently) eagle-eyed editor, Sara Porter.

And, as always, thanks to my pal Patrick Riley for coping with this Luddite's website.

Most of all, thanks to my Susan for her excellent editing and . . . well, for everything that matters more.

ONE

Three minutes and twenty-three seconds before the skeleton came at him with an axe, the candidate for US Senate stood grim, trim and confident behind a mahogany lectern set on the freshly hacked weeds of an abandoned farm. The wind hurled the first of the autumn's dead leaves across the lenses of the television cameras. A storm approached in the darkening sky. It was to be fine campaign video on the dire plight of the Illinois farmer.

'It's time to build new farms and barns and silos,' Timothy Wade intoned rhythmically for the dozens of admirers that had been bused in to applaud for the television news cameras. On script, he then turned and strode purposefully to the crumbling silo, picked up a long-handled sledge and swung it at the discreet green dot painted by a campaign aide.

The cracked, carefully reassembled cement fell apart precisely as planned, opening a ragged hole on the side of the silo. Clumps of damp, dark grain, the size of fists, began spilling onto the ground. The candidate stepped back to prevent his glossy wingtips getting mucky and eyed the tumbling rotted wheat morosely. Absolutely, it would be excellent video.

The forearm and hand materialized white in the black cascade of lumpy grain. The flesh, ligaments and muscles were gone; they were now only disconnected beige bones, pressed together by the weight of the rotting wet wheat.

They clutched a small, shiny-headed hatchet, pointed straight at the candidate.

It was over in an instant. The wheat and the bones and the tiny axe broke apart, falling to the ground.

But that instant was enough for the television cameras. They caught the fleshless bones aiming the axe. Worse, they recorded what happened next.

The candidate panicked. Red-faced, sweating, he bolted through the small crowd to dive into the back of his black Cadillac Escalade, tugging the door shut behind him like a child spooked wild-eyed in the night.

Though his driver, a fresh-faced young volunteer, had the wits to race after him and speed them away, it was too late. The anointed candidate of the Cook County Democratic machine, sure to become the next senator from Illinois and, some said, a future president of the United States, had been recorded melting down.

The video went viral within an hour. Chicago television stations broke into their afternoon talkers and soaps to show clips. Cable stations and the national networks snagged snippets from the Chicago locals and a thousand Internet sites got it from them. By midnight, twenty million people across the country had seen the candidate in Illinois running from bones, as though fleeing the Devil himself.

That was the beginning.

TWO

Like most Illinoisans, I expected the sleaze of our politics to ooze on as placidly as always that October. Though our most recent ex-governor was in prison, his predecessor had been paroled and was available to advise the newest crop of looters making runs for state office. Available to counsel, too, was the usual number of congressmen facing certain indictment but whom, nonetheless, were considered shoo-ins for re-election.

All this was viewed as especially acceptable where I live. My turret is in Rivertown, the greasiest of the Cook County suburbs, stuck foul and festering to the west side of Chicago. Crookedness wasn't going to change there, just as it wasn't going to change elsewhere in the county or even in the whole corrupt state. It's too long-standing, too ingrained. So, like most in Rivertown, I paid no attention to politicians that October. I focused instead on heat.

My turret was the only part of a castle my lunatic bootlegger grandfather got built before he died. I'd moved in a few years earlier – a broke, recovering drunk felled by scandal, thinking to convert the five-floor limestone tube into a saleable residence. I evicted the pigeons, power-washed away the mounds and splatters they'd left behind and began restoring the place, and myself. I sanded, stained and sealed the wide planks of the first three floors, and caulked and painted the slit windows. I built new kitchen cabinets, though as yet I had no appliances other than a leaky microwave oven and a rusting, avocado-colored refrigerator. I built a closet on the third floor, in case I got a wardrobe.

It was comfortable, cool work in summers. But in winters, I froze. There was no furnace, just monstrous fireplaces on all five floors that required more wood than I could ever afford. I kept warm with sweatshirts, a blazer and a pea coat, often all at once.

At last, that was about to change. Earlier that summer, one of the insurance company clients I'd lost during my notoriety offered me two months' work investigating a backlog of false accident claims. Enough money blew in to dream of warm winters. In August I bought tinwork and began building a central duct to carry heat to all five floors of the turret. Now, just days before Halloween, I was about to take delivery of a furnace.

I was on the first floor, readying the base of the main duct, when the woman called. 'You trace people?' Her voice was crisp and hoarse, like she'd had nails for breakfast.

'Actually, I'm doing that for another client right now.' I was shooting for crisp, too, but the sugar high from my breakfast of Ding Dongs had begun to sag.

'Speak up!' she shouted.

My hand was crisscrossed with painful, shallow lacerations, the result of working with sheet metal that had cut me more than I'd cut it. I could only use my left thumb and ring finger to pincer my phone, as one might hold a rodent by the tail.

'I trace people, yes!' I yelled, to bridge the distance between hand and mouth.

'I'll see you at one o'clock,' she barked.

'Let me check my calendar.' It was a charade and I didn't bother to set down the phone. My stint with the insurance company had ended and I now had only one client, a sorority alumni club from Northwestern University that hired me, cheap, to update their membership directory. It should have been a simple Internet tracing job, something the ladies could have done themselves if they'd been less rich and less fond of liquored lunches, but the project had become a nightmare. The former coeds had been serious drinkers, even in college, and had simply called each other Bipsie instead of struggling to remember given names. That caused problems now. I was chasing the whereabouts of over a hundred women known to each other mostly as Bipsie. There was a Bipsie from Rockford, a Bipsie from Wilmette, two Bipsies with Zits, several Bipsies with Big Boobs and even more Bipsies Without. It was brutal work.

I levered the phone closer to my mouth. 'I'm available,' I said after a pause long enough to have checked a calendar. 'Ms, ah?'

'One o'clock.' She gave me an address.

'Your name?' I asked again.

She took too many seconds to answer. 'Reynolds,' she finally said. 'Rosamund Reynolds.'

Likely enough, she'd needed the pause to make up a phony name. Still, what she'd come up with offered relief. I couldn't have stood it if she'd chosen to call herself Bipsie.

THREE

Rosamund's address was in one of the old industrial neighborhoods on the near northwest that had half-sputtered into trendy. An odd mix of optimism and despair, a Starbucks and a stained-glass studio were nestled among a discount tire store, a closed-up candle shop, two burned-out bungalows and an abandoned eight-story condominium conversion.

Her building was a sooty brick and glass-block former factory on the corner, one of the thousands that had once thrummed, three shifts a day, everywhere in Chicago and its blue-collared surrounds like Rivertown until penny wages sucked all that thrum overseas.

My footsteps echoed loud and alone on new red quarry tile as I walked through the oak-paneled foyer into a glistening hall of empty offices awaiting prosperity. Rosamund Reynolds had said hers, number 210, was on the second floor. There was no listing for that space in the lobby directory.

The elevator, squeezed in during the rehab, was a wire-caged affair the size of an upright coffin. It groaned as it began raising me to the second floor.

I checked my hands. The left hand had the fewest Band-Aids, so I left that one out and put the right one in my pants pocket, thinking to saunter in like an old-time movie charmer about to dazzle tight-curled lovelies.

Room 210 was at the end of the hall. I knocked on the unmarked, frosted glass door and the frosty woman's voice that had phoned commanded me to come in.

I stepped into a room lit surgery bright by midday sunshine firing through the eight-paned window at the back. I slipped on my Ray-Bans and offered the shape blurred in the glare a smile.

She said nothing.

I stood waiting for a moment, and then another. By now my eyes had adjusted enough to make out a room wallpapered in beige stripes and trimmed with hard, dark oak ceiling and baseboard moldings that matched the paneling in the lobby. The drapes bunched at both sides of the huge back window could have been drawn if Ms Reynolds wanted to be seen clearly.

Despite the glare, I made out that she was trimmed hard, too, in a starched sort of way. She sat in a wheelchair behind the dark oak desk. She wore thick makeup, perhaps to conceal an unhealthy skin pallor but more likely to disguise features she didn't want seen. Her hair, if it was hers at all and not a wig, was thick, mostly steel gray, and fell down to eyes hidden by large, tinted glasses. She wore a severely cut dark suit, a white blouse so stiff that it looked bulletproof and white gloves. I supposed the gloves were meant to cover age spots or fingerprints and not wounds suffered from cutting tin ductwork.

There were no framed photos on the walls, no personal items anywhere. The desk was bare except for a single sheet of paper. A desk chair was pushed into the corner, another tip-off that the space was a daily rental. If she'd used the office regularly the wheelchair-bound woman wouldn't have wasted space on a desk chair she didn't need.

She told me to sit down in a voice so hoarse it sounded like an old man's. I did, with my right hand still in my pocket.

'What's the matter with your right hand?' she asked.

I pulled it out to show her the patchwork of Band-Aids. 'It got damaged.'

'Your Band-Aids have cartoon characters on them.' There was nothing wrong with her eyesight.

'I get these cheap at a discount place.'

She nodded, uninterested. 'You spend your time restoring an odd round building?'

'It's temporary. My business—'

'You forged documents for the defense team in some sordid mayor's trial. Your business was destroyed.'

'False charges. I was exonerated within days,' I said.

'That's neither here nor there.'

'Hard to tell what's anywhere in this glare,' I rhymed right back at her. The woman's arrogance was irritating. 'How close is "Reynolds" to your real name?'

'Does it matter?'

'That will depend on why you asked me here.'

'I want you to look in on three individuals.' She pushed the single sheet of paper across the desk. It contained three typed names and addresses. All were out west, in Tucson, Laguna Beach and someplace I'd never heard of in Oregon.

'I'm not looking for simple Internet browsing, Mr Elstrom,' she went on. 'I want fast, discreet, first-hand visits. Be efficient; verify the current arrangements of each of these men.'

'Living arrangements?'

'Of course.' She reached into the center drawer, pulled out an unmarked plain white business-sized envelope and slid it across. Inside was a cashier's check, payable to me, for two thousand dollars. There was no bank name or address printed on the check.

'This now, then another two thousand when you complete the assignment. Plus your expenses, but those you must keep reasonable.'

There was a quiver in her voice – an urgency. I wondered if this seemingly commanding woman was afraid.

A phone number was typed below the three names. 'I'll contact you at this number?'

'Yes. Check on these men in the order I've listed. Start in Tucson and report in from there. Similarly, notify me before you leave California for Oregon.'

There was one more thing to say, always. 'I'm not licensed to be an investigator. I work for insurance companies, photographing accident scenes, checking out phony claims. It's research.'

I always said it, and I always said it just that way. For the most corrupt of states, Illinois had oddly strict rules for licensing private detectives. A criminal justice background or a law degree is needed. I had neither, and the press had made much of my lack of a license when I'd gotten caught up in the phony evidence scheme – that and the fact that I'd been married to the daughter of one of the wealthiest men in Chicago. Recovering from all that remained arduous; I did not need a second brush with that sort of difficulty. Nor did Amanda, my ex-wife, who'd become one of Chicago's richest and most prominent business executives.

'We'll play along with your little game, Mr Elstrom,' the woman calling herself Rosamund Reynolds said. 'We're hiring you to do research.'

Her use of the plural was revealing. She had a partner. 'Who gave you my name, Ms Reynolds?'

'You'll head west immediately, of course.' She drummed her fingers on the desk, impatient, anxious.

'I have other client work,' I said.

The fingertips drummed faster. 'How long?' she snapped.

'I need today and tomorrow,' I said, as though I was committed to more than readying tinwork for the delivery of a furnace the morning after next.

She caught her breath. It was barely audible. I had no doubt the woman was frightened.

'See that you do,' she said.

I left, amazed that her office had remained bright amid the thick fog of lies we'd both sent up.

FOUR

I breezed into the shadowy old marble of Rivertown's only bank – a place purposefully kept as dark as the town's city hall – to see what I could learn about Rosamund's check. And perhaps to enjoy a bite of a chocolate chip cookie, if luck was holding.

The bank's president, a brother-in-law of Rivertown's city treasurer and a man who knew to do as he was told, sat at the only desk with his back to the lobby. Except for the ancient teller behind the old-fashioned gilded cage, who was his mother, the lobby was deserted. The bank rarely drew retail customers. It served mostly to launder cash bribes collected at city hall.

I wanted to know something – anything – factual about Rosamund Reynolds.

I set her check on the president's desk. 'What can you tell me about this payee?'

He looked up from a newspaper crossword puzzle entitled 'Just for Kids,' set down his stub of chew-pocked pencil and shrugged. 'It's a cashier's check. It's good.'

'Why is there no bank name printed on it?'

'Not printing a bank name makes customers think cashier's checks are private. It's phony baloney. The routing number at the bottom always identifies the bank.'

'What bank issued this one?'

He sighed and typed the routing number into his computer. After a minute, he handed up the check. 'Chicago Manufacturers Bank and Trust,' he said.

'Never heard of them.'

'They probably never heard of you, either.' His laugh was more of a squeal, appropriate for a man who spent his days with his mom in a deserted bank lobby. He picked up his stub of pencil, anxious to get back to the intellectual combat of the child's crossword puzzle.

I walked over to the teller window, filled out a deposit slip and handed the check to the ancient. 'I'd like a thousand in fifties back.'

My account contained twelve dollars. Rosamund's check wouldn't simply moisten the parched bottom of my well; it was about to drench it like a tsunami. I braced myself for the wave.

The ancient smirked, cutting a hundred more wrinkles into her wizened face. 'The check's got to clear first. You can have twelve dollars.'

'Your son said cashier's checks are solid. I want to deposit one thousand into my account and take a grand back in cash.'

'How do you want the twelve?'

'In twenty fifties,' I said, furious. The woman wouldn't know a tsunami if a hundred foot wall of water smacked her in the face.

She handed across a ten, a single and four quarters, slammed her cash drawer shut and shuffled away.

A last insult waited. One lone chocolate chip cookie lay in the discolored plastic dish by the window, but someone had taken a bite out of it and put it back, rejected.

I felt like the cookie. My trip to the bank had been no triumph.

Rivertown, being Rivertown, offered ready alternatives for getting cash. The handiest was the Discount Den, one of the hot goods emporiums in the darker blocks off Rivertown's main sin strip.

My friend Leo Brumsky bought his outrageous Hawaiian shirts and luminescent slacks there, but most of its offerings are of a more sporadic nature and depend on what has recently fallen out of a truck or rail car. Cash, though, is always in stock at the Discount Den. One does not purchase warm goods with Discover or American Express.

'Ding Dongs? Twinkies?' I asked in time with the dangling bells I'd set jingling, stepping into the gloom. The Discount Den also did a fine business in stale-dated sugary goods, thanks, in part, to me.

The crafty little owner, noticing the bandages flapping on my hands, set a box of happy-colored Flintstones bandages on the counter instead and shook his head. 'Can't keep them in stock since their bakery went bankrupt for a time.'

'Peeps,' a woman said.

I hadn't noticed her in the shadows in the back, bent over a carton. 'Pardon me?' I asked.

She straightened up and came to the counter clutching an armful of small, pastel-colored packages. Each contained marshmallow bunnies, lined up like bright little corpses preserved beneath cellophane. By now they would have hardened to rocks since Easter was seven months' gone.

'Peeps,' she said, 'for when there are no Twinkies.' She smiled, exposing one tooth. It looked to be dark yellow but in the gloom I supposed it could have been gray. For sure, it looked insufficient for rock-hard marshmallow.

Jangling the bells, stepping out, she paused. 'Microwave,' she said, and took her treasures out into the sunlight.

I am always interested in any research that involves sugar and beat it to the back for two packs of purple bunnies and one of the green. I set them on the counter next to the Flintstones bandages and took out my checkbook.

The owner knew me and knew my check for a thousand dollars

would be good. He only nicked me five percent, counting out nine hundred and forty-nine dollars, keeping a buck for the weakly adhesive Flintstones bandages. He threw in the Peeps for free, either because some small part of him wanted to make a grand gesture or because he figured I'd noticed that the stiff little rabbits, petrified like driftwood, were past their sell-by dates by not one, but four, Easters.

FIVE

B ack at the turret, I logged on to Google, the electronic nose. I expected to learn nothing of the disguised woman who'd just hired me and wasn't disappointed. Google reported that Rosamund Reynolds didn't exist. That was acceptable for the time being; her cashier's check was existence enough for me for now.

I then Internetted west to Tucson, Arizona. Gary Halvorson was the first name on the list. Satellite photos showed his address to be a small, white stucco ranch in south Tucson but the county assessor's website listed someone else as owning it. Halvorson was renting the place.

He had no other online mentions. Living under such relentless, giant magnifiers as Google means that making a donation, coaching a kid's team, signing a petition or simply owning a landline phone gets us posted onto the Web permanently. Even the most careful of recluses gets tagged for something.

Not Gary Halvorson of Tucson. He'd escaped notice completely, perhaps striving for the same anonymity as Rosamund Reynolds. I wondered how she'd found him when I couldn't.

I had better luck, of a sort, with the second name on the list. David Arlin of Laguna Beach was divorced, had owned a kitchen hardware wholesaler and lived in a four-million-dollar home set on a hill. In dozens of pictures taken at business gatherings and local charitable events he looked to be about forty, with hair so black it might have been dyed, and he had a good tan. He'd not worked at all on becoming invisible.

Except now he was dead. His house had blown up, with him in it, just four days earlier.

I creaked back in the tired red vinyl chair I'd found in an alley. Unlike Halvorson, Arlin was out there, Internet-wise. He'd been involved in his community, visible. And now he was dead. Surely Rosamund Reynolds had known that, yet she'd instructed me to check him out anyway. I doubted I could learn much of anything in the short period of time she wanted.

The last man on the list was Dainsto Runney. As with Arlin, the Internet offered up immediate results. He lived in something called The Church of the Reawakened Spirit, a nondenominational organization in Reeder, a small town along the Oregon coast. There were two pictures of him on the Internet, both taken about twenty years ago, which meant he was about the same age as the late David Arlin.

The first picture showed a short fellow with a pale face pocked by long-ago skirmishes with acne. He was dressed in a red vest and a straw hat and was standing cocked in a song-and-dance man's pose, a preacher trying too hard to be cool.

The second photo was taken from a greater distance and was even more comical. He was dressed in a flowing white robe, holding his arms outstretched as he blessed, or beseeched, a group of cyclists racing for some charity. Nobody was paying attention to him: not the racers, not the bystanders. He looked like a fool begging for attention.

Rosamund Reynolds had hired me to check out three men. One was invisible, one was dead and one was a preacher in a get-right, private church. They seemed an odd sort of trio for a secretive woman to be interested in.

My phone rang. 'Anticipating heat?' Amanda, my ex-wife, asked, though the 'ex' part, blessedly, seemed to be diminishing.

'And, perhaps, even an expensive, programmable thermostat. I'm employed again.'

She laughed. 'You already told me: Bipsies.'

'A second client,' I said. 'A woman who gave me a fake name. She wants me to head west to Arizona, California and Oregon to chase down three men. One has no Internet presence at all, another just got himself blown up and the third is a preacher in an oddball church who enjoys acting like a jackass.'

'Sounds like a match to your skill set. Lucrative?' asked one of Chicago's richest women.

'Two grand retainer and another two when I finish the job,' I said, wishing I were with her so I could pirouette.

'Huge, indeed.' Then she said, 'I have to cancel tonight.'

We were treading cautiously, focusing on our friendship. Careful dinners, only once a week and only in restaurants that had no past romantic associations for us was part of that.

'Business intrudes?' I asked, trying not to sound tensed for any worrisome inference in her words.

'Even worse. Politics. I've inherited too many of my father's friends in the Democratic Party. The elections are less than a month out and nervousness prevails. They've called another advisory meeting. We get a make-up dinner or two next week?'

It was a relief. I told her I'd call her from out west, set out my new package of Flintstones bandages and went back to slicing my fingers on tinwork.

SIX

My furnace arrived at eight o'clock two mornings later. The driver helped me to slide it into place behind the table saw and the two white plastic lawn chairs that were the first floor's only other adornments. After he was gone, I lifted off the cardboard box as gently as if I were unwrapping a giant Fabergé egg and sat in one of the chairs to imagine the squat beige wondrous thing humming come November, warming every cragged chunk of limestone on all five of my round floors. The thought continued to warm me in the cab all the way to Midway Airport.

The Halvorson address was ten minutes from Tucson International. I motored up silently, having rented a mostly electric Prius at the airport as a sort of cap-and-trade restitution for the occasionally oil-vaporizing Jeep I drove at home.

I'd gotten enough Internet views of the neighborhood to feel like I'd been on the block many times before. Type in an address and see enough in an instant to zero in a missile; such fast availability of images from satellite peepers used to bother me. Now I'm troubled more by how easily I get seduced by it and how little I worry about the future as drones seem set to darken the skies in unfathomable numbers.

The Internet photos had shown Halvorson's stucco cottage to be jammed in tight in a row of identical white cottages but they hadn't shown its dinginess. Its stucco-board siding was more gray than white, except close to the ground where it was brown from dirt splashed up by rain.

The front yard had no grass but rather a scrabble of gravel, hard dirt and three discarded Coke cans. A 'For Sale by Owner' sign was stuck in the middle of it, slapped with a 'Price Slashed' sticker. Both the sign and the sticker looked new.

I parked the Prius across the street and walked up like I was in a buying mood.

No one answered the bell. I knocked. No one responded to that, either. I headed around to the back.

There was a side window on the one-car attached garage. I rubbed away enough of the dirt to look in. An old beige Chevrolet Impala was parked inside. Both right-side tires were flat.

I walked around to the back. The window on the kitchen door was covered with fresh plywood. I knocked.

'You got to call the number,' a man said from next door. He was Mexican, hand polishing a steel car wheel on a portable workbench.

'I was just passing by and saw the sign.'

His eyes narrowed. The man knew how to smell a lie.

'You got to call the number,' he said again.

'There's a car sitting on flat tires in the garage. Is anybody still living here?'

'Call the number, man.' He bent back to the wheel but not so low that he couldn't keep an eye on me.

I went to the front and called the number on the sign. The owner said he lived close by and would be there in five minutes. He pulled up in a pale blue minivan in four.

He was gray-haired, wore a shiny tan shirt, black jeans and nervous hope on his face. 'You'll love this house.' His hands shook as he unlocked the front door.

'Nobody's home?'

'It's priced lower than right,' he went on quickly, like he was afraid I'd bolt. 'I know a banker. You got any kind of credit, you can move right in.'

We stepped into a small living room. The floor was glazed brown tile. A grease-stained, two-seat orange couch and a cracked black vinyl recliner better than the blue one I had at home were pushed against a windowless side wall. A low, plastic wood-grain table where a television might have once sat was set against the back wall, absolutely devoid of dust. Despite being in dry desert air, the house stunk of dampness and bleach. It had been scrubbed recently.

'Is the place unoccupied?' I asked.

'You can move right in,' he said. Then added, 'I just cleaned,' like my nose didn't work.

The smell of bleach was giving me a headache. No landlord was that thorough. He hadn't just cleaned; he'd tried to eradicate something. I wondered if that explained his bad nerves.

'You had a tenant?' I asked, trying to sound casual.

'Gone.'

'When did he leave?' I started toward the back of the house. The smell of disinfectant was strongest there.

'Recent,' the owner said, following.

I got to the kitchen. The refrigerator door was rusted at the bottom and a ragged corner of the white laminate counter was broken off. 'What about those?' I asked, pointing to tiny scratches on the brown-painted back door an inch above the threshold. The exposed wood was raw and clean. The scratches were fresh.

'I can fix.' His eyes were restless, looking everywhere but at the scratches.

'And that?' I pointed to the fresh plywood screwed to the kitchen door.

'Punks broke in. I got to get new glass.'

'Does the Impala in the garage come with the house?' I smiled like I was making a joke. A car sitting flat, not drivable, was bothersome.

He forced a smile so broad it must have hurt his ears. 'I'm having it towed this afternoon.'

'You want nothing to do with it?'

'Ain't mine to do nothing with.'

Except to tow, to make it go away. 'You're sure your ex-tenant doesn't want his car?'

'Maybe it don't run.'

No tenant leaves behind a car. Even as scrap, cars were always worth something.

There were two bedrooms. The largest held a double bed stripped to its stained mattress and a chipped dresser. A spot on the beige carpet was almost white. It had been scrubbed recently.

I went to the closet. Not even a hanger remained. Maybe that was odd, maybe it was not, but it seemed like further proof that the whole house had been hurriedly emptied and scrubbed down in a panic.

'Place comes with the furniture,' the landlord said.

'Yours?'

He nodded.

The second bedroom was completely empty, too, except for the lingering smell of much bleach.

We walked to the front door. 'How much?' I asked, because I remembered it was what potential buyers asked.

'I'll cut you a huge deal.' Faint sweat had broken out on his forehead.

'Throw in the car?' I asked, again like I was joking. The car nagged. It shouldn't have been left behind.

His face remained tight. 'Like I said, it'll be gone.'

We drove away at the same time. When he turned left, I turned right and doubled back. I wondered if he'd remember he'd been too nervous to give me a sale price.

'What do you know about the guy who lived here?' I asked the man in the back yard next door.

'You ain't interested in buying anything, are you?'

I pulled a fifty out of my wallet and handed it across the chain-link fence. 'Just information.'

He took the fifty but kept it visible in his hand like the deal was still pending. 'About what?'

'Anything you know about the guy who lived here, Gary Halvorson.'

'That his name? I don' even know that and I been here a year. He wasn't sociable.'

'The landlord says he's gone.'

'He's always gone. Salesman, maybe.'

'What does he look like?'

'I never seen him, but the guy who owned my house before me seen him once or twice a long time ago. He has bright red hair. There is something strange, though . . .' He let the thought dangle, like bait.

I produced another fifty but held onto it.

It prompted more words. 'A couple of weeks ago, about three in the morning, I hear glass breaking outside. I put on pants, a shirt, go out front. Next door, the front door is wide open and two kids, teenagers, are running down the street. I called the cops.'

'Sounds like they didn't stay inside long.'

'From the time I heard the glass until I was out the front, seeing them running away, was only a couple minutes.'

'Why break in only to run out so quickly?'

'Maybe nothing there. Maybe not.' He paused to let his eyes caress the fifty in my right hand.

'Halvorson never came around, afterward?' I asked, not ready to pony up more.

'Just the owner. Next night, he's there with mops, buckets, you name it.'

'That was two weeks ago?' The house must have been shut up tight ever since for the bleach to still smell that strong.

'Then there's that other thing . . .' He let his voice taper away so I could focus harder on him eyeing the fifty in my hand.

I held tight.

'The owner, after the break-in . . . real strange, you know?' he said, coaxing.

I didn't know, and wouldn't, unless the second fifty changed hands. I handed it over.

He jammed the second bill into his jeans. 'The owner, he's in there for hours, but after all that cleaning he hauls out only two plastic garbage bags. And he don' leave the bags at the curb, even though pick-up is the next morning. He puts them in his van to get rid of them elsewhere.'

'He didn't want someone poking through them?'

'That's what I'm thinking.'

I had an inspiration. 'Did the house go up for sale right after the break-in?'

He rubbed his right thumb against his first two fingers, looking for another fifty.

'I gave you a hundred already,' I reminded him.

He grinned; he'd tried. 'Sign went up the next day.'

'Without asking Halvorson?'

'Maybe he did, maybe he didn't. Maybe there's no lease and it don' matter.'

'I might take one more look inside.'

He shrugged and bent back down to the wheel he was polishing; the hundred dollars I'd passed over would also buy blindness. I popped the back lock with a credit card and went inside.

I headed into the garage first. It smelled faintly of gasoline. The Impala's driver's door was unlocked. The inside dome light didn't go on when I slid inside. The battery was dead.

The glove box contained nothing but a bill of sale dated almost twenty years before. The car was almost ten years old when Halvorson had bought it from a private party. I put the bill back.

I went back through the kitchen, into the master bedroom and turned on the light in the closet. Things can get forgotten in closets when not even a coat hanger is left behind. I felt along the top shelf and came away with dust. The landlord must have been in too much of a hurry, cleaning, to think of the shelf.

There was dust on the second bedroom's closet shelf as well but the rest of that room had been scrubbed like all the others.

I went back to the kitchen. The fresh scratches on the base of the door could have come from anything. So, too, could the tiny reddish brown residue caught against the threshold beneath them. I ran my rental car key over it and came up with enough to tap onto the white counter. It could have been ketchup or a hundred other normal red-brown things.

I looked around the kitchen floor more closely. There were several other faint traces of the same brown or red residue along the cabinet baseboards.

Maybe if the next-door neighbor hadn't said he'd never seen Halvorson. Maybe if the kids who'd broken in hadn't run out almost right away. Maybe if the Impala hadn't been left behind. Maybe if the landlord hadn't been in such a hurry to scrub away whatever he'd found. Maybe if he hadn't hauled away what little had been left behind, rather than leave it at the curb. Maybe if the dust wasn't so thick on the closet shelves, as though it had been ages since anything had been placed on them.

Maybe if the next person on Rosamund's list hadn't just been blown up.

I looked again at the tiny speck on the counter.

I began opening cabinets. Unlike those in the closets, the kitchen shelves had been wiped down and smelled strongly of the bleach. Fortunately, one held a paper towel core with one last sheet stuck to it. I used it to pinch up the little clump of reddish brown material from the counter, folded it twice over and put it in my pocket.

Maybe I wouldn't have, if it didn't look so much like blood.

SEVEN

Despite the dozen Halvorson questions batting at my brain, and despite the aftershocks from the taco and two burrito grandes I'd just eaten at the tin-sided roadside stand, I felt tired enough to think I could sleep anywhere. The first motel I came to, a Valu-Lodge at the edge of Tucson International, looked good enough. Others certainly thought so. A dozen cars were parked there, though all were nudged up to the rooms in the back, away from the street.

The desk clerk, a kid of nineteen, asked for sixty dollars cash and no identification, then handed me a plastic key card.

For sure, he didn't flinch at the thunder of what sounded like a jetliner descending onto the roof.

'Things will quiet down?' I shouted.

His face clouded, though that could have been caused by the shadow of the plane darkening the window. 'No problem!' he yelled.

Another plane roared over, low.

I was too tired to look for a room elsewhere. 'Is mine the quietest room you have?' I asked when I could.

He laughed. 'There are none quieter.'

Even when I saw that my room was at the end of the building, right below where fuel would get dumped by a plane landing in crisis, I figured I'd sleep. Unlocking the unmarked door – a No

Smoking sign would have been prudent, given the possibility of high-octane rain – I tossed my duffel on the king-sized bed and stretched out next to it, ready for oblivion.

A plane roared over, low. And another. And another.

Sleep didn't come. Each thundering plane brought the possibility that a fatigued pilot might misjudge and leave a tire mark on my forehead. But more, I was agitated by the possibility that Gary Halvorson, a recluse living a hidden life, might have been hunted down, leaving behind his car, his meager belongings and maybe enough of his blood to require gallons of bleach to scrub away. Killed, like David Arlin had just been out in Laguna Beach.

The thought triggered the queasy notion that Rosamund Reynolds, an anonymous operator, had sent me to Tucson not to report whatever I could learn quickly of Halvorson's life, but rather to verify that he was dead.

EIGHT

A t nine o'clock the next morning, fresh from three hours of intermittent sleep, I called the number Rosamund gave me. Likely it went to a burner phone that could be discarded once she'd finished playing her cagey game.

'Did you tell anyone I hired you?' she shouted, right off, hoarse and out of breath.

'What's happened—?' A plane came in low.

'No matter—!'

'I've learned nothing, and perhaps a good deal more!' I yelled quickly. Another plane was approaching.

'Call me from a quieter—'

I showered, packed my duffel and stepped outside. Only three other cars were in the lot and they were parked down by the office. No one lingered, mornings, at the Valu-Lodge.

I dropped my duffel in the Prius and headed down to the office in search of alertness.

The coffee was on a small table next to a blue bowl containing four bruised yellow apples. I pumped a cup and silently conveyed sympathies to the wounded fruit; no doubt they'd been wounded being bounced about by the decibels thundering above. A middle-aged man stood behind the counter, chewing on his lip.

I told him I was leaving and that relaxed his face a little. I might have been the only guest that stayed the whole night, making him suspect I was Immigration or IRS.

He didn't offer a receipt, nor did I ask for one. His was a cash operation, employing illegals to tend to trysting lovers. It was a way to get along in hard times. I understood hard times.

I called Rosamund back once I'd driven far enough north to escape the flight paths. 'Gary Halvorson might have disappeared. He's never been seen by his newest neighbor. He left behind his car and enough dust to make me wonder whether he ever used his closets. And he might have left behind blood that needed lots of bleach to get rid of.' I paused and added, 'He was living under the radar. I should poke around, see if I can find out the last name he used from utility bills and such. Or, if you like, I can see what the cops know about him.'

'No idea where he might be?'

'Halvorson's landlord was evasive. I should question him again. Why did you ask if I'd told anyone you'd hired me?'

'Go next to Laguna Beach, and quickly.'

She hung up before I could ask why speed mattered, since the man there was dead.

I would have also liked to press her about why she didn't want me to try to learn more about Halvorson, but she was the client and she'd forked out over two thousand dollars. That was a good enough reason to take a drive.

I took I-10 north toward Phoenix, then west into a desert of beige rocks and brown rocks, some of which were big and some of which were small. It went that way, rock after rock, for almost four hundred miles, except for when a green glass-and-cement-block truck stop rose up like a shimmering mirage, a fantastical oasis offering gaso-line, gristly hot dogs and hardened pastries set amid the never-ending landscape of rocks.

Oddly, close by on the other side of the interstate was a gathering of at least fifty mobile homes – more than would be needed to house workers at the truck stop. It was a ragged cluster, loose and asym-metrical, and I had the thought that the trailers had been dragged there by people pushing back against the stuff and clutter of their previous lives. Things were seductively simple out in the desert, there being only rocks to look at. When folks tired of a particular view they could simply tug their homes a few yards up the gulch and have entirely new rocks to enjoy until it was time to move another few yards again.

I got to the lush of Laguna Beach late in the afternoon. There were plenty of rocks there, too, but those glittered on the tanned hands steering the expensive Benzs, Bimmers and Bentleys cruising the South Coast Highway. All those rocks were big – several carats at least – and none were small.

Sparkling, too, were the enormous houses high on the hills to the east, their bronzed windows reflecting bright pinpoints of the waning sun. Everything seemed to glitter in Laguna Beach.

I thought of Amanda. The murder of her father, an immensely wealthy Chicago businessman, had drawn her into his world, a world of power and privilege and glitter very much the equal of Laguna Beach. She seemed to be faring well, this former writer of art history books, but the challenges she faced running his enormous conglomerate all seemed as big and unmovable as the largest of the rocks I'd just seen in the desert.

I came upon the Sun Coast Hotel, a genuine pink stucco throwback to California's golden days of the mid-nineteen forties and fifties. More essential at that moment, the sky above it was blue and clear and free of planes. I parked next to a long black Audi and went in.

The office had two types of saltwater taffies in glass jars on the counter and two types of blondes behind them. One was tall and tanned. The other was short and tanned. The short one smiled first with teeth that naturally sparkled, it being Laguna Beach.

She said they offered three types of accommodations. 'One faces the beach, the other the courtyard. Three hundred and two hundred, respectively.'

'And the third type?' I asked, taking a taffy from one of the jars. It was a perfect caramel color, as though it had spent time on the beach with the blondes.

She tried not to be obvious as she studied my wardrobe. Though I was wearing my best blue button-collared shirt and my best khakis, she'd probably seen better on the local homeless. She nodded, very slightly, and said, 'One hundred and twenty per night, but it's real close to the road.'

'No planes, though?' I asked, remembering my previous night at the Valu-Lodge.

'Just the occasional private jet.'

'Then it will be fine with me,' I said, mindful of the dour Ms Reynolds' wallet.

'Here visiting friends?' she asked, keying up her computer screen with my credit card number. Unlike the Valu-Lodge, there would be no cash changing palms, not in this joint.

'David Arlin's place?'

Her face softened with as much empathy as her guileless young life experience could summon up. 'Be careful driving up,' she said, giving me directions. 'The explosion blew sand and dirt everywhere and it still washes onto the road after it rains.'

'Have they found the cause of the explosion?'

She took the lid off the jar of the darkest, most mournful of the taffies and slid it closer to me. 'It's been less than a week. No one's saying much of anything,' she said.

NINE

The street followed the gentle curve of the hillside. The houses were expansive, California-perfect edifices of timber and glass, stucco and stone. Their bushes were tightly trimmed, their lawns relentlessly watered to attain unvarying shades of deep green. Only the mound of scorched wood and stones behind orange plastic link fencing marred the beauty of the street. The rubble was Arlin's.

Grit crunched under my shoes when I got out of the car. It would take many more rains to wash the last of it from the pavement.

'I called city hall three times but nobody will tell me when this mess will be removed.'

I turned. An elderly woman with a smear of lipstick that matched her red hair had walked up with a tiny dog on a leash.

'They're probably being cautious, still investigating,' I said.

'Well, they ought to find that man who asked me if this was the Arlin house.'

'When was that?'

'Night before the explosion.'

'Did you tell the police?'

'Of course I did. Creepy fellow. His car had dark windows and he powered them down only a little but I could see him good enough. Red-headed man.' She touched her own hair as she looked down at the pavement. 'Poor David, blown to smithereens. The blast woke up the whole town. The thought that parts of him are still . . .' She scraped a shoe on the pavement. 'Horrible, horrible.'

She tugged at the dog's leash, also a red affair with bits of glass sparkling along every inch. Then again, they might have been real gems, it being Laguna Beach where everything glittered.

I got directions off my phone and drove to the police department. The lieutenant in charge of the Arlin case met me in the foyer and led me back to a gray metal desk in a small office. He said his name was Beech. He was slender, pushing fifty, and had close-cut graying hair that almost matched the color of his desk.

'Insurance, you say?' He frowned as he studied my card.

'I work for the smaller companies. I'm on an extended west coast trip and was asked to look into the Arlin matter. He was badly burned?'

'Your insurance company can hold off until we complete our investigation, if that's what you're asking. That should make them happy, delaying payment.' He leaned back in his chair and studied me. 'Who is the beneficiary?'

'You're thinking the explosion wasn't accidental?'

'Too soon to suspect anything at all. Who was the beneficiary?'

'A lady with a dog told me she talked to a stranger looking for Arlin the night before he was killed.'

'Old lady, hair dyed fire-engine red, lipstick and dog leash to match?'

'She said a red-haired man drove up the night before the explosion, asking where Arlin lived . . .' I let my voice trail away, knowing what he was going to say.

He said it exactly as dismissively as I expected: 'The woman sees red everywhere, right?'

'Maybe,' I allowed, thinking it wasn't the time to mention red-haired Gary Halvorson.

'So, who benefits, Elstrom?'

I put on one of my stupid faces, of which I have several. 'They don't tell me things like that. I'm just supposed to stop in, find out if there's an investigation and, if so, how long it will take.'

The dumb face worked. He let it go. 'Arlin was divorced two years ago, no children,' he said. 'His ex-wife moved back east, free of his financial mess. He got stuck with the mortgage on the house, which is upside down by eight hundred thousand, and business debts. He was a kitchen and bath hardware distributor. The last housing downturn stuck him with inventory he couldn't sell.'

'No sign of a wrench near a loose gas fitting?'

'You're asking whether Arlin blew up his house to get out from under that mortgage and accidentally blew himself up as well?'

'It happens.'

'Call your employer; get back to me with the beneficiary on his life insurance.'

'You wouldn't want to know that unless you're thinking this was no accident.'

'I expect to hear from you within forty-eight hours.'

Outside, the setting sun was beginning to gild the waves in the ocean. I found a Whole Foods grocery, got a vegetable salad and a tuna sandwich on seven-grain bread because they were healthy, and a box of chocolate-dipped butter cookies because they were necessary, and drove back to the Sun Coast Hotel.

And then I sat, in the Prius, in the parking lot, wondering whether Rosamund Reynolds was gaming me by sending me off to learn information she already knew. What I couldn't figure out was why.

Calling her, I got her voicemail. 'I've just visited David Arlin's house, or rather what's left of it and, I suppose, of him. The cops are playing things close to the vest, saying only that they're investigating. I'm thinking you know more than they do, just as you must know more than I could learn about Gary Halvorson. Call me with truths before I waste more of your money.'

I leaned back behind the wheel and shut my eyes, hoping to be calmed by the sound of the surf, but all the water did was pound in my ears, one wave after another. I waited fifteen minutes, then fifteen minutes more. There was no call. There was no calm.

The same short blonde looked up when I entered the office. 'I'd like to upgrade to a room on the beach,' I said.

'A water view would triple your rate,' she said, casting a new glance at my old clothes.

'Excellent,' I said, sticking my hand into the jar of the more lightly tanned taffies.

She gave me a quizzical look and a key to a room that overlooked rocks, some of which were big and some of which were small. But these had an ocean beyond them and a big-dollar veranda from which to enjoy them, all at the expense of the wily Rosamund Reynolds. Upgrading seemed such a perfectly petty gesture.

By now, the sun was almost gone. I slid open the door and stepped outside. The surf had softened. Little silver lines shimmered in the shallows along the beach.

'Nothing is as it appears,' a voice said.

A man stood on the next veranda, smoking a cigarette and looking down at the water. 'Bioluminescence,' he went on. 'Microorganisms. Phosphorescence. Things you can't see, moving beneath the surface. That's what's making those silver lines.'

'Couldn't prove it by me,' I said.

'Some things can't be proved by anybody,' he said and went back into his room.

It sounded like a California sort of attitude. I ate the salad, the tuna sandwich and three of the cookies as I watched the last sliver of the sun disappear. Then I took my cell phone down to the beach to walk among the silver lines shimmering even brighter in the moonlight. I thought of Amanda in Chicago and the moonlit beaches we'd shared and were working toward sharing again. And I thought of Jenny Galecki, so much closer up in San Francisco yet now so much farther away, and of the beaches that likely would never be. Jenny and I had come together at a time when Amanda and I were so very far apart. But then a better professional opportunity came for her and Jenny, ever the vigilant newswoman, left Chicago television for San Francisco. We'd stayed loosely in touch, thinking we'd become closer in mind should times change.

I got cold. I went up to bed, hoping the surf would pound loud enough to drown out everything I didn't know.

TEN

Ibrewed lousy coffee in the room the next morning and took it with a lousy attitude out onto my three-hundred-dollar a night veranda to call Rosamund Reynolds again. Once more I was routed to voicemail.

'What's left of your two-thousand-dollar retainer is stuck, confused and unnecessary, in an expensive room on the sands of Laguna Beach,' I said to her recorder. 'The cops won't tell me anything. To learn more will take time. Call me.'

I went down to the lobby, got better coffee and more of the superb saltwater taffy, and used the guest computer to Google Dainsto Runney, the preacher in Oregon. Nothing new was posted. If he'd been killed or disappeared unnaturally, news of it had not yet been sniffed by the Internet.

I called his Church of the Reawakened Spirit from the sidewalk and was surprised when an articulate, businesslike woman answered instead of some drugged-up dreamer of the lost sixties. It proved, for the first time, that I shouldn't judge a church by its name.

'Dainsto Runney, please.'

'He's not here.'

'When will he return?'

'May I ask who is calling?'

'It's regarding an insurance payout,' I said, because even reawakened spirits love free money.

'If it's personal, you should send him a letter.'

'It's a sizable amount.'

'A letter would be perfect,' she said, and hung up.

And perfect, too, was Runney. He fit seamlessly into Rosamund's ragged puzzle. He'd either gone away like Halvorson or gone dead, like Arlin. I had no doubt Rosamund knew Runney was missing before she hired me.

I called her again, and again got sent to voicemail. 'Runney's missing. I'll waste more of your money to verify that in Oregon.'

I got my duffel from my room, grabbed a last fistful of taffies from the lobby and headed north to the airport and the safest direct route north to Oregon.

But I slowed, as I knew I would, a mile before the turn to Los Angeles International. I'd been talking to myself above the Prius's silently sanctimonious electric motor, reminding myself that I had other business in that part of the world, business that demanded more than a simple telephone call. A face-to-face conversation was so very necessary, I told myself.

What I didn't need to tell myself, I devoutly hoped, was that I had to be careful, that there was rarely even one Amanda for the dumb-luckiest of men and that the odds of getting second chances with such a woman were smaller than moon shots attempted with basement-built rockets.

I blew past the turn-off to LAX and continued driving north.

ELEVEN

Jennifer Gale, as she was known to her television viewers, had come to Rivertown to report the arrest of one of its municipal lizards. Our zoning commissioner, Elvis Derbil, had been caught slapping fake labels on bottles of out-of-date salad dressing, and the symmetry of that was undeniable for television. His was an oily scheme, altering an oily product in an oily town.

Being a good reporter, she'd sought to brighten the odd story with a minute-long color piece on the oddball – me – who lived in a turret across the lawn from city hall. She'd dropped that notion when she'd discovered I was working on a case for one of Chicago's most prominent socialites. She'd attached herself to my investigation like a limpet mine and led us, on a hot July day, to a fly-covered corpse in a trailer off a dune in Indiana. And that had led to an almost supercharged night back at my turret. But she had been coming off the trauma of her reporter husband's death in the Middle East and I was descending from the flameout of my marriage to Amanda Phelps. Our ghosts, those who haunted us – hers dead, mine so very alive – had pulled us back.

Jenny left Chicago for better assignments in San Francisco and we didn't see each other for months. She remained transfixed, though, by the crookedness in Rivertown and when she got tipped off to a Chicago-based Russian gang's plan to slip their fingers around the greasy necks in Rivertown she took a leave and returned to Illinois, hoping for a career-raising series of reports on new sorts of mob crime in America. Still tethered by our ghosts, we reconnected, warily at first. And then less so.

She returned to San Francisco. I returned to scrambling for insurance company work or, absent that, rounding up semi-coherent sorority alumni to inhale again the vapors of old times.

And I was returned, too, to the periphery of my ex-wife Amanda's new world.

Her father, Wendell Phelps, had run Chicago's largest electric utility. Later in his life, he'd sought to build a bridge to the daughter he'd ignored when she was growing up. He'd enticed her to quit teaching at the Art Institute and instead manage big-buck philanthropy through his company. It was an offer to do much good, and one no conscientious person could refuse.

Mindful of his majority stock position in the utility, the company's need for a ready successor as CEO and her status as his only heir, he'd enticed her to enter his boardrooms as well. It was a prudent, business-like preparation for when the time came.

The time came too soon. Wendell Phelps died. The circumstances of it had brought Amanda and me closer together, and then even more so as she became one of Chicago's wealthiest and most powerful people. We talked on the phone two or three times each week and shared dinner, usually on Thursday evenings. At first it was business – her business – and her splashdown into Wendell's Machiavellian world of corporate politics. But then, little by little, we began to let our past return. We began reminiscing over the little things we'd shared in our brief marriage. There'd been much good in those days.

Amanda was, and would always be, my ghost.

I called Jenny two hours north of Los Angeles. 'Care to have dinner?' I inquired.

'Oooh . . . you're here?' She'd dropped her voice to an exaggerated seductress level.

'Almost,' I said, adding, 'I'm on my way to Oregon,' because I wanted the call to feel more casual.

'I'm on the TV this afternoon at five. Big expose: someone's been juicing up pumpkins, making them bigger and brighter on a supposedly organic farm. Say six o'clock?' She named a restaurant close to her apartment.

I told her that would be just about right, because at the time I believed it.

TWELVE

The usually malevolent California freeway gods must have been on new meds, for it was exactly six o'clock when I walked into the restaurant she'd named. It was in the Marina District, the kind of out-of-the-way place that she sought. Whereas television's dark-haired and voluptuous Jennifer Gale was professional enough to welcome interest in her and her station, Jenny Galecki, a no-nonsense Polish girl from Chicago's northwest side, sought privacy in her personal life. She chose restaurants where Jennifer Gale wouldn't be stared at.

I knew to look in the darkest corner. She was there, in a beige suit that must have paled even the brightest oranges of the inorganic pumpkins she'd reported on that day.

We kissed, but not as long as the last time we'd seen each other.

She'd ordered me a single Scotch, neat. 'I've been on the road for seven hours,' I said. 'This might knock me out.'

'That's OK. I live one block up. I can drag you there.' She said it half-jokingly, watching my eyes to see my reaction.

I hid behind my drink, taking a small sip, though to my shame part of me wanted to wonder what it would be like to gulp the thing down and be dragged up the block.

'You're angry,' she said after a moment. Jenny's antennae were so very finely tuned.

'Unsettled. A lying client.'

'So, heading to Oregon?' she asked.

'The third of a trio of men I've been hired to look up.' After
making her promise that not one word of what I said would make
the news, I told her about Rosamund Reynolds, Gary Halvorson,
David Arlin and Dainsto Runney.

She leaned forward. 'You think the third man, the preacher
Runney, has also disappeared?'

'The woman at his church was too vague about when he'd return.
Until I see what I can learn up there, the only solid lead about the
trio seems to be Arlin in Laguna Beach. There's a cop there, a
Lieutenant Beech . . .'

'Beech, of the Beach?' She laughed.

I laughed, too. We always laughed well together, Jenny and me.

'Perhaps a delicate inquiry . . .?' she asked.

'From a foxy TV lady in San Francisco . . .?'

'Might yield a little more information.'

'Only as long as the foxy TV lady doesn't go too far, or public
– at least until I get up to Oregon.'

'What can this mysterious Reynolds woman be up to?' she asked.

'It's all I can think about.'

She began circling the rim of her own Scotch with a slow,
suggestive forefinger. 'Really? Nothing else?'

It was a perfectly formed forefinger, attached to a perfectly formed
hand. 'Well, perhaps something else did flit in and out of my mind.'
It was true enough; I can be a weak man. And though ours was an
unformed relationship, we did have good history, Jenny and me.

The forefinger slowed. 'Flit? That's all it was, a flit?'

'Perhaps a little more extended.'

The forefinger picked up the tempo just a little, ever so tantaliz-
ingly. 'Extended?' she whispered softly, teasing, sensing triumph.

'Absolutely,' I said. I had to look away from the mesmerizing
forefinger.

'What is it, Dek? What else is wrong?'

'Not so much wrong.'

'Amanda?'

'We're in touch,' I said.

'Your ever-present ghost.'

'Yes.'

She reached across the table to touch the back of my hand. 'I
dream about my husband every night, especially about the last time

I saw him. I told you once, remember? I was late for work and he was racing around the apartment packing, late himself to get to O'Hare, to a plane, to Iraq, to his death. I wake up in tears.'

'You can't do that, you know.'

'Punish myself for brusqueness?' She made a small laugh. 'You know the difference between us, Dek? The only way I can live is in the present. No future. And God knows, my past hurts too much to want to think about. Yet it comes so very alive when I'm unguarded in my sleep. But you . . . you have a past that can become a future, a past that can become real again. Your ghost isn't really a ghost, and that is very fine.'

My cell phone shattered the mood, whatever it was. 'My elusive client, no doubt,' I said, a man of dedicated professionalism and suddenly renewed self-control.

It wasn't Rosamund calling. It was my pal, Leo Brumsky. 'You're not alone?' he asked.

It was an odd thing for him to say. 'Actually, no.'

'Hmmm . . .' He paused, as he does when he's slithering toward something salacious. 'That explains the turret's being dark and my banging fruitlessly on your door for five minutes. You're otherwise engaged. With Amanda?'

He was making no sense. Leo, always a romantic, always a believer in the possibility of righting old wrongs, thought I was inside the turret with my ex-wife.

'I'm in California.'

'No, you're not. You're here. You must be here.' After the briefest of instants, he asked slowly, 'Where . . . in . . . California, exactly?'

I could envisage the look spreading across his face. Five foot six, one hundred and forty pounds and no doubt garbed as always in a preposterous Hawaiian shirt and neon-colored trousers, the man knew how to offer up the filthiest of smirks no matter how ludicrous his costume.

'Middle of the state.' I was speaking to the phone but I couldn't take my eyes off the forefinger. It had paused, barely moving side to side, but still restless, teasing, promising. I doubted Jenny was aware she was doing it.

'San Francisco!' he announced.

'As a matter of fact, yes.'

'Tell Miss Galecki I love her.'

'Leo says he loves you,' I said to Jenny.

'Tell him I love him, too, and that I'm waiting for him to come and rescue me.'

'Listen,' Leo said, 'it's nuts leaving this thing in your Jeep. People steal them for their copper content.'

'What are you talking about?'

'Your furnace. It's so small anyone can get at it. All they'd have to do is peel off some of the duct tape you've used to patch your top—'

'Leo! Make sense.'

'The furnace you left in your Jeep. It's in a cardboard box that's marked "Furnace," an invitation to any thief—'

'My new furnace can't fit in the Jeep,' I cut in, trying not to shout.

The restaurant had gone silent. Every head had turned toward me.

'I'm looking right at it,' he said.

'A cut-down furnace box stuffed inside . . .' My mind flashed through the possibilities of why I'd been sent out of town. The most horrible of set-ups suddenly seemed probable.

'Get out of there, Leo!' I yelled into the phone. 'Get out of there fast.'

THIRTEEN

I reserved a last-minute seat on a nine o'clock flight to Chicago as Jenny raced me to the airport in my rental.

'You'll talk to that cop in Laguna Beach?' I said as I got out.

'Discreetly, as I promised,' she said, offering a small smile up at me through the open window. 'I'll see you again?' she asked.

'You betcha.' I pulled my duffel from the back seat. It felt like it weighed a hundred pounds. It wanted to be an anchor, to tug me back into the car.

She eased me away. 'Remember, I want to know about Halvorson, Arlin and your mysterious preacher, Dainsto Runney,' she said. 'I want to know the true identity of the mystery woman who hired you. But first, I want to know what's in the back of your Jeep.'

There was so much more to say, and I said none of it. I bent down to quickly kiss her and then closed the car door. She gunned the engine and sped away. She'd drop off my rental and take a cab back to her apartment where she'd wait breathlessly, she said, for news I'd made her promise to not break on television.

The flight, luckily enough, was not full and I managed to find a window spot with an empty space between me and a fat man spilling out into the aisle. He had a bad cold and wanted to chat between wet coughs.

'*No habla ingles*,' I said, which I hoped meant, in Spanish, that I didn't speak English. I closed my eyes. I needed to dare to think.

I was being set-up.

It now seemed so obvious. A woman behind a fake name and a thick mask of make-up and half-truths had played me for a chump. She wasn't interested in learning much about Halvorson and Arlin and Runney so much as she wanted me noticed asking around about them. Clearly I'd been hired for my history and my susceptibility. I'd made a big splash in the Chicago papers, starring as a moron who'd gotten suckered into authenticating phony evidence for a crooked suburban mayor, Evangeline Wilts. That I'd been quickly exonerated made no ripple at all; it got one paragraph buried in the back pages of Chicago's main newspapers and there'd been no mention at all on local television. Rosamund Reynolds had likely hired me for my ripeness to be made gamy again, perhaps for murder. After sending me away she could have filled my Jeep with something that might be the corpse of Gary Halvorson or Dainsto Runney. I'd even left her a cardboard box.

But I'd gotten lucky. Leo Brumsky, my pal of pals, had alerted me. And that bought me time. Rosamund believed I was still on the west coast, headed up to Oregon. With more luck, I could dispose of whatever was in the box before she'd anonymously tip the cops that I was returning from doing bad out of town and that I had a surprise in my Jeep.

It seemed so paranoid. It seemed so probable.

The fat man on the aisle seat beside me coughed wet into the flesh of his fist. It seemed so wonderfully ordinary.

I stepped out from Chicago's Midway Airport terminal at two in the morning. Leo's pale orange Porsche roadster was idling at the curb.

I jumped inside. 'How long have you been waiting?'

'I came straight here . . . almost. I didn't know where else to go,' he said in too small a voice. 'The cops keep making me move.'

He stared straight ahead as he pulled us away from the curb. His hands were shaking, squeezing the steering wheel too hard. Two hundred yards down, the transmission whine was deafening; he'd not shifted out of first gear. I told him to pull over. He complied, a wooden man. We switched places and I started us up again.

'I'll take care of things, Leo.'

'I already did.'

I slowed down. 'Tell me.'

'I dis-dis-disposed,' he said, stuttering in that same small voice. His teeth chattered as though it were winter.

He was in some phase of shock. I'd seen him that way once before, though that time had been more severe. He'd just fired a revolver at a killer.

'Damn it, Leo.'

'You'd have done the same for me,' he said, shivering.

'I would not.' I reached to turn up the heater.

'You al-al-already did,' he said, still chattering.

He was right, but I hoped never to confirm it. I'd done my own disposal of the man who'd come to kill him.

'You returned the Jeep to the turret?' I asked as we approached Harlem Avenue. I'd take it north, up to Rivertown.

'Back again, okey dokey,' he said in a strange, sing-song voice. He turned to look at me, working up a smile. As always when Leo smiled at night, his huge teeth lined up ghostly white, like cemetery markers in a row. That night, there was something wrong in his eyes. They were too dark, like black windows looking in on an empty room.

I backed off from asking him anything more. One thing was certain: I couldn't return him to his mother's bungalow; he'd be too much for the septuagenarian Ma Brumsky. I turned around, caught I-55 east to Lake Shore Drive and headed up to the high-rent district north of the Chicago River. We rode in silence for ten minutes. I doubted he was aware that he was out in the night.

I called Endora, his girlfriend. A former model and current researcher at the Newberry Library, she's brilliant, like him. She'd be capable.

She answered the phone sleepy-voiced. 'I'm bringing Leo to you,' I said.

'What's wrong?' she asked, instantly alert.

'He did me too much of a favor. He needs a safe night's sleep, out of sight.'

All the while, Leo said nothing. I drove faster.

She was waiting on the sidewalk outside her high-rise condo building when I pulled up.

'I'm fine,' he managed, getting out of the Porsche.

'I'll pick you up tomorrow,' I said. 'We'll have lunch. We'll talk.'

He nodded, uncertain. Endora smiled, uncertain.

I headed west to whatever waited in the night.

FOURTEEN

'Rescue me, you cur.' It was Leo calling, and it was ten-thirty the next morning.

'You sound perky.' It was a relief.

'Deservedly. My swift brilliance saved your bacon.'

It had, for sure. I'd gotten home to find the furnace box in the back of the Jeep blessedly empty.

I was outside Endora's building in thirty minutes. 'Where's my Porsche?' he asked, through one of the newer rips in the passenger-side plastic curtain.

'Parked in front of your bungalow. I slipped a note to Ma through the mail slot, saying you were with me.' He got in and I pulled away from the curb.

'How'd you get from my place to the turret?'

'Hoofed.'

'At four in the morning?'

'The hookers were home; the cops were drunk. There was no one to notice.'

He turned to look at the cut-down furnace box lying collapsed in the back. 'The box is still there.'

'You emptied it.'

'Residual DNA. Get rid of it, you idiot.' He closed his eyes.

I am an orphan, of sorts – the product of a Norwegian sailor who might have been named Elstrom and an unstable high-school sophomore who'd taken off the day after I was born. Her three older sisters raised me haphazardly, passing me among themselves, bungalow to bungalow, a month at a time.

Diminutive Leo Brumsky had been the one towering pillar in my life, growing up. He latched onto me in seventh grade, on a day when an aunt had again forgotten to pack me a sandwich. He brought me home for lunch, and from then on the three Brumskys: an always silent, rarely seen Pa; irrepressible, bustling, quirky Ma; and Leo were my backstop. Whenever one of my mother's three sisters, meaning well enough but sullen about it, forgot it was her turn to get me to a doctor or to a dentist, or even to jam a sandwich into my coat pocket for lunch, the Brumskys were there. Every time. Always.

'Care to tell me where you made your disposal?' I asked.

'Kutz's,' he said. Kutz's Wienie Wagon was one of his most sacred destinations. It would be a calming place to decompress.

'Tell me everything on the way over, so you don't choke on the hot dogs,' I said.

He took a breath. 'I dropped by your place last evening. The lights were off but I figured you were home because the Jeep was there. I even dared hope you might be in bed with your delectable former—'

'Amanda and I aren't edging back together that closely.'

He sighed. 'So I gather, since I caught you rutting out in San Francisco. Anyway, I banged on your door. No answer. Banged louder. Still no answer. I started to walk down to the bench by the river, to see if you were outside, stealing better clothes from the winos dozing by the river, when I saw the box in the back of the Jeep.'

He made a vague motion at the box behind us and went on. 'You'd been bragging about getting a furnace so I figured that was it, though it looked awfully small. And like I said, very much a target for thieves. When I didn't find you by the river, I tried your door once more. Then I called you, thinking you'd fallen asleep in your La-Z-Boy. Surprise, surprise; you were in California, yelling at me to get the hell away from the Jeep.' He managed half a smile. 'That piqued my interest, of course. I peeled back one of the many pieces of silver tape holding your rear window together, reached in and pulled back the top flap of the box.'

'Get to it, Leo; what did you do?' He was taking such a long time.

'There was a large plastic bag inside, done up at the top with a twist-tie.' He took another deep breath. 'There was a smell, Dek, even through the bag. Still, to be sure, I undid it.' He shuddered. 'I felt hair; oh, jeez, I felt hair. You were in trouble, big time, and I could help. Since I keep the turret key you gave me in my glove box, I let myself in and got your spare Jeep key from the hook in your kitchen. I was thinking clearly; I was in control. I would drive far out to the woods, unload the cargo – minus the box, of course, which maybe had your name on it – and get rid of whatever was meant to burn you.'

He slumped back in the seat and closed his eyes. He needed a break. We drove the rest of the way without speaking.

At Rivertown, I turned onto the old river road that led down to the viaduct. Kutz has been selling hot dogs in a trailer down there for more than half a century.

We drove onto the rutted ground, long bereft of gravel, that Kutz offers as a parking lot. Leo gasped. He'd turned to look at the river beyond the trailer.

A white Cook County sheriff's car was parked down by the Willahock. Ordinarily, that wouldn't have been a surprise. Cops, too, liked Kutz's lukewarm hotdogs and soggy French fries.

Not this day. The two deputies weren't at the picnic tables; they were standing close to the water, looking down at the branches, empty anti-freeze jugs and other trash trapped along the bank.

Normally pale, Leo's face had gone faintly green. Big beads of sweat had popped up on his forehead. 'Oh, jeez.'

I focused on pulling to an easy stop well away from the trailer. 'Please tell me the woods where you dumped the bag were far from here, Leo.'

He jerked around to look at me, his eyes wild and wide. 'We've got to get out of here!'

'And draw attention to ourselves? No chance. We're going to stay and eat like nothing is wrong.'

'I thought he'd be long gone by now, way downriver,' he said, apparently meaning the previous passenger in my Jeep.

'We'll be calm. We'll eat; we'll leave.'

'You can't imagine,' he said, his words coming high and fast, 'driving with a corpse jammed behind my head. I was heading to the forest preserve east of us, in Chicago, but I swear he grunted every time I hit a bump. I freaked. All I could think was getting rid of the body. I swung in here, backed down to the water, opened the rear door and slid—'

'Being careful to not pull out the box with it,' I said, trying to sound approving, 'because it had my name on it?'

'See? I was thinking clearly. I slid the plastic bag out of the box and pushed it into the river.'

'Right where those deputies are standing?' I asked.

He moaned. 'That would be the exact spot.'

'You saw the bag sink?'

'It didn't.' His voice had risen even more. 'It bobbed; the poor bastard bobbed like he was in a balloon. Body gases, maybe. Oh, jeez.' He wiped at the saliva on his lips. 'I told myself he'd bounce right over the dam and be long gone by now.'

I looked down the river. Blue lights were flashing by the dam.

He'd followed my eyes. 'Oh, jeez,' he said again.

'Oh, jeez indeed,' I said.

FIFTEEN

'We really, really can't be here,' he said as I got out. 'We're innocents, here for hot dogs. You're going to consume your usual load.'

'No chance,' he said, but he did get out.

'Find us a table before people start to stare.'

He shot me a contemptuous look, for no one was sitting at the pigeon-strafed picnic tables. They'd carried their lunches to the Willahock and were lined up like crows on a telephone wire, watching the blue lights flashing down by the dam. And turning, occasionally, to glance at the two sheriff's deputies just a hundred yards away, inspecting the river bank for marks.

My cell phone rang as I walked up to the peeling trailer. It was Jenny. 'What's shakin'?' she asked.

'I can't talk,' I said.

'Bad?'

'Manageable.' It was more wish than truth.

'Call when you can,' she said, and clicked off.

Young Kutz lowered his grizzled gray head to see beneath the greasy film on the order window. 'The midget can't order for himself, Dickweed?' he asked, watching Leo sit at a table.

There was nothing young, or nice, about Kutz. He was on the wrong side of eighty and had seen little good along the way. Certainly there was little good in the food he served up. His hot dogs weren't hot and his carbonated drinks had long lost their fizzle, but Leo and I had been eating there since we were kids, and that made it good enough for us.

'Leo needs to sit down,' I said. 'His bowels knotted up as we drove in. They sensed the age of the grease surrounding this place and knew they were going to be punished.' With Kutz, it was best to battle charm with charm.

He looked over at Leo, sitting with his back turned resolutely to the river, glaringly uncurious. 'He don't want to know what's going on?'

'Obviously there's been a drowning.'

'Possible floater,' he said, squirting a small cardboard tray of shiny red fries with the yellow stuff he passed off as liquefied cheese. I'd tried one of Kutz's special barbecue cheese fries once and could only hope the yellow stuff was disinfectant, but Leo loved them.

'Possible floater? No one's sure?' I asked.

'Someone saw a big black garbage bag banging against the dam, all blowed up, maybe from rotting inside.' Kutz slid the cracked plastic tray under the order window, with effort. The counter has been sticky for years.

Leo looked away as I set down the tray and took my hot dog and diet cola. I'd bought his usual six hotdogs, barbecue cheese fries and the forty-eight ounce cup of semi-fizzed root beer that too strongly resembled the faintly bubbling water in the often fermenting Willahock River.

'Eat,' I said.

'Can't.'

'Then turn around and pretend you're interested in what everyone else is looking at down the river.'

He picked up a hot dog instead. It was an achievement of sorts. The two sheriff's deputies left the riverbank and walked up to the order window.

'They gave up,' I said. 'I'll bet the ground is too hard to find tire marks.'

He nodded. In the instant I'd looked away he'd finished the first hot dog at his usual warp speed. 'So tell me,' he asked, his voice stronger as he picked up a second, 'how does a body happen to get stuffed in your Jeep?'

No doubt there was something restorative in Kutz's grease, or perhaps in the secret red and yellow squirtable substances that were dissolving his fries. Leo had been resurrected and was looking at me now, normal and curious about the latest mess I'd gotten myself into.

I started with Rosamund Reynolds, told him of my futile search for Gary Halvorson, the demise of David Arlin and the purportedly traveling Dainsto Runney.

'You think the preacher's the one I dumped in the river?'

'Him, or Halvorson, since Arlin's dead in Laguna Beach, for sure.' I picked up my own hot dog and felt my youth in its reliable chill.

'Why would the Reynolds woman want to get you arrested for murder?' His eyes were unblinking. For sure, he was back in control.

'I'm easy. I'm broke enough to work anywhere for a few thousand dollars and still tainted enough by the Evangeline Wilts trial to get readily blamed for something new and nasty. I like that explanation better than thinking that it's personal, that someone's really got it in for me.'

'You'll go back to the day-rate office where you met the Reynolds woman?'

'I'll start there but I'll be unable to trace her. She was too careful covering her real identity.'

'And then?'

'I don't know. I'm not ready to risk going to Oregon, for fear of also getting linked to Dainsto Runney, especially if he's met a bad end here. The bank where Rosamund got the cashier's check won't tell me anything.' I nodded downriver. 'The best I can do now is wait to see what pops up.'

He winced at my word play. 'Any chance the police from Tucson or Laguna Beach will ask the Rivertown coppers to pick you up for questioning?' By now, red sauce and yellow cheese encircled his ample lips like clown's make-up, but the set of his mouth was dead serious.

'I didn't leave my name in Tucson. I left a card with a lieutenant in the Laguna Beach police but I was careful to come across as a plausible insurance man, merely following up on Arlin's policy.'

'But . . .?' He let the question dangle, unfinished.

'That parcel left in my Jeep was only the first round. Someone, likely Rosamund, wants me tagged for murder. She'll figure out a way to try again.'

He'd started to nod glumly when a small ruckus rose among the people standing by the river. Several were pointing toward the dam. I got up and tried to look casual as I walked down to join them. Four flashing red lights had joined the blue ones.

An ambulance had arrived.

Someone had indeed popped up.

SIXTEEN

Even Rivertown cops know to scrutinize whoever shows up when a body is discovered, in case one might be an offender, so I pushed away any thought of going right down to the dam. I dropped Leo at his bungalow and headed into the city, to the building where I'd met Rosamund Reynolds. My footsteps echoed alone in the empty, glossy halls. Like before, it was a slow day for temporary rentals.

The lock on the office she'd used popped easily with a credit card. A good lock wasn't necessary; no one left anything in a day rental.

Except for the desk chair being returned to its rightful place behind the desk, the office was the same – spartan and anonymous, empty and ready for anyone who needed a space for a day to impress. Or to fool.

The management office was at the rear of the first floor. A pert young woman in her mid-twenties sat behind a glossy white desk.

'I had an appointment with a woman in Two-Ten but no one's answering my knock,' I said.

She frowned, and then keyed something into the small computer on her desk. 'No one is using that space today,' she said after a moment.

'I met Rosamund Reynolds there just a few days ago.'

She smiled. 'The offices on the second floor are for short-term rental. Miss Reynolds is not currently renting.'

'It's about insurance,' I said. 'She's owed some money.' I looked around as though I were afraid someone else was listening. 'Actually, she's owed a great deal of money.'

'I'm not surprised,' the young thing said. 'It was obvious that she'd recently lost a loved one.'

'Pardon me?'

'Her voice was rough, from crying.'

I nodded, remembering the hoarse voice. It could have been affected, a contrivance.

'The black clothes and hat, the veil . . .'

'She wore a veil?'

'Black lace. Old fashioned, huh?'

Rosamund had taken no chances in disguising herself when renting the office, though for me all she'd needed was bright backlighting from the sun.

'I don't suppose anyone accompanied her to help with the wheelchair?' I asked.

'She managed by herself, poor dear.'

'Even in the elevator? It seems too small for a wheelchair.'

She stood up. 'It meets all building codes.'

I supposed it did, and was especially suitable if one was able to fold the chair and stand to ride up. I wondered if the woman calling herself Rosamund Reynolds had needed her wheelchair only as part of her disguise. I thanked the young woman and left.

As I was about to drive away, I got a call from Lieutenant Beech in Laguna Beach.

'I'd like you to stop by,' he said.

'I'm no longer in California.'

'Back in Rivertown, Elstrom?'

'Yes.'

'Why did you come to Laguna Beach?'

'As I said, one of my carriers learned of the explosion. I was already in California. They asked me to look into the matter.'

'How long ago was the policy opened?'

Something had gone wrong with his investigation. He was no longer simply interested in the beneficiary. 'What's your interest in that, Lieutenant?'

'How long ago was the policy opened?'

'I'd have to check.'

'What's the name of the insurance company? I'll call them myself.'

'I've got to get their permission to tell—'

'Cut the crap, Elstrom. What's the name?'

'Why?'

He took a breath and spoke more calmly. 'We've become more interested in Mr Arlin's past.'

'Because . . .?'

'Because he doesn't have one, damn it. It appears Mr Arlin, one of our most respected citizens, re-invented himself with a new name when he arrived here twenty years ago. I need to know what your insurance company knows about him and I'll subpoena you to find that out.'

'Surely his ex-wife would know quite a bit.'

'She knew him as David Arlin said she had no reason to question what he'd told her of his past.'

'I'll pass this along to the insurance company,' I lied.

'Also, find out who I can talk to about the physical they gave him.'

'Any specific medical concerns?'

'Have that insurance company call me immediately,' he said.

'I'll see,' I said.

'Here's what I'm beginning to see, Elstrom: a guy who might not represent an insurance company at all, a guy who came nosing around not so coincidentally, a guy who knows one hell of a lot more than he's saying.'

'As I said, I'll see what I can do.'

I hung up. I couldn't very well tell him that my client had given me a phony name and that I had no idea as to her real identity.

Or that she was trying to frame me for killing whoever was just found bobbing in a plastic bag, down by the dam.

SEVENTEEN

B ack at the turret, I meandered casually down to the Willahock like I was intent only on savoring the rainbow of plastic debris caught in the muck and fallen branches on the opposite side. I keep my own side clean, though no one in Rivertown notices, except Leo.

Lights still flashed down by the dam, but there were only two now and they were blue. The reds belonging to an ambulance had disappeared, the body snagged and taken away. I went inside to kill an hour on the Internet until it got dark.

Several news sites reported the discovery of the body in a bag at the dam but none offered anything more. Elsewhere, there was nothing new about David Arlin or Dainsto Runney, and nothing at all about Gary Halvorson.

I crossed the hall to the would-be kitchen, put two Peeps – one green and one purple – belly to belly in the microwave and turned it on. In no time they puffed up to more than twice their size and then their round, beaked heads completely disappeared into their bloated bodies. When I shut off the microwave the inflated creatures collapsed into flat green and purple smears that came within an inch of leaking out of the gap at the bottom edge of the ill-fitting glass door. I ate what I could unstick from the bottom of the microwave. The Peeps tasted excellent and the carnage fit my mood.

By now it was dark. I drove to the dam, stopped fifty yards in front of the flashing blue lights and walked the rest of the way.

No cop was visible until I got right up to the cruiser. And even then, no cop was visible. It was Benny Fittle who sat reclined behind the steering wheel, mouth agape, eyes closed, sound asleep.

Dressed in his usual rock band T-shirt and cargo shorts, Benny clattered around Rivertown in an aged orange Ford Maverick as the town's parking enforcement officer. The town treasurer prized his PEO's productivity, for Benny didn't waste time waiting for meters to actually expire. Rather, he wrote tickets based on his intuition that they might flash red before being replenished with coins. In this manner, Benny contributed mightily to the town's coffers, and for that he was cherished.

I cleared my throat. Benny's unshaven jowls quivered but his eyes did not open. I cleared it again. This time his right eye opened, but it went first to the Dunkin' Donuts box lying on the seat beside him. Once it satisfied itself that the box was empty, the eye closed.

'Wake up, Benny,' I was forced to say.

'Huh?'

'Wake up.'

He pushed his bulk a little forward, but not upright, and gave me a powdered sugar grin. 'Hey, Mr E, what's shakin'?'

'What are you doing down here, Benny?'

'Keepin' a watch for who shows up.'

'What for?'

He yawned. 'Suspicious behavior.'

'They pull a body out?'

'Floater in a bag, pretty banged up. Nobody knows nothin' yet.'

'Then why were you assigned to watch the dam?'

'To see who shows up, like I tol' you.'

'You know your lights are flashing, right?' I asked.

He yawned again and nodded as best he could, being reclined so far back on the tilted seat.

'Those flashing lights would alert any criminal that an officer of the law was waiting, ready to pounce,' I said, though the idea of Benny pouncing on anything other than a doughnut was laughable.

He took a long moment to process my observation before summoning the energy to switch off the lights. 'Good thought, Mr E,' he said, slumping back.

'Any identification on the guy?'

'Nah,' he said. 'Just a Jane Doe.'

My mouth went dry, like it was chalked. 'A woman, Benny?' I managed. 'The floater was a woman?'

He tried to nod, gave it up and closed his eyes.

I don't think I said another word. I only remember concentrating on walking away.

EIGHTEEN

Leo called me at seven the next morning, out of breath and half out of his mind. He was yelling something about the *Argus-Observer*'s website. The *Argus-Observer* was the cheesiest of Chicago's gossip rags and the fastest at reporting the city's most torrid news.

'Speak slowly,' I said. I was half out of my mind, too, but it was from worrying most of the night that the corpse stuffed in my Jeep had been my client and that I wouldn't figure out who was coming at me until it was too late.

'The body they found in the Willahock . . .'

'A woman,' I said. I stuck legs into jeans, arms into a sweatshirt and beat it down barefoot to the second floor to switch on my computer. 'They have a name?'

He spoke a name too fast for me to understand.

'Who?' I asked.

'Marilyn Paul.'

I didn't know the name. I told him I'd call him back in an hour. The *Argus-Observer* website had come up. In its usual big point type, the headline screamed loud: BAGGED BABE BOBBER SLASHED!

Underneath was a grainy black-and-white photo of the dam and beside it Rivertown's own Benny Fittle lounging against the hood of a police cruiser. The picture had been taken when the body was first discovered, when it was still daylight and there were still doughnuts. His mouth was closed but his cheeks bulged; he'd been snapped mid-chew. Surprisingly often, the *Argus-Observer*'s photographer caught the essence of any given moment.

The short paragraph that followed was written in the *Argus-Observer*'s typical, terse, details-to-follow style. The sheriff's police theorized that Marilyn Paul, fifty-four and wrapped in a large black plastic bag, had been dumped into the river somewhere east of the Rivertown dam and was carried downstream. The police were investigating. The county's medical examiner was examining. Cause of death was preliminarily thought to have been from a slashed throat. Details to follow.

Google had fourteen listings for Marilyn Paul. Only the *Argus-Observer* reported her death, which wasn't surprising since Chicago's other news sites insisted on double-checking stories for accuracy before posting them. The other thirteen were old mentions of her full-time, professional political work for the Democratic Party, most memorably as a call center manager during the Illinois gubernatorial campaign that elected the mop-haired jackass who was now doing time in a federal prison.

There was one picture of her, taken at a gathering of former workers from that campaign. Two dozen of them, loyal Democrats to a fault, had drafted a letter requesting leniency at an appeal of the mop-head's sentence. The men were done up well in conservative dark business suits and reasonable neckwear. The woman were done up even better, in bright dresses and glittering jewelry. By the tight look on most of the faces, the event had the frivolity of a wake.

Marilyn Paul was round-faced and had brown, softly spiked hair. She wore a blue business suit, a white blouse, no jewelry and projected no nonsense. She was the only attendee who had not forced a smile for the camera.

I tried to imagine a gray wig, lots of thick makeup, tinted large glasses and cheeks puffed with cotton. It could have been her in that day-rate office. Or it could have been any other woman, disguised just as heavily, backlit so blindingly in such a bright sun.

What I couldn't imagine was why such a woman would have obscured her identity to hire me.

And whether someone had wanted to kill her for that.

NINETEEN

Prairie Hill had sat, mostly unchanged, for a hundred years alongside the railroad tracks that ran northwest out of Chicago. Most people knew the small burg only as a blur to blow through on their way to weekends on the Chain O'Lakes along the Wisconsin border.

Not me. I knew Prairie Hill better. Amanda and I had stopped several times at the Dairy Queen there, summers when we used to go boating on Lake Marie. Those days, I was a magnificent blur of my own, breezing in my stick-shift Jeep while consuming cherry-dipped, double scoop, soft-serve chocolate ice cream. Only once did I launch the ice cream from the cone, and then only because a fresh pothole appeared unfairly out of nowhere. Fortunately, little was lost. The glob of ice cream had lingered, stuck to the windshield, long enough to be mostly retrieved by my smooth and swift upward scoop of the cone, leaving only a smear of cherry and chocolate, which I removed within days. Amanda was enchanted by my dexterity.

I was headed now to Prairie Hill to talk to Lena Jankowski, a woman standing next to Marilyn Paul in one of the photos taken at the mop-headed jackass's leniency petition gathering. I'd called, saying I had an urgent matter to discuss that involved one of her fellow campaign workers. She asked which one. I said Marilyn Paul. She asked if I were a cop. I said no. She said she didn't know Marilyn well, that she'd been a volunteer and Marilyn was a career professional. I said anything would help. She said I could come to her home, but only for a few minutes. I said yes.

She lived four blocks behind the Dairy Queen in a white clap-board single-story house on a block of identical small white houses. That sort of lapsed architectural imagination reminded me of Rivertown, though the unvarying bungalows where I grew up were gloomier, made of brown brick darkened even further when the factories were alive and pumping soot into the sky. Prairie Hill looked to have a more vibrant pulse. Her block was littered with tricycles and small plastic wagons, the stuff of a new generation keeping the town alive. An oversized child's white plastic baseball bat lay on the lawn next door.

I recognized Lena easily when she came to the screen door. She was in her early forties, younger than Marilyn. She wore her dark hair short, and that reminded me of Amanda, as so many women did.

'Insurance investigator, really?' she asked, opening the door to take my card but remaining inside.

'Regarding Marilyn Paul, as I said when I phoned.'

'I'll go along with this, but you'd have to tell me if you're a cop, right?'

It was myth; cops lied about not being cops all the time. 'I suppose, but I'm not a cop,' I said anyway.

'Marilyn is dead,' she said, watching my face. 'They just found her in the Willahock River, in Rivertown, where you live.'

She'd checked me out, so easy in the Google age. 'Yes,' I said.

'What do you know about her death?' she asked, her eyes still steady on mine.

'Not enough. It's why I'm here,' I said.

'You didn't say who you're working for.'

'I can't divulge that.' It sounded smarter than saying I wasn't sure. 'I saw a picture of you and Marilyn on the Internet, taken when you were petitioning to get the ex-governor's sentence reduced.'

'Last May,' she said.

'Rocky evening?'

'The man we helped elect turned out to be corrupt. Even so, his fourteen-year sentence was excessive.'

'You knew Marilyn long before that?'

'We met on Delman Bean's congressional campaign twenty years ago.'

'Delman Bean?' I remembered the name vaguely.

'He lost, narrowly. He should have won, narrowly.'

'How did she seem last May?'

'She acted normal, which is to say testy and self-righteous. To her, being a Democrat was holy work. Our ex-governor violated her sense of ethics.'

'Do you know this man?' I pulled out an Internet photo of David Arlin taken in Laguna Beach.

She reached out to take the photo and studied it for a full minute before passing it back. 'The caption calls him David Arlin.'

'You know him?'

'That's John Shea, not David Arlin. And that's troubling.'

'Why?'

'Because two weeks ago Marilyn called, asking about the whereabouts of two other musketeers. I sort of keep track of the old gang, updating addresses when they bother to let me know.'

'Other musketeers?'

'We called them the Four Musketeers – four young guys that volunteered on the Delman Bean campaign. They hung out together. John Shea was one of them.'

'Was Gary Halvorson another?'

Her eyes narrowed. 'What are you here for, really?'

'I'll tell you when I'm sure.'

She considered it for a moment and nodded. 'Yes, Red was one of them.'

'Red?'

'Everybody called him that because of his hair. I told Marilyn I get a Christmas card from him every year. He lives in Tucson.'

'How about Dainsto Runney?'

'Who?'

'Just another name on my list. Who was the other musketeer Marilyn asked about?'

'Willard Piser. He went west with the others. The three of them – John, Red and Willard – got huge paying jobs working on an oil rig on the west coast. Apparently that fell apart almost right away. Red sent me a Christmas card from Tucson a few weeks later and Willard went to Oregon.'

'You have an address for Willard Piser?'

'Nothing so specific. Willard had been sweet on one of the girls in the campaign and sent her a Valentine's Day card three months after he left. The girl saw it was from Oregon by the postmark. He'd written no return address.' Then she asked, 'Why would John Shea change his name?'

I couldn't answer that, like I couldn't tell her my gut was sure that Willard Piser had changed his to Dainsto Runney. All I was sure of now was that Marilyn Paul had pressed Lena for information about Halvorson, Shea, and Piser, and then, as Rosamund Reynolds, she'd hired me to find out more.

'You said there were four musketeers? Who was the fourth?'

She smiled. 'He didn't have to head west. He didn't need money. He was Tim Wade.'

Timothy Wade, dubbed the Grain Man by many in the press: the candidate who'd fled a skeleton in a silo.

'It's a shame, him freaking out like that,' she said. 'He's such a sweet guy.' She stared at me through the screen. 'Marilyn was working for him this season, you know.'

'Working for Timothy Wade?'

'His run for the senate is the most important Democratic race this fall. She was assigned to manage his call center. It's in Chicago, on the west side.' Then she asked, 'That couldn't have anything to do with Marilyn's death?'

I told her I'd be in touch.

She told me she didn't believe me.

I told her that was probably wise and walked down to the Jeep.

TWENTY

His name was Anton Chernek but everyone referred to him – often whispering – as the Bohemian. I called him from the Jeep. As always, he said he'd see me right away. And, as always, I was amazed. Except for Chicago's mayor, certain top-tier titans of local industry like my ex-wife and a smattering of big-name philanthropists, also like my ex-wife, few were allowed to drop in on the Bohemian. He was a counselor to the area's elite, the go-to man when things got too dicey, embarrassing or tragic for normal retainers. And, ever since my divorce, a counselor to me, whenever I plummeted into a big-time jam.

It was only midday but traffic heading into the city was jammed on the too-narrow expressway. It's like that in Chicago. Millions of dollars get approved to improve things but the 'things' – the roadways, elevated train lines and schools – rarely get improved as much as the bulges in the pockets of the shiny-lipped supplicants that move in the shadows of Chicago's city hall.

The Bohemian knew all about that. He knew about the things that happen in the dark of Chicago, the gray of the Cook County that surrounds the city like a greasy collar and the murk of the entire state beyond that. He knew who moved, he knew who shook and he knew who trembled. He'd know Timothy Wade.

His offices were on the top floor of a ten-story yellow-brick factory rehab in a trendy outskirt of Chicago's Loop. Riding up in the elevator, I glanced down at my clothes – the rumpled khakis, blue button down shirt, and blue blazer that have been my uniform since my life went to hell after the Evangeline Wilts trial – and thought of the time, not so very long before, when I'd ridden up in that same elevator wearing the same uniform, except that day I was smeared with blood and likely to be accused of murder. The Bohemian had taken efficient charge of me. He'd hustled me into a private conference room, dispatched someone for fresh clothing and called the city's best criminal defense lawyer. I'd walked out of the Bohemian's office three hours later sporting a much-calmed outlook and better duds than I'd ever owned before.

Now I was returning, likely to be accused of murder again. It was just like old, damned times.

The elevator opened into a dimly lit reception area of reassuringly creased old green leather, dim lamps and earnest young portfolio and fund representatives anxious to have an audience with one of the people who reported to one of the people who reported to the Bohemian. Because of the high quality of its client list, Chernek and Associates was the most prominent unknown financial management firm in Chicago. If I'd had a net worth beyond what I just invested in a brand new furnace I'd have tried to hire them.

The receptionist was new, and like all of her predecessors was young, taut and tanned. The Bohemian had an eye for perfect assembly, as did his most discerning clients. His receptionists got hired away regularly to adorn other fine reception desks, and always with the Bohemian's blessing. It was simply another of his services to the city's elite.

Chernek's long-time executive assistant came for me in an instant. Helmet-haired and creased as deeply as the leather in the reception area, she was less of an adornment than a barbed necessity. She wore a dark navy suit buttoned all the way up to her neck and the grim countenance of someone who might have just buried Jimmy Hoffa with a small shovel without so much as smudging a knuckle. Her name, preposterously, was Buffy, and that was the only giggle she offered the world. She marched ahead of me to the executive offices, tapped on the jamb of the open door in the corner and faded backward toward the cubicles, all without giving me a flicker of recognition or a single word.

The Bohemian was resplendent, as usual. His shirt was pale lemon, the tie navy and subtly patterned to perfectly complement his chalk-striped gray suit. Every silver hair on his head was brushed neatly back and his tanned skin spoke of a summer spent on the most expensive fairways in northern Illinois.

'Vuh-lo-dek!' he pronounced from behind his mahogany desk,

elongating the two syllables of my Bohemian first name – Vlodek – into three. As much as I found the name irritating he saw it as evidence of our being kindred ethnic, if not financial, spirits. He pointed to one of the burgundy leather guest chairs.

'Someone is trying to frame me for murder,' I said.

'Marilyn Paul's?'

It wasn't a surprise. 'You do stay informed, Anton.'

He smiled, though not as broadly as I would have expected, having made such an accurate guess. 'Given that the woman was found in the Willahock, just downriver from your, ah, circular abode, it seemed possible I might hear from you.'

'And when I called . . .?'

'It could have heightened my self-regard,' he said, but his eyes didn't crinkle with amusement. Something else was going on behind them.

'Somebody alerted you,' I said.

He smiled more broadly. It must have been Amanda, the only client of his that would have cared.

'Marilyn Paul, heavily disguised and calling herself Rosamund Reynolds, might have hired me. It was an odd assignment—'

'Aren't they all, with you?'

'It paid two thousand dollars up front to look in on the situations of three men in Arizona, California and Oregon. The men in Arizona and Oregon have disappeared. The man in Laguna Beach, who changed his name to David Arlin, also disappeared but into fragments when his house blew up. I passed myself off as representing Arlin's insurance carrier to the cops out there. It was a mistake. They want to know the details of the mythical insurance policy, which does not exist, including medical records. Apparently they have questions about the corpse.'

'You've tangled yourself up in quite a web.'

'I thought, for a time, that Marilyn Paul, if it was Marilyn Paul, hired me to take the rap for one or more of their murders.' I slumped deeper in his chair. 'I changed my mind when she got stuffed in the back of my Jeep, dead, while I was out in California.'

'You did the transfer to the river cleanly?' The Bohemian was never indelicate.

'Yes.' There was no sense in mentioning Leo's involvement.

He sensed it anyway. 'Someone else helped?'

'Someone who can be trusted.'

'No idea who is trying to frame you?'

'None.'

I told him of going to see Lena Jankowski. 'David Arlin's real name is John Shea. The man in Oregon, perhaps born Willard Piser but passing now as Dainsto Runney, is a man of God, or maybe he's just a hustler in a sham church. He's either in the wind like Halvorson or dead like Arlin. As for Halvorson, he's the only one of the three who never changed his name. He's simply lived underground for as far back as I can find out.'

'These three – they're linked, how?' he asked.

'They were friends, part of a quartet calling themselves musketeers, working on the congressional campaign of a man named Delman Bean. They quit the campaign to take oil rig jobs out west, though I don't think those jobs ever really materialized.'

'Your client, perhaps Marilyn Paul, knew all this before hiring you, of course?'

'As would the fourth of those old musketeers, Timothy Wade.'

'The candidate for US Senate?' he asked. His well-tanned forehead had not wrinkled. He was masking his surprise. 'I suppose you're here to ask me to arrange a meeting with him?'

'He can explain the links between the other three.'

'I can't set that up.'

I knew enough to not ask if Wade was one of his clients. 'Because he's still avoiding personal contact with everyone after that barnyard meltdown?'

He nodded. 'His sister has put out the word that it's a matter of his personal safety.'

'His sister?'

'Theresa Wade is directing the campaign and she wants him protected until they find out who planted those plastic bones and rubber hatchet in the silo.'

'They were plastic and rubber, not real?'

'Harmless for sure, but a real threat all the same.' His eyebrows arched. 'You know, of course, who's gotten close to the Wade campaign?'

'You're referring to one particular member of his Committee of Twenty-Four?'

'Two dozen very influential people he assembled to serve as an advisory committee. Their financial contributions are large, but their concerns and hopes are also considered respectfully. That one particular member might be able to arrange such a meeting.'

'I won't ask her.'

He nodded, approving. He was always on full alert for anything that might threaten Amanda. She'd been a client of his since the moment she was born, because of her father.

'She can't be involved,' I said. 'Do you know anyone other than the Wades who might remember the Delman Bean campaign from twenty years ago?'

'I might know just the man.'

My cell phone rang while I was driving back to the turret.

It was Lieutenant Beech from Laguna Beach. 'You live on the Willahock River in Rivertown,' he said, right off.

'Come out sometime. We'll fish for trash.'

He didn't laugh. 'And corpses. A woman was just found downriver from you.'

'Don't believe everything you find on the Internet. Floaters are rare.'

'I'm close to having you picked up for questioning.'

'I'm working on the insurance records,' I lied.

'You'd better hurry.'

'Why?'

'A television reporter from San Francisco is getting interested in this case. Before she can embarrass me I'll feed you to your local cops to sweat you for things you won't tell me. Play ball, Elstrom.' He clicked me away.

My cell phone rang again, just a minute later.

'Dek Elshtrom?' a woman slurred.

'Who's this?' I asked, like I didn't know.

'Bipshie,' she said, with a gin-swollen tongue. 'Howsh our sishters?'

'Going great,' I said 'I just found another one.'

'Whatsh her name?'

'Bipsie,' I said.

'Schwell,' she slurred. Her phone clattered and went dead.

I wanted to laugh but I was too worried about who was still out there, building a new frame to hang around my neck.

I called Jenny's cell phone. 'Beech from the Beach just called. You were going to call me right after you talked to him.'

'And you were going to let me know what was going on as soon as you got back to Rivertown,' she countered. 'It was a woman found dead in your . . . in your river?' she said, catching herself before she said 'Jeep.' 'The story's in the Chicago papers. It's fair game for all reporters now.'

'No one knows the things I told you.'

'Except the killer.' She sighed. 'Don't worry, I got nothing from Laguna Beach. The good Lieutenant Beech was very tight-lipped. He told me to contact their press officer and hung up.'

'Did you?'

'I called back. They don't have one.'

'He keeps pressing me for the name of Arlin's supposed insurance company. He wants medical records. Something's wrong with the corpse.'

'I should poke around?'

'Use your wiles, discreetly.'

'Ah, those wiles,' she said, dropping her voice. And then she, too, hung up on me.

TWENTY-ONE

I swung by Leo's ma's bungalow. Leo knew I knew the Bohemian and he'd relax more knowing Chernek was involved, if only peripherally. The Bohemian could fix so many things.

No one answered my knock. I called him from the curb.

'Give me good news,' he said tersely, amid thunderous whoops and shrieks that sounded like kids playing in a cave.

'Let's not talk on the phone. Where are you?'

'Health club.'

'You've joined a health club? Exercise is good for stress.'

'Not me. Ma and her friends won free memberships at bingo.'

'Free? Where, Leo . . .?' An ugly thought reared up like a stallion spooked by a snake. 'Certainly not in Rivertown,' I ventured, needing to be wrong.

'It's free,' he repeated, with what sounded like defensiveness amid the background whoops.

I paused to think the unthinkable, that he'd brought his own mother to the Rivertown Health Center. Built decades earlier, when young Christian men, new to town, needed cheap rooms, Rivertown's YMCA was disenfranchised for filth, locker-room theft and drunken inhabitants even before the last of the town's manufacturing companies toppled to foreign competition.

The lizards that ran Rivertown wanted the land. They seized the property, much as they'd seized my grandfather's, but when they found the building too expensive to demolish they dubbed it a health center and kept it running on a shoestring, though those few seeking exercise were far outnumbered by the welfare winos living upstairs and the hoodlums lounging in the parking lot. The health center was no place to bring Leo's septuagenarian mother and her friends.

'The lizards can get federal funding if this place qualifies as a rehabilitation center for seniors, so they're handing out free memberships,' Leo went on as I sped along Thompson Avenue toward the health center, passing the usual handful of daytime working girls, veterans all and some seriously arthritic, milling along the curb.

'Your ma will get tetanus from the rust on the equipment,' I yelled into the phone. It was why I used only the duct-taped running track that surrounded the exercise machines.

There was silence.

I thought perhaps he hadn't heard. 'Leo? The machines? Tetanus?'

By now, I'd gotten to the parking lot. I shifted the transmission down into low four-wheel drive, the hill-climbing gear, to creep over the potholes. Leo's Porsche was nowhere to be seen but a brand-new silver Dodge Ram window van with a temporary handicapped card was parked in the restricted zone.

'No worry,' he said. The odd echoes in his background remained deafening and confusing. The fitness room had never sounded like a cave to me.

An impossible thought flared into my head as I came to a stop in my usual spot next to the doorless Buick. 'Not the pool, Leo. You didn't put your mother in the pool.'

'They assured us it's been power-washed,' he said, adding, 'three times.'

I paused only for a second to make sure the Jeep's doors were unlocked, in case the younger hoodlums – the thumpers – needed to verify they'd already boosted my radio, and hurried inside. Three residents lounged on the torn vinyl chairs in the lobby, filling the portal to health and fitness with blue cigarette smoke. I hustled past them and down the stairs with my phone still pressed to my ear.

'They didn't just use Lysol and bleach,' Leo was saying. 'Industrial etching acids, too.' He sounded proud of what he'd not overlooked.

No amount of Lysol, bleach and acids could eradicate the memory of why the pool had been closed ten years earlier. One of the upstairs residents had gone missing. No one thought much of it; residents often wandered off and were usually found semi-upright near one of the town's liquor stores, asleep on one of benches along the Willahock or propped up against my turret. But this one particular fellow remained missing for a full week, until at last a hardy swimmer, having lost his goggles, dove deeper into the pool's murky water to retrieve them and touched something soft. It was the missing resident, spongy but mostly intact. Wags said he died of malaria.

The county health department made the town's lizards drain the pool and for ten years it remained dry, if not particularly clean. But now, according to Leo, there was an opportunity for federal tax dollars if they filled it back up. The lizards always seized opportunities, even when they were legal.

'Aren't you concerned the locker room attendant is rifling their purses?' I was just a few feet from the pool door now.

'*Au contraire*,' he said, slipping into French, a language he does not know. 'I'm watching the purses.'

And so he was. Looking through the glass door, I saw Leo sitting on a folding chair in front of a row of purses lined against the wall. Water was puddled at his feet. I opened the door and went in.

'Welcome to my world,' he said with no trace of a smile.

'Where's your Porsche?'

'At home, in the garage. Ma made me buy a stretch van to bring the ladies here to get healthy,' he said, with no trace of irony on his face. He motioned for me to grab the stool next to the door.

I brought it over, sat down and looked around. There was no lifeguard.

'There's no lifeguard,' I said, observantly.

'That's another reason I'm here.'

Six gray heads bobbed in the water as a seventh – Ma's octogenarian friend, Mrs Roshiska – pulled herself up on the ladder beneath the diving board, grabbed her wheeled walker and began pushing it toward the board. Her one-piece black bathing suit was wool and looked to have been enjoyed more than once by hordes of moths. Dime-sized spots of puckered white flesh protruded everywhere.

'She's not going to dive . . .' I let the thought dangle.

'Oh, but she is.'

It took Mrs Roshiska five excruciating minutes to negotiate the twenty feet to the diving board. When she got alongside it, she threw her walker at her friends in the water, rolled her ample belly onto the diving board and began crawling toward the end of the board. Five feet from the end, she pushed herself up to a shaky standing. The whole process wanted to trigger thoughts of the moment ancient life first slithered from the sea.

'She might fall, Leo.'

'Time to retreat,' he said, getting to his feet. I didn't understand, but I moved backward to the purses.

'Now, behold the transformative power of youthful exuberance,' he said.

Mrs Roshiska staggered the last few feet to the end of the board, bounced up with startling power, grabbed her knees and executed a perfect cannonball into the water. A huge wave shot over the edge of the pool.

The gray heads in the pool shouted, elated. Leo clapped, grinning for the first time since I'd come in. I did, too. Mrs Roshiska's head rose above the surface to cheers.

Leo motioned for us to bring our seats forward again. His grin had faded. 'Any news?'

Another gray head appeared at the side of the pool, tossed Mrs Roshiska's walker up onto the tile and climbed up the ladder.

'That's a man,' I said, surprised. I'd assumed all the swimmers were Ma's lady friends.

'Say nothing.'

The aged gent pulled himself out of the water and began walking on stiff-kneed legs toward the diving board.

'He's not wearing a suit,' I whispered.

Leo nodded.

'Can't they see?' I asked, gesturing at the women in the pool.

'They invite him because he's forgetful.'

'Surely they're not optimistic?'

'Who knows what aquatic exercise might revive?'

The old gent made it up to the board, walked to the end and belly-flopped off the edge. He hit the water perfectly flat.

'Ouch,' I said.

'At his age, it probably doesn't matter . . .' He let the thought fade away. Too many lines had formed around his eyes. 'Who the hell is Marilyn Paul, Dek?'

'A full-time Democratic worker,' I said. I told him about my trip to Prairie Hill.

'That's all you know?'

'The three men that Marilyn Paul, if it was Marilyn Paul, hired me to look up were friends. They worked together on a congressional primary twenty years ago with Timothy Wade.'

'The Grain Man?'

'Yes, indeed.'

'How is that relevant?'

'I don't know.'

'I shouldn't have dumped her into the Willahock.'

'Not dumped, Leo; relocated to keep me from getting charged with her murder.' Then, 'I went to see the Bohemian this morning.'

His face relaxed, but only a little. 'How can he help?'

'I'm hoping he'll put me in front of someone who knows about that congressional campaign.'

There was faster movement in the pool. The ladies had swum up to surround the naked man, hands alternating between flailing to stay afloat and stabbing beneath the surface. I looked away from the roiling water. The swim party was getting ugly.

'Have fun,' I said, standing up.

'Did you get rid of the box? Cadaver dogs can smell the faintest trace of decomposed human remains.'

'I'll burn it when I get back,' I said.

And so I'd planned.

TWENTY-TWO

I'm still surprised at my luck in spotting it at all, that barest pinpoint of a flashlight aimed so briefly inside my Jeep. It was two in the morning and three stories below my bedroom window. If I'd been looking in any other direction, or simply not gotten out of bed, I'd have missed it.

I'd lain awake for hours, dancing worries in the darkness. Marilyn Paul's killer had known to leave her dead in my Jeep to get me blamed for her murder. He'd found a file, or notes, that had my name on them. Or maybe she'd kept a copy of the check she'd given me. Whatever it was, it had been enough for her killer to plot to point the cops at me.

I worried, too, about how it all would affect Amanda. She'd been tough enough to survive my falsified document scandal and her father's murder, but she was on new turf now – moneyed turf. High stakes, big business, accountable-to-stockholders turf. Surely she could do without being linked to an ex-husband accused of murder.

At some point in the night, I decided I might thrash more efficiently standing up, in front of the microwave, nuking a Peep or two. I got out of bed and, as is always my habit, I went first to look out the window.

The pinpoint of light darted about for only a few seconds inside the Jeep, and for those seconds I wasn't worried. Someone poking around inside would find only Burger King wrappers, my gym duffel and a rats' nest of loose wires from the ripped-out radio.

And the box, I realized, in the next heart-thudding moment – the cut-down, folded-up furnace box I'd forgotten to destroy. A box that surely contained some last bit of Marilyn Paul's DNA. And mine. And likely Leo's.

Now someone had come, most likely a cop, tipped to the existence of the box by someone keeping an eye on the turret. Stupid, stupid me.

Unless the visitor was not a cop but Marilyn Paul's killer.

I slipped on jeans, a sweatshirt and running shoes, and went down the wrought-iron stairs in the dark to the first floor. I am no hero. I was not about to charge out to confront a prowler. Nor was I anxious to converse with a cop. I peeked out the window closest to the Jeep. For a moment I saw nothing, but then a vague shape moved away from the Jeep and started hurrying toward the short street that led to Thompson Avenue.

I flipped on the outside light, a lantern-shaped affair as old as the turret, and ran out the front door. The shape of whoever was out there began running. A few instants later, headlights lit the short street. A car pulled away, too fast for me to see what kind it was. All I saw were taillights.

It was a relief, of sorts. And not. The prowler had been no cop. Rivertown detectives can't run. They're overweight from the free booze they lap up along Thompson Avenue.

That meant whoever had come in the night was there for the frame.

I opened the Jeep's tail door. The flattened furnace box was still inside; it had not been taken. I brought it inside and put a match to it in the second-floor fireplace. It caught nicely.

I went into the soon-to-be kitchen, made coffee and was about to irradiate a Peep when a new thought twisted nasty. No one but a cop would want the box. My intruder had come not to take something but to leave something behind.

I ran out into the night to paw inside the Jeep. I felt it, almost right away, in the mess of Burger King wrappers under the passenger's seat. It was an eight-inch serrated kitchen knife. I held it up to my outside light. It was covered with dried blood. Having failed to frame me with her corpse, Marilyn Paul's killer had returned with the blade that had killed her.

A blade I'd just made more incriminating with my fingerprints.

There was no time. My visitor had surely called the cops. I scooped the knife and the wrappers out from beneath the passenger seat and ran down to the Willahock. The river is wide where it passes the turret. I threw the knife as far as I could into the rapidly moving water. It splashed in the middle and sank.

I knelt to plunge the Burger King wrappers deep into the frigid muck at the shore, then released them to float free with the rest of the debris headed downriver. I grabbed more muck and rubbed it around my fingers and deep under my fingernails. Only after a full five minutes did I rinse my frozen hands in the water. Then I went inside and up to the kitchen, where I scrubbed my hands with dishwashing detergent, scalding water and a touch of bleach.

My breathing had calmed, but only a little. I'd stopped whoever was coming at me for a second time, but that worry was for later. For now, the second act was sure to play out in what was left of the night.

TWENTY-THREE

I put on my pea coat, took a travel mug of coffee up the stairs and the ladders and eased through the trapdoor out into the night. I keep a lawn chair on the roof for when things haunt too closely for sleep.

Across the spit of land, the gas was being let out of the greasy old balloon that was Thompson Avenue. The neon lights were flickering off; the cruising headlamps were speeding away. Curbside girls were wobbling home, a few bucks richer, a few hundred years older.

My night, though, had surely just begun. I pulled my pea coat tighter, sipped my coffee and waited.

Twenty minutes later, headlamps turned onto the short street off Thompson, turned again onto mine and began weaving toward the turret. Plenty of people, tipsied, used the short street and my street in the middle of the night. Frugal, last-hour johns liked them because they were dark and saved the cost of a room. And night-shift cops used them because they led to the police station, hidden at the back of Rivertown's city hall, where its pretense of law and order wouldn't give pause to the commerce of the town.

The car bumped softly to a stop against the curb below. It was a Rivertown police cruiser. Two uniformed officers pushed themselves out.

I bent over the wall and called down. 'Good evening, or perhaps it's good morning by now, gentlemen!'

'What the . . .?' one of them shouted as they both looked around, confused.

'Up here!' I saluted them with my travel mug.

They looked up to see me backlit by the moon. 'That you, Elstrom?' one called up.

I had history with the Rivertown police, going back to when I'd been briefly suspected of murdering my girlfriend at the end of high school. 'I'll be right there,' I shouted and went down the ladders and the stairs, stopping at the second floor to check the fireplace.

The cardboard had burned down nicely. Only ash remained. I continued downstairs and opened the timbered door.

'What's up?' I asked, like I didn't know.

'Cook County got a tip-off – asked us to help check it out,' the one who'd been driving almost steadily said.

'Yesh,' his partner slurred.

'Regarding?'

'Someone said you got evidence in your car about that broad floater.'

As if on cue, an unmarked police car drove up followed by a white sheriff's forensics van and a flatbed car hauler. My nighttime visitor had been persuasive, no doubt from a disposable cell phone.

A woman got out of the car and a man with a dog on a leash got out of the van. Pulling on purple plastic gloves, the man sidestepped the whiskey-misted Rivertown cops and followed the dog, straining now on its leash, directly to the Jeep. The woman came over to me. She was about forty, had short blonde hair and grim tidings on an otherwise pretty face.

'The door's open,' I called over to the man with the dog. There was no point in locking a door that had so many rips in its plastic window.

He switched on a flashlight and pulled open the door. The dog jumped up into the Jeep like it was rocket propelled and began thrashing around in frenzy. The handler tugged at the leash, trying to restrain the agitated animal. The dog snarled, desperate to be free. It took the man ten hard pulls at the leash to drag the beast out of the Jeep. He swore, slamming the door.

The blonde officer turned from the spectacle. 'You're Elstrom, of course,' she said. Behind her the dog kept on barking at the Jeep's closed door.

'And occasionally proud of it,' I said.

The two Rivertown cops, uninterested in any of the goings-on, strolled back to their cruiser and bumped their way along the curbs back to Thompson Avenue.

The flatbed driver backed up to the front of the Jeep and tilted back the bed.

'Got a warrant for my car?' I asked the woman.

'That a deal breaker?'

'Nah,' I said. If I demanded a warrant she'd simply phone someone to have one forged and delivered within the hour, it being Cook County. I gave her the key.

She walked the key over to the flatbed driver and came back, looking up toward the top of the turret. 'I smell fire,' she said.

Chains clanked as the flatbed driver began attaching them to the Jeep's bumper struts.

'I thought a fire might help me sleep,' I said. 'Want to come in and look around?'

'Probably too late, if you've had a fire. Besides, the Jeep's what we want.'

'Why is that?'

She shrugged. 'Oh, just curiosity.'

That and an anonymous telephone call, I thought.

The driver began winching the Jeep onto the flatbed. Behind him, the handler was still tugging at the dog's leash. The beast was desperate to follow the Jeep up onto the flatbed.

The blonde cop smiled. 'We'll let you know if you can have your vehicle back,' she said and headed for her car. In a moment, she, the flatbed and the van were gone.

I walked inside. The fine ash in the second-floor fireplace was stone cold but there was no doubt that things were about to get hotter.

TWENTY-FOUR

It took the Bohemian little time to find someone familiar with the congressional campaign that Marilyn Paul, Piser, Shea, Halvorson and Timothy Wade had worked on together twenty years earlier. Nor did he settle for a minor operative. He arranged for me to meet the failed candidate himself, Delman Bean, in a small anteroom at the Chicago Enterprise Club at eleven-thirty the next morning.

I had to take the train into the city because the Cook County Sheriff's Police had my Jeep. That was worrisome. Experts might well find transfer traces of Marilyn Paul's DNA in the back, where the box had been, and her blood under the front seat, left by the knife.

The train was almost empty. I sat by a window. It didn't relax my mind. The day was dark, wanting to rain. It matched my mood.

I arrived at the lobby of the Enterprise Club early. It was a place of brass elevator doors, veiny gray marble and veiny gray old men.

The former candidate rolled down the marble staircase twenty minutes late, presumably from the bar two flights up. 'I can give you five minutes,' Delman Bean said.

He was power dressed in a light gray suit, white shirt and solid purple tie, and smelled strongly of musky cologne overlaid by too much whiskey. According to the Internet, he'd used his political connections to make a fortune fronting for a road construction contractor, certainly much more than he would have gotten chiseling as a US congressman from Illinois.

'Marilyn Paul,' I said.

'So Anton told me. Bossy bitch in charge of our phone bank but not bossy enough to get out the vote.'

'John Shea, Gary Halvorson, Willard Piser.'

'Punks. They bailed on me just before the election.'

'All three at the same time?' Lena Jankowski had said merely that they'd taken jobs on an oil rig, not that they'd quit so abruptly as to leave the campaign in a lurch.

'Quit with no notice, the three of them. We'd rented vans for them to pick up old people and get them to the polls. They were reliable votes, those old people. Hell, we thought of everything, right down to putting goody bags in the vans, soft chocolate, apple sauce – the crap old people can eat. We gave our drivers routes all planned out, names and addresses of people to be picked up and when. But we didn't think of our drivers quitting so sudden, taking with them the lists of people to be driven. And there went the whole shootin' match. We didn't do much with computers back then and nobody else had the lists. We lost by a lousy five hundred votes.'

'Timothy Wade volunteered for you in that campaign?'

'And now the Wades are a shoo-in for the senate because they're worth millions and self-fund his campaign. Once in they will be solid party supporters. No worries about them.'

'You're including his sister?'

'She calls most of the shots. Reclusive, an invalid, probably half-insane from never leaving her house. But everybody says she's sharp as a tack.' He looked at his watch. He'd respected the code he shared with the Bohemian – to supply a minimum of information without asking why anyone would need it. Now he was done.

I was only beginning.

TWENTY-FIVE

The first few drops of rain fell as I ducked into Union Station. I called the Bohemian. 'You're sure I can't get in front of Timothy Wade?'

'You got nothing from Delman Bean?'

'He's angry with Marilyn Paul and jealous of Timothy Wade. But he's downright furious with Halvorson, Shea and Piser. They quit his campaign just before the election. He blames their desertion for his loss.'

'You'll never get in front of Wade.'

'Isn't staying incommunicado a big risk?'

'Especially after running scared from a toy axe and plastic bones? I would think so, but Theresa Wade knows more than I do about politics. As I said, she's passing it off as a security issue, which it probably is. And, don't forget, he's polling twenty-five points ahead of his Republican opponent. Tim Wade's your next senator.'

'Can you get me in to see the sister?'

'To discuss a twenty-year-old congressional race?' He laughed. 'I'll see if I can find someone who knows her and forward your request, but she'll say no.'

My cell phone had beeped with a missed call. I called back. A Sergeant Bohler of the Cook County Sheriff's Police answered. I recognized her voice from the middle of the night.

I took a breath, waiting for her to tell me to come in for questioning. Instead, she said, 'We're done with your vehicle.'

'I'm downtown, at Union Station, not at home.'

'There's a train stop four blocks from us.'

Thunder sounded in her background as she gave me her address. I stepped out and looked at the sky. It was black in the west. 'It's raining there?'

'If there's to be justice.'

A fast-driving rain was beating down by the time I got to her stop. There was no station building, just a flat, unprotected platform. And there were no cabs.

I got drenched running to the overhang of a gas station across the street. I called the sergeant. 'It's raining buckets,' I said, so she could say she'd send a car.

'That's the least of your worries,' she said, and hung up.

I remained under the overhang, worrying about what she'd just said. She sounded like she'd found ripe evidence, blood or DNA traces. I tried to tell myself that was impossible, that she'd only had the Jeep for a few hours. And then I told myself I'd only grabbed the knife and a few Burger King wrappers. I hadn't looked for anything else Marilyn's killer might have left.

I ran the four blocks to the gray cinderblock, six-bay garage and would have stopped short, to swear, if it wasn't pouring.

My Jeep was parked in front, red, glistening even where it was rusted. And topless. My vinyl top, which I'd not dared lower in years for fear of disturbing the artful mosaic of silver tape that held the rips closed, lay in a crumpled heap on the ground a few feet away, its mending strands loose and curling upon it like a tangle of shiny gray snakes trying to slither away.

I ran inside. Sergeant Bohler sat at a desk in a glass-windowed office. She smiled delightedly when I sloshed to a dripping stop in her doorway.

She tossed two overstuffed, clear plastic bags at me, one after the other. 'Know what those are, Elstrom?'

I'd recognized the contents even as the bags were in flight, and understood the reason for her pettiness. 'Memories,' I said.

'Excellent,' she said, nodding approvingly at my sodden clothes.

I stepped up to her desk. She pushed her chair back from the torrent of drops that fell from my hair, face and shirt. 'Damn it, Elstrom.'

I upended the contents of both bags onto the papers on her desk. 'What we have here are Burger King wrappers,' I said, speaking softly so we could both enjoy the gentle patter of me dripping onto the wrappers and other papers on her desk.

'Step back, for Pete's sake,' she said, lurching up from her chair.

'Not just ordinary Burger King wrappers,' I opined, a tropical rain forest standing pat. 'But Whopper-with-cheese wrappers, to be precise.'

By now, her work papers and my wrappers lay sodden on her desk like leaves pasted lifeless to a sidewalk by a hard autumn rain.

'There were eighty-four of those damned wrappers inside your Jeep, Elstrom,' she said, pressed up against the file cabinets at the back wall.

I remembered the cadaver-sniffing dog going berserk inside my Jeep. To its nostrils it must have seemed like a meat paradise.

'They ruined the dog's nose,' she said. 'He can't differentiate between scents anymore.'

'Perhaps counseling?'

'I like you for Marilyn Paul in the Willahock, Elstrom. Our dog may have given up, but I won't.'

'No blood, no hair, no murderous weapons?' I asked, feigning outraged innocence, for clearly they'd found nothing.

She stepped forward to open a side drawer, grabbed my key and tossed it at me. 'I'm not done. Do not leave town.'

I went out into the rain, hefted the vinyl top into the back and took the slow way to Rivertown. I didn't dare risk the speeds needed on the expressway. It was challenging enough to drive even slowly while wiping my eyes constantly to see through the rain falling between my face and the windshield. I got plenty of honks from other motorists. Some smiled; in shock, I supposed. Most sped up to pass, tight-faced, anxious to escape an obvious crazy driving a topless Jeep in a thunderstorm.

I shivered, from the downpour and in relief that Bohler had found nothing. But mostly I shivered from the certainty that I now had a cop who was going to be relentless in tagging me for Marilyn Paul's murder.

Despite all that, I was mindful that I owed a homage. My usual Burger King outlet rests at the extreme western edge of Chicago, right at the Rivertown city line. They know me there.

I turned into the drive-through lane, dripping and grinning in the rain, and paid the delighted teenage window attendant with a drenched bill.

I ate as I drove through Rivertown, savoring as always the magnificent taste – even sodden – of my cheese Whopper.

Yet that day, I savored the wrapper even more.

TWENTY-SIX

Leo, bright in a tropically orange shirt festooned with frolicking red parrots, yellow slacks and black-and-white wingtip shoes, looked through the rain at the Jeep parked at the curb. 'Odd day to be driving without the top,' he opined, like it was wisdom.

'The sheriff's department seized the Jeep in the middle of the night, looking for evidence.'

His thick eyebrows snapped together into a thick line of furry worry. 'Please tell me you got rid of the box.'

'Yes, but they'd gotten tipped to something else. Before they came I spotted somebody who put a bloody knife under the passenger's seat. It's now in the Willahock.'

'Can't there still be DNA or blood residue?'

'My lifestyle mostly saved the day,' I said. 'Their cadaver dog's nose went haywire from sniffing cheeseburger wrappers. Their own noses must have gone just as haywire from finding no blood or anything else. They reacted petulantly. They left the Jeep out in the rain with the top off.'

'Petulant, but cleansing all the more?' His smile lit the dark gloom of the day.

'I can only hope. I'd like to reattach the top in the shelter of your garage.'

Relieved, he hurried back through the house and had his Porsche out before I pulled around to the alley. Reattaching the top took ninety minutes because it was slippery and wet and had separated, like an unraveled patchwork quilt, into a dozen smaller pieces where the strands of duct tape had fallen away.

'I'll go to the Discount Den for more silver tape,' he said.

'No need. I'm going to leave the rips open for now. They'll help circulate the air once the sun comes out.'

'I'll get you seat covers.' He ran inside and came out a moment later to slip two clear plastic garbage bags over the front seats. I doubted they'd matter. I was already drenched.

Back home, in dry clothes, I was nuking a modest rainbow of three Peeps – two green, one lavender – when the phone rang. It was the Bipsie who'd hired me to track down the other Bipsies in her sorority.

'Long time no hear, Mr Elshtrom,' she said slowly, straining to enunciate each word perfectly. It was well past lunch.

'We just spoke,' I said, picking little Peep splats out of the microwave and sliding them into my mouth.

'Refresh memory. Am doing the newshletter.'

A thought teetered. 'You've put my name in your newsletter?'

'Lasht time, too,' she slurred. 'Tell everyone you're tracking ush down. Whatsh new?'

'Bipsie Paul,' I ventured.

She snorted. 'Don't bother. High and mighty, pain in the ash.'

'She's moved on anyway.' I clicked the liquored woman away with a fast forefinger. Later, perhaps, I'd feel like a crumb, getting angry with a foolish drunk who obviously didn't know that Marilyn Paul had been murdered.

I pulled out the old records the sorority women had given me for updating and found Marilyn listed at the same address in Oak Park I'd gotten from the Internet. She'd learned of me through her sorority newsletter and now she was dead.

I went to the kitchen and microwaved another Peep until it collapsed into a vaguely green slick that resembled nothing of its original chick-like state. And that reminded me that Beech in the Beach wanted medical information on David Arlin. Jenny was going to try to find out why.

I called her. 'You were going to use your wiles to find out what's wrong with the corpse in Laguna Beach,' I said.

'I took a day and did drive down there, but I got sidetracked when I got back by a crooked councilman in one of our suburbs,' she said.

'Sounds like Rivertown. You learned nothing?'

'I didn't try Beech again but I did manage to get a stool at a diner next to a younger cop at lunchtime. You were right. There's something wrong with the corpse, beyond it not being intact. My new young friend said they're contacting every doctor in Laguna Beach, looking for Arlin's records.'

'No idea what's wrong with the body?'

'He didn't know; only that it's wrong.'

'I'm surprised they haven't yet sent my local cops after me for the name of Arlin's insurance company. They won't be happy when they learn I lied.'

I then told her what I'd learned since we last talked.

'I can understand all three quitting that old campaign at the same time,' she said, 'if it meant snatching great-paying jobs.'

'The jobs didn't work out, and they didn't work out awfully quickly. All three stayed out west, though they didn't stay together. Arlin went to Laguna Beach, Runney to Reeder. Both changed their names.'

'Now we're getting to an intriguing part,' she said.

'Because since the third musketeer, Halvorson, didn't change his name. He became invisible instead and has stayed that way ever since.'

'You think one of the three killed Marilyn Paul?'

'Could be, because of what she knew. But there's another wrinkle. The three young men were good friends twenty years ago, thought of as three of four musketeers.'

'Now I'm sensing something really big.'

'The fourth musketeer was Timothy Wade.'

'The Grain Man? Your next senator from Illinois? He figures in this?'

'I don't know.'

'Oh, boy. This could be huge.'

'Not a word about any of this yet,' I said. 'Likely as not, Wade's totally uninvolved.'

'Bigger than big,' she said.

At the time, neither of us knew what we were talking about.

TWENTY-SEVEN

The rest of the afternoon dribbled into evening. I spent a fraction of it lacerating my hands with ductwork but mostly I peeked out the window for whoever might come at me for the murder of Marilyn Paul.

At eight-fifteen, it paid off. And not.

A white Ford Explorer pulled onto my street and parked in the dark, a hundred yards away. That wasn't unusual for bargain-seeking Johns. Nor was it strange he'd turned to face heading out. Knowledgeable Rivertown revelers desired speedy exits, should a Rivertown squad car come weaving at them. It wasn't arrest they feared – nobody ever got arrested for lewdness in Rivertown – but rather a hard-to-explain collision, while parked in the company of a hooker, with a drunken cop.

I watched the Ford SUV for too many moments before I left the window, telling myself I was simply jumpy. Two attempts at a frame for murder will sandpaper even the calmest of nerves.

Thirty minutes later, I was back, looking again. The Explorer was still there and I had the thought it might belong to one of Sergeant Bohler's people, keeping me under surveillance. I padded down the wrought-iron stairs, turned off the lamp I'd set on my new furnace so it could be admired after sunset by peeping toms or worse and slipped out the door. The interior bulbs in the Jeep don't work and I eased in without flashing any light.

A twist of the key, a quick U-turn and I came up on him fast, ready to flash on my headlamps.

He was faster. He shot forward, made a right turn and another onto Thompson to head west. He was no john, and he was no cop.

Night-times, cars crawled along Rivertown's seediest half-mile. Drunks poked along to avoid the hallucinations that jumped at them from the shadows and johns drove slowly to inspect the meat working the curbs.

The driver I was chasing wasn't mindful of any of that. He darted recklessly in and out of the slow parade, causing a dozen drivers to hit their horns and swerve. In no time he'd gotten six car lengths ahead. I worked the tangle as best as my nerves would allow, but no matter how craftily I drove, he was better. Soon he was at least ten car lengths ahead.

The drunks and the johns fell away at the outskirts of town. I sped up, hoping to close some of the distance. But his Explorer was a rocket compared to the lump that was my Jeep. He gunned his SUV up to an almost suicidal ninety miles an hour.

And then he got stuck behind a slow-moving tractor-trailer. By then there were only three cars between us. I pressed down on the accelerator, hoping to pass to get closer.

The bubble lights of a cop lit up the opaque yellow of my plastic rear window. I had to back off and pull to the side of the road.

The plainclothes cop came up to my side window, flashing a badge. 'Trying to outrun me, Elstrom?' she asked.

'You just cost me, Bohler,' I said. 'The person who likely killed Marilyn Paul was watching my turret. You just helped him get away.'

She smiled. 'Your fantasies won't change my mind. You killed Marilyn Paul.'

My heart finally quit pounding by the time the Bohemian called at ten. 'No dice, Vlodek,' he said. 'According to my contact, Theresa Wade insists on running the lives of her brother and herself like she runs the campaign, entirely through her address on his website. The best you can do is request an interview through that.'

'She's keeping as low a profile as her brother.'

'Supposedly, she's severely agoraphobic.'

'Delman Bean inferred something like that. She's afraid to leave her house?'

'She hasn't ventured out for years. Plus, she's paralyzed from the waist down, from an accident when she was very young.'

'Wheelchair-bound,' I said, remembering my meeting with the woman calling herself Rosamund Reynolds.

'You're thinking it could have been Theresa, not Marilyn Paul, who hired you?'

'No,' I said. 'Marilyn Paul got my name through a sorority newsletter. The real question is why she wanted to impersonate Theresa Wade when she hired me.'

'To leave a trail to Timothy Wade?'

'That seems most likely. Wade was the fourth musketeer. One of the other musketeers is dead and two are missing. He's got to be involved, either as a perpetrator or a target.'

'Because he's the only musketeer still standing? That's a reach, Vlodek.'

'Marilyn Paul worked for the Wade campaign. She knew his schedule,' I said.

'And planted those bones to publicly embarrass Wade, the very candidate she was laboring to elect?'

'Whatever the intent, it didn't work. The press dropped the story.'

'As we discussed, Theresa has convinced the press that Tim was reacting to a very real and imminent threat and that he's safest remaining in seclusion. She's wise, and that's wise, until they catch the perpetrator.'

'If Theresa is as sharp as you think, she suspected Marilyn Paul right away.'

'You're imagining she had Marilyn Paul murdered? For that simple prank? That's crazy.'

'Not necessarily,' I said, 'but I'm still stuck wondering if Marilyn Paul suspected Theresa or Timothy Wade of something.'

I told him I was going to poke around a bit on the Internet and he hung up, sounding tired but no doubt grateful that he wouldn't have to listen to more of my nonsensical rambling. Not me; I wasn't tired and I wasn't too impatient to chase more nonsense. The man who'd likely killed Marilyn Paul and wanted me framed for it had come again. I went to my computer to find Theresa and Timothy Wade.

They came from a line of rum runners and politicians, which in Chicago was considered a doubly golden pedigree. Their great grandfather, Samuel Wade, Sr made his fortune during the Prohibition years, operating a construction company with excellent ties to Chicago's city hall. By most accounts, the company did build a scattering of tiny municipal buildings – warming huts at ice rinks and such – but mostly it made deliveries. News reports of the day marveled that his trucks, presumably loaded with lumber, were a familiar sight in the city and in Cook County. Later, it became accepted that because Wade Sr owned a distillery in Canada it was likely his trucks delivered things more liquid than lumber.

I creaked my tilting red vinyl chair back from the screen and allowed myself an irony. We shared Prohibition-era histories, the siblings Wade and me. My own grandfather also ran alcohol through Chicago during Prohibition, though his was lowlier – beer made in local garages. And alas, our ancestors invested their incomes differently. Whereas Wade, Sr constructed an expansive estate close to the magnificent shore of Lake Michigan, my grandfather never got further than one turret of a castle along the greasier shore of the Willahock River – then, as now, more of a drain than a desirable waterway.

Samuel Wade, Jr brought the family new sources of revenue. He entered politics. The profession had always been a moneymaker in Illinois, making multi-millionaires of thousands that dedicated their lives to the public good. Wade, Jr was no slouch at it. He multiplied the family fortune ten-fold in the years he served in the state senate.

Jared Wade, Samuel Jr's son, sought to use the ancestral money to buy the family respectability. He sat on several charity boards, contributed heavily to the Chicago democratic machine and married a dazzling blonde socialite from Kenilworth. They had dazzling children. Theresa was their first born, followed by Timothy, two years later. Pictures of them enjoying charitable events with their parents appeared regularly in Chicago's newspapers.

At the age of six, Theresa showed promise as a gymnast. At ten, she landed wrong on the edge of a trampoline. It put her in a wheelchair. The family remained upbeat, and pictures from then on showed a smiling, pretty young blonde girl resolutely participating in all sorts of events with other kids her age. Theresa Wade was no recluse at that time in her life.

Jared Wade and his beautiful blonde socialite wife were killed in a boat explosion on Lake Michigan when Theresa was twenty-one and her younger brother, Timothy, was nineteen. A photo of the two young siblings showed them smiling bravely at their parents' funeral, where Theresa announced their intention to live on at the family estate.

A second showed them six months later, sitting in the family's older Cadillac Eldorado convertible with its top down, enjoying a polo match in Oak Brook, Illinois. Life was going on.

Theresa Wade graduated magna cum laude from Northwestern's Medill School of Journalism the next year. She'd never intended to go into any form of journalism, for reasons that did not become clear for several more years.

Fresh from graduating, also from Northwestern, Timothy Wade almost immediately became prominent in Chicago's political and philanthropic circles. He became an aide to the president of the Cook County Board, and then to the speaker of the Illinois House of Representatives. He attended ribbon cuttings, taxpayer forums and open government meetings of every sort, always visible but in the background, assisting, learning. He was photogenic, a comer in Illinois politics destined for the national stage. Never, though, did he bruise himself in campaigns for small office. There'd been little doubt his future was in the US Senate. And then, likely, a run for president.

And all the while, he did serious social good, chairing or serving on boards devoted to helping young, disadvantaged children, often willing to brandish his own inheritance. Roadblocks disappeared when young Timothy Wade's checkbook appeared.

The press on Timothy Wade was overwhelmingly favorable. And, by then, it had long been apparent that Theresa had gone to Medill to learn how to manage media, for the political career of her brother, Timothy. They were long-term planners, the Wades.

As photos of Timothy began appearing everywhere in the press, pictures of Theresa had completely disappeared. She'd backed away completely from public notice. One columnist speculated that Theresa had suffered some sort of delayed depression over the deaths of her parents. Nobody else speculated much at all. Tim's star was rising by Theresa's design. She best served their ambitions by staying out of the limelight.

I found only one picture of her taken in recent times on the Internet, and it was worthless. It showed her in profile, sitting behind a sheer lace curtain in a second-floor bedroom of the Wade house. It looked to have been taken with a long lens from a hundred yards away. Theresa Wade was a blur, much as Rosamund Reynolds had been the day I'd met her in the day rental office.

Fatigue found me at three in the morning. I went up to bed, numbed finally by enough information and adrenaline withdrawal to hope to not dream of the living or the dead. Of Amanda, and of Jenny.

That night, only one dream came, but it came hard. It starred the white Ford Explorer I'd chased earlier. I hadn't seen much except its taillights but it had been enough. I was almost sure they were identical to the ones I'd seen on the car that had sped away, the night an intruder had left the serrated knife in my Jeep.

I dreamed the driver wore a black hood and was death himself.

TWENTY-EIGHT

I broke in the next morning because I figured enough time had passed for the cops to quit watching her apartment.

Marilyn Paul had lived in a beige brick, two-story, four-flat apartment building three blocks from the Eisenhower Expressway. I parked a block away and walked up the alley, slowly. I saw no one who looked like Sergeant Bohler, or any other cop.

The building was old and didn't have electronic locks. I couldn't see any security cameras.

It had a center hall. I came in from the back. Twenty feet ahead, yellow police tape crisscrossed the door on the right. There'd been no follow-ups in the newspaper on the case; certainly there'd been no mention that she'd been murdered in her apartment.

I probed the lock with a credit card. The door was locked tight.

I went out to the back. She'd had a small, low-walled patio. A dozen red clay pots were lined on the cement along one wall. Some held curled flowers that had been dead a long time. Others just held dirt. She hadn't been a gardener.

One green webbed chair and one small metal table were set in the center. She hadn't entertained, either.

There were deep gouges and dents on the aluminum sliding door. They looked fresh, made by someone who'd been in a hurry. The bent metal prevented the door from locking. I slid the door open and walked in.

The small living room was a mess of dumped drawers and scattered papers. Until she'd gotten her head bashed and throat slit, Marilyn Paul had prized an ordered life. The only picture on the wall was of President John F. Kennedy. She'd been a reader, but of nothing fanciful. A tall bookcase contained books of history and of fact, biographies of great men and accounts of great wars.

The bedroom was at the end of a short hall. The bed was rumpled, the rust-colored stain on the carpet beside it dry. It wasn't hard to imagine her last couple of minutes. She'd been jerked from her bed and cut right there, defenseless in her nightclothes. I hoped she hadn't had time to fully wake up.

The drawer on the night table had been spilled. A nail file, a sleeping mask, a tube of hand cream and a pair of reading glasses lay on the floor next to a thick volume of Winston Churchill's memoirs.

The clothes in the closet had been yanked from their hangers and tossed on the floor. She hadn't had many clothes, and most of them were beige and black. A gray wig also lay on the floor. The sun at the day rental office had bleached the color out of everything, but I'd have bet she'd worn that wig the day we met.

I went back into the living room and poked my toe at everything that had been tossed on the floor. They were ordinary papers, though I suspected she'd had a file of some sort on the four musketeers. If the cops had discovered it, they would have paid me a visit before Bohler got tipped that something was in the Jeep. Chances were, Marilyn's killer found the file. It was how he'd known where to leave her body, and the blame.

Everything in the kitchen had also been dumped on the floor. Even the smallest boxes of her dry food had been spilled out. Her milk and orange juice containers had been emptied in the sink. Somewhere in that mess, or the messes in the bedroom and living room, her killer had found her burner phone. He'd done me a favor by taking it away before the cops could check its incoming call history.

The door to the front closet was ajar. Likely her killer had paid no mind to the contents of the box on the shelf. I guessed the cops ignored that box, too.

It was black, with a ghoulish white skeleton pictured on it, dancing in front of a jack-o'-lantern face on a blood-orange moon. The description said the whole thing could be easily assembled in minutes with the wire clips provided.

Marilyn Paul hadn't been interested in assembling the whole thing. She just wanted the few bones of a forearm, wrist and hand to put in a silo. I looked inside to make sure. Those plastic parts were missing.

I went back out the patio door and slid it shut behind me. I headed down the alley toward the Jeep sure of only one thing.

Marilyn Paul should have left those plastic bones in the box.

TWENTY-NINE

I drove north and west again. Lena Jankowski said on the phone it was either face-to-face or no discussion at all. She said she wanted to watch my face when I lied.

'One fib and the door gets slammed,' she said, stepping out onto the concrete stoop.

'Sometimes truth is the only recourse,' I agreed, affably enough.

'John Shea is dead,' she said. 'I Googled the name he was using, David Arlin, after you left the last time. John got blown up in a house explosion.'

'I don't know all the details. The Laguna Beach cops are playing things cagey.'

'And Willard Piser has been passing himself off as a preacher, Dainsto Runney, in Oregon.'

I'd mentioned Runney's name the last time. 'You Googled him?'

'It figures, Willard pretending to be a preacher. He liked to talk, and being a preacher means he can lock the doors and trap people into listening. I called that church of his. A woman said he'd left town.'

'You then checked on Halvorson?' The woman was thorough.

'I thought I'd have better luck with him since he sends me Christmas cards, but the Internet shows nothing.'

'Did Halvorson have relatives in Chicago?'

'Willard and John were from out east, though they didn't know each other before the campaign. But Red is a Chicago boy. He had a brother in the city somewhere, though he said they hardly ever spoke.' She studied me for a moment, then said, 'Zero for three, Elstrom. Three musketeers have disappeared or died. That's why Marilyn hired you?'

There was no doubt; the woman was sharp. 'I'm not sure what she was up to. She disguised herself to meet me.'

'She was afraid of getting killed?'

'She sat in a wheelchair, where she could be obscured by bright sun.'

'Marilyn didn't use a wheelchair.'

'Theresa Wade does.'

'You're saying Marilyn disguised herself as Theresa Wade? That makes no sense.'

'Maybe she was trying to point a finger as insurance in case something went wrong.'

'At Theresa Wade? No chance. She and Tim are saints, philanthropists. They do good all the time and they're rich enough to be destined for big things. Next month, Tim will become our senator-elect and then he'll get tapped to run for president.'

'How well do you know Theresa Wade?'

'I don't know her at all. Tim used to call her every night from the Bean headquarters, asking her to come down, to hang out, stuff envelopes, go out for beer and pizza afterward. He was trying to get her out of the house. He was afraid she'd become what . . . well, what she did become – a total recluse.'

'To be sure, when you talked recently with Marilyn Paul she never expressed any concerns about Theresa or Timothy Wade?'

'Never. What aren't you telling me?'

'Delman Bean blames Marilyn Paul for his loss,' I said, changing the subject again. 'He said she wasn't prepared when John, Red and Willard quit suddenly. He said lots of sympathetic voters never got to the polls because there was no one to drive them.'

'Those guys were fresh out of college and broke. John worked in an appliance store and Red stocked shelves somewhere. I think Willard worked part-time at a grocery store. Naturally, they jumped at a new opportunity. Nobody could see that coming.'

'But it was sudden? They didn't talk about it beforehand?'

'They certainly didn't say anything the night before. I'm sure of that because we were so shocked the next evening at campaign headquarters when Tim said they took off for great jobs out west.'

'You were all out together, that last night?'

'Not Marilyn, just the volunteers. We went out most nights for pizza and beer.' She laughed, remembering. 'Truth is we volunteered in that campaign more for companionship than out of any mission to improve the world. Well, most of us except Tim. He was always high-minded and purposeful. He really did want to change the world through politics.'

'Did anything unusual happen that last night?'

'Not that I recall. It would have been too much beer as always. Probably, we staggered—' She stopped, frowning in concentration. 'No, we didn't stagger out like always. We got thrown out, I think. We must have gotten obnoxious.' She laughed. 'It happened some-times. We were young.'

'Where was your usual place?'

'We had several usual places, all within a couple of blocks of Bean headquarters, depending on whether we wanted pizza, burgers or just cheap beer. Mostly it was about the beer.'

That would prove true enough.

THIRTY

There were over thirty Halvorsons listed in the online white pages for Chicago. The woman who answered the phone at the seventeenth number said, 'Try Tucson,' before hanging up. Her address was just east of O'Hare Airport. I drove over.

'You the one who called an hour ago?' the woman demanded through the glass louvers on the front door. The house was about forty years old, made of gray bricks and was jammed tight on a twenty-five-foot wide lot. She looked ten years older than the house but just as solid, and her hair was just as gray. She wore a pale blue cleaning company shirt and dark blue slacks and rubbed red eyes like I'd just woken her from a nap.

'The very same,' I said, beaming like I was proud of it. 'I just have a couple of questions about your brother.'

'This look like Tucson to you?'

'I only need a minute.'

'Gary is my brother-in-law, not my brother, and I ain't seen him in years,' she said, starting to close the door.

I leaned against the wrought-iron railing like I was prepared to wait.

She held the door half open. 'Is Gary in trouble?'

'I thought everyone called him Red.'

'Everyone called my husband Red, too. Same color hair.'

I gave her a card. 'An insurance matter,' I said. It was always such a handy lie.

'Can't help you. Like I said, I ain't seen him in years.'

'How about your husband?'

'My husband is dead. Heart attack, six years ago.'

'They were close?'

'They never saw each other, but that doesn't excuse Gary from moving out of state without telling us. Upset my husband no end. A Christmas card was the first we heard.'

'From Tucson.'

'You're sure this is really about insurance and not some old political campaign?'

'Why do you ask about a campaign?'

'I don't believe in coincidences. A very rude woman called the week before last, saying she was an old friend of his from a congressional campaign twenty years ago and needed to get in touch. She didn't sound like she'd ever been a friend to anybody. She said he angered a lot of people because he quit the campaign right before the election and asked if I knew why he quit that sudden. I told her what I just told you, that we didn't know he'd even moved to Tucson until we got a Christmas card from him in December.' Her face tightened. 'He never called, he never wrote a letter. He just sent us a card, printed with just his name and a computer addressed label on the envelope, like you insurance people use.'

'Did you try to contact him?'

'The second and third Christmases, I sent a card with a note to his return address, also on a printed label, but Gary never once replied. Just kept sending the same old printed card, year after year. I still get one, addressed to the Halvorsons, every Christmas. After five or six years I quit bothering to send him one back.'

'Did you try calling?'

'Directory assistance said no phone.'

'You mean his number was unlisted?'

'I mean no phone period. Maybe he has a cell phone by now.'

'Are there other relatives he might have stayed in closer touch with?' I asked, trying to sound casual. 'Blood kin? A cousin or an uncle?'

She shook her head. 'Gary's the last of the line, unless he has kids.'

And there went any hope of identifying the reddish-brown scrapings from the Tucson house as Gary Halvorson's blood spill, though certainly something bad must have happened there for the landlord to have used so much bleach to clean the place up.

I thanked her, started down the steps, stopped and turned with a new thought. 'Did you send him a note when your husband died?' Surely Red Halvorson would have responded to that.

'Yeah. The jerk never replied.'

'Yet you still get a card every Christmas?'

'Yeah.'

'Addressed to the Halvorsons, like always?' Meaning both of them.

She understood. 'He didn't bother to change his computer program, even knowing his brother was dead.'

I started for the Jeep.

'Don't bother to call if you learn anything,' she called after me.

I nodded without turning around. By now, I didn't think I was going to learn anything she'd want to hear.

THIRTY-ONE

The next morning I followed the shore of Lake Michigan north.

It was one of the finest of the October days we get in Chicago, crisp at sixty degrees and so deeply colored with magnificent reds, oranges and yellows in the trees that we almost forget the excesses of our other three seasons. It even made me forget that I was the target for a murder frame and I found myself whistling in counterpoint to the rhythmic flapping of the loosened shreds of my vinyl top.

In seemingly no time at all, I got to the college town of Evanston. A homecoming football weekend was approaching and the season's bright hues were joined by an abundance of the purples and whites of the Northwestern Wildcats. Staggering among them, I supposed, were more than a few returning Northwestern sorority Bipsies, though they were deeply purpled year-round, from lives of long lunches.

My cell phone rang. I clicked it on.

'You there, Elstrom?' a woman's voice yelled.

'I am!' I screamed back.

'This is Bohler. I can barely hear you.'

I dropped it on the passenger seat. 'In accordance with Illinois law, I'm operating a motor vehicle and therefore unable to pick up a hand-held phone to communicate,' I shouted to the policewoman. 'Plus, you separated my vinyl top into many pieces. Each one is flapping and slapping now, letting in deafening traffic noise.'

'Pick up the damned phone!' she shouted.

I picked it up. 'How's Sniffy?'

'Who?'

'Sniffy, the wonder dog.'

'I like you, Elstrom.'

'Me, too,' I said, agreeably.

'No. I mean I really like you. For Marilyn Paul's murder.'

'The woman in the river?'

'Don't act dumb.'

There were ninety-nine ways to respond to that, most of them truthful, but I chose the hundredth and said nothing.

'You dumped that woman in the river,' she said.

'What lies have you manufactured to prove that?'

'You screwed up. You bagged her watertight. She's giving us DNA to compare to those bits of hamburger we took from your Jeep. Plus, someone called who can tie you to Marilyn Paul's murder weapon.'

'The same anonymous tipster that sent you to grab my Jeep?'

'A charge of destroying evidence material to a murder investigation will be just for openers.'

'What evidence, exactly?'

'The knife that killed Marilyn Paul. We'll be dragging the river.'

Whoever I'd scared off after he'd planted the knife in the Jeep hadn't run very far. He'd circled back to watch and had seen me throw the knife into the river.

I figured recovering it, even so close to the turret, would only offer circumstantial evidence. Fingerprints and blood evidence are fragile. On cardboard furnace boxes, they don't withstand fire. On knives, I doubted they'd withstand long immersion in polluted water, even if the knife was recovered from the debris at the bottom of the Willahock.

Nonetheless, Bohler's cheery certainty turned my mouth to chalk. For a day or two, I'd been thinking about what I hadn't thought about at first: carpet fibers. Some could have gotten trapped in the bag Marilyn had been put into and compared to samples from my Jeep. They, too, would be circumstantial, but evidence nonetheless that Marilyn Paul's body had spent time in a Jeep very much like mine. Circumstantial evidence, piled high enough, can become damning evidence.

Bohler coughed. I'd gotten so lost in the newest of my worries that I'd forgotten she was still on the phone.

'Anything else, Sergeant?' I asked, in what sounded like a child's voice.

She laughed and hung up.

The Wade estate in Winnetka was on familiar turf, a few miles of multimillion dollar homes south of my ex-father-in-law's ex-digs in Lake Forest. Though the Wade grounds only backed down to a road that ran along Lake Michigan and were not on it, like the late Wendell's, the Wade property looked to be many times more valuable. The thickly wooded grounds covered at least twenty acres of prime North Shore real estate and had to be worth tens of millions.

The house was set in a clearing at the top of a rise along another road, across from more woods nestled between two upscale housing developments. The Wades' was a rambling white-frame affair with black shutters and yellow awnings landscaped with precisely trimmed yews fronted with those little yellow and purple flowers rich people buy in small cement urns to let die on their front lawns after the first frost. The rich are odd ducks.

I got stopped at the curved drive by the black-iron gate I'd seen in the satellite photo. The small white security hut behind it looked to have been painted as recently as the house, which might have been that morning, such was its sparkle.

I thought again of the only photo I'd found of Theresa Wade as an adult. It had been snapped with a long lens through the rightmost, second-floor window. Then, as now, a gauzy curtain hung behind the glass. It had obscured the woman sitting behind it into a blur.

A guard walked up to the gate. I stuck my head out through the shreds of my own gauzy curtain, though mine was of yellowed plastic, slashed on several different occasions at the health center by thumpers too stupid to remember they'd already boosted my radio.

'I'm here to see Miss Wade,' I said to the unsmiling fellow. He wore a gray uniform and a Glock semi-automatic holstered on his hip.

'Appointment?' he asked through the gate.

I got out. 'Nah; I was just in the neighborhood and thought I'd drop in for coffee.'

'Get back in your vehicle.'

I complied and he opened the gate just enough to step out. I handed him the envelope I'd brought. 'Miss Wade will want to see me after she's read this.'

'Stay in your vehicle.' As he reached for the envelope his jacket sleeve slid up enough to reveal the edge of a gold wristwatch, and for an instant I was reminded of the last time I'd seen Amanda's father, who'd lived not so far away. He'd been wearing a gold wristwatch almost the same color as the guard's, though Wendell Phelps' timepiece had been a hugely expensive Rolex.

The guard pulled out a cell phone and made a call. A moment later, another gray-uniformed man came down the drive to retrieve the envelope. The inspiration for the letter was a long shot, but long shots were all I had to fire.

I remained behind the steering wheel as instructed, though the day was warming the interior of the still-drenched Jeep to the humidity of an Ecuadorian jungle. Ten minutes passed, then another ten. I would have played it nonchalant by listening to the radio but I was sweating too hard and the radio had been stolen years before, leaving nothing on the dashboard to look at except the multicolored wires Amanda had braided the time we'd come up to see her father. It was one of the last times I'd seen him alive.

So it went, the guard looking at me sweating inside the Jeep and me looking at the little yellow and purple flowers, destined for death at the first frost. The purple ones were the same hue as the sweatshirts and sweaters worn by the Northwestern alumni I'd spotted on the drive up, as well as the Peeps I'd been nuking lately, and that got me wondering how many other colors the Discount Den might begin offering once they'd gotten too old to be sold elsewhere.

The second guard returned and bent to my slashed plastic window.

'Plastic garbage bags for seat covers? Clever,' he said, no doubt in admiration.

'The interior is drenched,' I said.

'I don't wonder,' he said, glancing at the rips in the top. 'Miss Wade doesn't want to see you,' he added.

'Does she ever see anybody?'

He handed me a small notepad and then entrusted me with the kind of pen even the cheapest motels leave lying around every-where, knowing they won't be stolen. 'She'll email you,' the guard said. 'Or not.'

'Did she read my note?' I asked, writing down my Gmail address.

'I put it in the mail slot and then waited for a few minutes. Nothing.'

'Maybe she's a slow reader.'

'Winter's coming. Your seats might ice over before she gets to it.'

I gave him back his paper and pen and drove away like I'd been victorious.

THIRTY-TWO

It had begun raining by the time I drove back south through Evanston. It happens that way, to the wild palette that is Chicago, every autumn. October rolls in warm and glorious in her bright paint, seeming like it is going to last for forever. Then, in a heart-beat, the winds shift to blow in frigid from Canada and the plains and swirl around the Great Lakes, hunting to suck up water to hurl at the trees. And in a day, maybe two, all the reds and oranges and yellows suddenly become sodden, turn brown and fall heavy and dead from the trees.

The purple people had fled Evanston's sidewalks to seek shelter. I was quickly becoming sodden myself from the rain sheeting in through the tears in the top. I wanted shelter, too, and warmth. I called Amanda's office number. 'It's a fine day for dinner,' I said.

'He calls!' she said.

'I've been busy.'

'No; you've avoided calling because you knew I'd pester you about that body in the Willahock.'

'There is that, yes,' I allowed.

'I'm having one of my "How could my father stand this?" sort of days,' she went on, 'so dinner sounds great.'

'Your father was born to be a tycoon.'

'As you were born to dodge a subject,' she said, meaning the woman in the river.

'So, dinner?' she asked, after I said nothing.

'Pizza,' I said. Gush as so many do about Chicago's magnificent skyline, its museums, orchestras, and opera, what truly makes the city sparkle is the grease on its sausage and pepperoni.

'Perfect.'

'I'll bring excellent pizza and reasonable beer.'

She hesitated for only a second. 'To my place? I thought we were treading carefully.'

'Careful it will be. I'll even keep your oven mitts on my hands.'

She didn't laugh. 'Why not a restaurant?'

'I have an ulterior motive.'

'With oven mitts? Sounds kinky.'

I reached to wipe the inside of the windshield. 'It's raining like crazy now and your building has indoor parking.'

'That makes all the sense in the world,' she said.

'It will, when I bring the pizza. Pizza makes sense of everything.'

The guard outside the garage at Amanda's building remembered me and remembered my Jeep.

'You're not, ah . . .?' He let the question trail off as his gaze shifted from the maze of rips in the vinyl to the box on the passenger's seat.

'Delivering pizzas? No; I'm having dinner with Amanda. This is the cuisine.'

'Hold up here for a second,' he said, picking up the wall phone to call Amanda. A moment later, he raised the door that led to the guest parking. A second guard, just inside, stepped back to allow me through.

Amanda's Lake Shore Drive condominium was in one of the most protected buildings in Chicago. She moved there after her home, and many of her neighbors', was blown up in Crystal Waters, a gated community west of Chicago. Coincidentally, my business and professional reputation had blown up not so many months before, along with our marriage. It was a time of explosions all around.

Amanda chose the high-security condominium not to safeguard her few, cheap furnishings, nor her jewelry, of which she had very little. She had art, specifically a large, never-exhibited Monet, a small Renoir and a bronze Remington, paid for with the entirety of an inheritance from a grandfather. They were her passion, worth millions, and they needed the highest level of protection.

Her father's recent murder passed down an inheritance of all of his business, real estate and other investment holdings. She'd become worth hundreds of millions of dollars and now it was her very self that had to be protected. Her choice of residence had been prophetic.

A man in a suit cut large enough to conceal a gun stood a discreet few feet from the elevator door on her floor. Amanda was chatting with him when I walked up bringing pizza, beer and residual raindrops.

'The hunter-gatherer returns, damply,' she said of my rain-spotted clothes as she held her door open with a flourish.

I hadn't been in her place since we'd met with a rigidly officious federal agent days before her father had been found dead. Nothing had changed. The scratched, chipped enamel table she'd had since college still looked like a lost pauper in the high-end, stainless-steel and black gloss kitchen. The expansive beige sofa in the living room was still oriented to face a gallery wall. And the dining-room furniture she'd reluctantly bought for the Art Institute donor dinner parties she'd laughingly called 'gab and grabs' still looked too new and out of place.

The art, of course, was unchanged. I'd gone into her collapsing house to rescue that art.

We sat at the kitchen table, opened cans of Coors and for a moment simply savored good beer and the best pizza on the planet.

It was only as I was reaching for my second slice that she asked, 'What's going on with you?'

'Bipsies,' I said, because she knew about my sorority clients.

'Baloney,' she said, grinning just like old times.

'Bohemian?' I asked.

'Barely.' Chernek had told her nothing of the case I was working on, though she was a client. He respected everyone's confidences in complex relationships.

'Blessfully,' I threw out.

She pounced: 'I win! That's not a real word.'

It was a game we used to play, one-word give-and-takes beginning with the same letter. Indeed, they were good old times.

'A woman, passing as one Rosamund Reynolds, hired me to look in on three men out west,' I began. 'The first, Red Halvorson, of Tucson – nicknamed for his red hair – appears to have not lived in his rental house for quite some time and is nowhere to be found. The second, David Arlin, of Laguna Beach, got himself killed in a gas explosion at his house just days before Rosamund hired me. The cops out there are playing close to the vest but something about Arlin's body has raised questions. Interestingly, a red-haired man was seen outside Arlin's house the night before the explosion.'

'Red Halvorson?'

'Or someone trying to appear as Halvorson,' I said. 'The third man, Dainsto Runney, was a one-time preacher. He's disappeared from his church in Oregon. I'll go out there, see what I can learn.'

'Two men have disappeared and at least one is dead? How are the three linked?'

'They were friends twenty years ago, volunteering on a political campaign here. All three quit just days before the election, supposedly to take oil rig jobs in California. They did not. They scattered – Halvorson to Tucson, Arlin to California and Runney to Oregon. Arlin and Runney changed their names. They were known here as Shea and Piser. Their buddy, Halvorson, did not change his name. He went underground, became invisible, perhaps for all of the past twenty years.'

'Any clue to what made them scatter and change their names?'

'Rosamund Reynolds suspected something but she didn't share it with me. Her real name was Marilyn Paul.'

'The woman found downriver from your turret?'

'And the very same woman you called Chernek about, to ask if I was somehow involved.'

She merely smiled.

'She worked with those three young men on that old campaign. She's worked for the Democrats ever since.' I paused, then said, 'She rigged those bones and toy axe in that silo that so unnerved Timothy Wade.'

'My God! Why?'

'She wanted to send a message to the future senator. My rootling around in the fog surrounding her murder to find out what that was might come back at you because of your membership in Wade's Committee of Twenty-Four. I could cause you embarrassment.'

'And that's why you brought pizza and beer?' Her smile widened.

I raised and lowered my eyebrows swiftly in a most lascivious fashion.

'We agreed to wait, remember? No fever to cloud our judgment?'

'They were such glorious clouds.'

'Tell me what you're going to embarrass me with,' she said.

'The three young men were part of a tight little group called the Four Musketeers. Know who the fourth was?'

'Obviously, you're about to say Tim Wade,' she said, 'since you just mentioned my membership in his committee.'

'Marilyn Paul worked for his campaign, she planted the bones and axe at his speech and she hired me to look into three of his old friends. It seems obvious she suspected him of being mixed in something.'

She thought for a moment, then said, 'No way Tim's involved in anything gamy. I might have inherited my father's political obligations but I didn't take them on blindly. I checked Tim out. Despite his abysmal response at that farm, he's a level-headed, good guy. And speaking of commitment, what's yours now? If your client is dead, why go on? Leave this investigation to the cops.'

'For one thing, there seems to be only one cop interested in the Marilyn Paul murder at all – a sheriff's deputy who runs an impound garage, of all things.'

'And for another thing . . .?' she asked. She knew me well enough to know there was more.

'Whoever killed Marilyn Paul wants me framed for her murder. He put her corpse in my Jeep.'

She set down her beer too fast, spilling some onto the chipped enamel.

'The surest way to stop any investigation is to put the jacket on me as the killer.' I filled her in on most of the details.

'Leo,' she said, smiling.

'Lucky for me he came along before that Cook County sheriff's deputy was tipped about the corpse.'

'Still, according to your own timeline,' she said, 'you were out in California, dining with the extremely attractive Jennifer Gale, when Marilyn Paul was killed. Isn't that a good enough alibi?'

'I think there's a problem with establishing time of death if a body's been submerged for any length of time. The cops could say she was killed before I left for California.'

She pursed her lips. 'But the Willahock is a long, wide river. Seems to me a cop would have to assume the body could have been dropped anywhere upriver.'

'Agreed, and the killer realized that. So once news came that Marilyn had been found by the dam, he came back to put the murder knife in the Jeep. This time, he called the sheriff right away and stayed around to keep watch. But again, I got lucky. I saw him plant the knife. I threw it into the Willahock. He must have been frantic, having now struck out twice. After the sheriff's cops showed up to impound my Jeep, he called them back to say I'd thrown the knife in the river.'

'Creepy, him watching you so closely.'

'This could be much worse than the Evangeline Wilts mess.'

'No. Last time was the worst. It cost us our marriage.'

For a moment, we hid behind the pizza and beer, saying nothing. And then I said, 'Earlier today I dropped off a vague note for Theresa Wade, saying only that she and I had a similar interest in my being framed in a recent matter. It's a long shot, that note.'

'No chance she'll respond. Tim is cunning but well-meaning, outgoing and friendly. Theresa's secretive to a fault, obsessive about her own privacy. I've never met her, never even talked to her, but I know she'll never let you get close to her or to Tim.'

We got up and headed for her door. I lingered for a moment and told her about the man I'd chased the previous night.

'Your stalker,' she said.

'You'll keep your own guard close by?' I asked, gesturing to the hall outside.

'Maybe I'm not the one who needs him,' she said.

The building's security guard had a surprise for me when I got off the elevator by the garage. 'You might be attracting the law, Mr Elstrom,' he said.

'Occupational risk,' I said.

'I think a cop followed you this evening. Plain-clothes. She walked in a half-hour after you got here, flashed her badge and asked to look around the garage. She didn't say why and she didn't mention you by name.'

'Good looking, short-haired blonde?'

He nodded.

'Did you let her in?'

'I thought it best. She had a badge. But she only stayed a minute. She seemed most interested in your Jeep, though she tried not to show it. I made a joke. I told her the top had always been ripped up like that. It wasn't funny. She laughed. I told her the owner left it here to dry out indoors, that he caught a cab out the side door. She gave me a look like she thought I was lying.'

'If I had any real money, I'd give you a tip.'

He laughed. 'Save it for a new top,' he said.

THIRTY-THREE

The rain had stopped and I drove back to Rivertown leisurely enough to keep an eye on the road behind me. One particular pair of trailing headlamps mimicked my every lane change, speed-up, slow-down and turn. The guard at Amanda's building had been right. Bohler hadn't fallen for his story.

Likely enough, too, Bohler wanted another chance to examine my Jeep.

I drove to the Rivertown city garage. Booster Liss operated there. Daytimes, he worked for the city, for cash, cleaning the fleet of Cadillac Escalades that the city purchased, for cash, for its elected officials, who drew modest paychecks but prospered mostly from bribes, in cash.

Night-times, Booster and a small crew used the city facility for private work, cleansing vehicles of fingerprints, identification tags, and worse. Some cars were freshly stolen, on their way to being disassembled for saleable parts in one of the chop shops in the abandoned factories across town. Other vehicles were tainted differently, with evidence of hit-and-runs and gun-shot murders. Those were headed for even more careful disassembly and the crushing of their more worrisome parts. In either case, a wash by Booster was always the first step.

After I knocked, he peered through the small dark glass set in the steel side door and then eased himself outside. He was a big bear of a man, clean shaven, likely scalp-to-toes, so as to not leave his own incriminating evidence, and wore a surgical mask, scrubs, little cloth booties and thin latex gloves. Such caution inspired confidence among his understandably nervous clientele.

'Dek! Long time, man,' he said, grinning.

He always welcomed me like an old friend. We'd gone to high school together, or at least until the end of our sophomore year when he dropped out to join the legion of thumpers being mentored at the health center parking lot by seasoned thieves. Ultimately, but not unfortunately, that led to a short stretch in a prison downstate for grand theft auto, which in turn led to a broader circle of acquaintances and a new career. Already a devotee of colon cleansing, Booster saw the possibilities of extending that devotion to stolen automobiles. He began cleansing cars.

'I've been followed here,' I told him, though the trailing headlamps had vanished after my last turn. They'd probably just been switched off.

'You're worried I'll duck inside and bolt myself in?' He laughed. He operated with impunity, being connected not only by blood to the lizards that ran Rivertown but also by the services he provided to others even better connected throughout Cook County. Should a clueless cop arrive, Booster would remain safely locked inside until the proper corrective phone calls sent the cop away.

'I need a cleanse,' I said, looking up and down the street.

He noticed. 'In a hurry?'

'The tail I caught is police. I didn't see the vehicle, only the headlights.'

He stepped up to finger the shreds of the vinyl top. 'Full cleanse?'

'The best, starting with a long power wash.'

He opened the door to look inside. 'Already wet in here.'

'Rain, through the rips.'

'When we're done with the shampoo, we'll bake it in the paint booth to get rid of anything organic.'

I supposed by that he meant skin, or blood.

'Two hundred, ready at dawn.' It was a bargain rate. He got in the Jeep, tapped the horn and started the engine. The big garage door shot up fast; someone was watching from inside. Booster barely got across the threshold before the door began to drop, just as quickly.

Efficiency can run rampant in Rivertown.

THIRTY-FOUR

I'd just stepped out at nine the next morning to walk to the bank and then to the city garage when two sets of flashing police lights turned off Thompson Avenue. I tensed, thinking they were sheriff's cars, coming for me.

But when they got closer, I saw they were Rivertown cars, not Bohler's, and a different worry took hold. The two squad cars were boxing in a silver Dodge Ram window van between them. I knew that van. It was Leo's.

He passed by, the middle of a tiny parade, staring straight ahead, his arms straight out and tense on the steering wheel.

Sitting beside him on the passenger's seat, Ma Brumsky stared straight ahead as well. Her face was every bit as rigid as her son's.

Never since seventh grade had Leo not flashed one of his huge-toothed grins if he was within a mile or so of my eyes. For sure, he couldn't have missed seeing me standing so close to the curb. Something was wrong.

I ran across the broad lawn that separates city hall from my turret. It had all been my grandfather's land once but the lizards that ran the town had seized most of the land after he died. They'd seized the enormous pile of limestone he intended for his castle as well and used it to build an enormous city hall of dark hallways and shadowed rooms.

I got around back to the police station door, just as the three vehicles pulled to a stop. The two officers in the rearmost car got out quickly, as though anxious to avoid whatever was coming next. They reached into the back of their car, tugged out huge armloads of wet garments and ran into the front door of the station without a glance at either the van or the leading squad car.

The two officers in the lead car were in no such hurry. They stayed in their car, facing one another. They shook their heads and waved their arms; they were arguing. Finally, they got out and began moving, with zombie-like slowness, back to the Ram van. The younger of them suddenly stepped in front of his more senior partner and reached to open the front passenger door.

The move infuriated the older cop, who shouldered the younger man aside so he could pull open the passenger door himself.

Ma Brumsky began pivoting on the passenger seat slowly because of her arthritis and turned her knees toward the open door. Her hair was damp and she'd wrapped herself in one of the yellowish thread-bare towels they set out – rarely washed, just refolded by someone wearing thick gloves – at the health center.

Sliding down from the seat caused the towel to ride up higher on Ma Brumsky's hips. And as it rose, it became obvious that she was wearing nothing underneath. Mercifully, she paused to yank the towel down before proceeding. And so it went, for a few more minutes and many more tugs, before Ma inched down enough to get her bare feet planted on the sidewalk. Without a glance at anyone, she headed for the police station door, clutching the towel safely around her.

The younger officer, having witnessed this at close range, stood frozen, as if in shock, until the older officer, pressed safely behind the still open front passenger door, yelled at him: 'Open the damned sliding door!'

The young cop raised a trembling arm, grasped the handle and slid the center door back.

Mrs Roshiska, Ma's best friend and the woman I'd recently seen cannonballing at the health center, stood bare-legged and bare-footed just inside the opening, hunched like a precision sky diver about to hit the silk. She was older than Ma by at least five years. More relevant that day, she was fifty pounds heavier.

The health-center towel could not completely encircle such girth. The two frayed edges were separated by at least a foot of puckered, white, septuagenarian skin.

Bless the woman; she tried. She tugged both sides of the towel as close together as she could before aiming a bare leg down toward the running board. But then she teetered and had to let go of one edge of the towel to shoot an arm out onto the shoulder of the young officer. The towel fell limp and dangled uselessly in her other hand like a flag drooping on a windless, humid day.

'No!' the young cop shouted, desperate to duck out from under the suddenly naked old woman's hand pressing down hard on his shoulder.

'She's turning!' shouted his more experienced partner, who'd doubtless seen other, perhaps equal, terrors.

And indeed she was. Still maintaining a steel grip on the young cop's shoulder, Mrs Roshiska grinned at all the eyes on her and released the towel from her other hand, to reach behind her for her walker. Turning back, she dropped the aluminum contraption gently to the ground in front of her, stepped almost daintily down to the pavement and aimed her walker toward the front of the station, covered by nothing but autumnal air.

The young cop looked like he was about to cry.

The rest of Ma Brumsky's swim-club ladies emerged. All wore towels, and only towels. The elderly gent I'd seen swimming with them exited last, ever a gentleman.

There was no need to wonder further about the police escort. Rejuvenated by whatever hung suspended in the health-center pool, Ma's happy little group had been busted for ditching their suits in youthful abandon.

Once the last of the swimmers and the cops had disappeared into the police station, I walked around to the driver's side of the van. Leo had not moved from his perch behind the steering wheel. His normally pale face, now as red as if he'd spent some hours being boiled, was buried in his hands.

I pulled open his door. 'Surely this isn't as bad as floating a corpse,' I whispered before I noticed that his lips were moving. He was murmuring into his phone.

I left him there, slumped forlornly in his brand-new silver Ram van, and headed off to the bank.

THIRTY-FIVE

I spotted no police surveillance tagging along as I walked on to the bank. I could only think that Sergeant Bohler had given up in fatigue and headed home to sleep.

Inside the bank, it was business as usual, meaning there was no business, as usual. The gloom; the ancient behind the teller window; the son sitting, indifferent to the lobby at his back as he puzzled over a child's crossword puzzle; even the bitten, lone chocolate-chip cookie lying unclaimed on the plastic plate were all as they'd been the last time I was there. This time, the ancient could find no reason to deny me my cash, so I withdrew the last of Marilyn Paul's retainer and headed down the few blocks to the city garage.

The Jeep was parked outside. Its lower half glistened red and rusty and normal in the morning sun, but higher up things had changed. The faded black tatters and discolored plastic windows were gone, replaced by a new vinyl top with new, clear windows. The new top was bright green.

Booster must have seen me walk up. He came out, bleary-eyed. 'Nice, huh?' he asked, a bit tentatively.

'Christmassy,' I said.

'Ah, the red . . . and the green, I get it.' He managed a hopeful smile. 'Your Jeep is a work in progress,' he said, pointing to the rust. 'That will eat up more of the red paint, and in four or five years your Jeep will be mostly green and brown, like camouflage, in the woods. Then it won't be so Christmassy.'

'Why?' I asked, warming to the notion of motoring about in something that was itself more warming than the flapping shreds of my previous top.

'We drove the Jeep out back and removed the seats and the carpet for the power-washing phase. The kid doing it was new, and not

practiced with a nozzle, though in fairness your vinyl had deterior-
ated past fragile and was mostly a collection of ribbons. The kid
blew your shreds right off the metal bows. Some of them went in
the river and, well . . .' He pointed up into an old oak by the water.

I followed his gaze. There, flapping proudly high in the tree, was
a strip of sun-faded vinyl, a remnant of my former top.

'Fortunately one of my clients had an inexpensive replacement,'
he said, meaning a chop shop.

'Green?' I asked him. 'I've never seen a green top. And won't such
an unusual one be easy to trace, and tie my Jeep to another crime—?'

He stopped me with a raised hand. 'Out of state situation,
Dek. The owner and what's left of his green-topped Jeep are long
gone.' Then he added, 'I'm only charging an extra fifty for the top,
and that includes installation. Plus, you can now see out of windows
that are clear and not fogged like severe cataracts. You'll be dry
and safe for years.'

The improvements were a bargain, indeed. I peeled off two
hundred and fifty dollars and gave it to him. 'Did a tail ever show
up last night?'

'That's another reason why installing the new top was wise, if it
was a cop. Someone pulled up across the street after you left.'

'Unmarked sedan?'

'Someone in a bad-ass black Ford pick-up truck, thousand dollar
chrome wheels with big off-road tires. It was a fifty-thousand-dollar
ride, at least.'

'Too flashy for a cop?'

'Cop or not, whoever was watching maybe thought you brought
your Jeep in for a new top instead of a cleanse, so that's a good thing,
too. Speaking of cops, we put your Jeep up on the hoist to do the
underside. Want to guess what else we blew off with the power washer?'

'A button?'

He nodded. 'A nice little GPS transmitter – expensive, better than
the cops typically use to keep track of someone. I threw it in the
river. Don't get cocky. They'll find a way to attach another one.'

I drove home, red bodied and green topped, tempted to break out
singing 'Silent Night' in salute to my wonderfully silent new top.
And when I pulled up to the turret, things were even better. Amanda's
old white Toyota Celica was parked at the curb.

I found her sitting on the bench down by the river. 'You still have the Toyota,' I said in obvious admiration. It was the car she'd owned when we first met.

She gestured at the water flushing debris to the west. 'I've missed this.'

'I've missed you missing this.'

She leaned closer to me. 'I'm playing hooky,' she whispered, as though someone might be listening.

Her breath warmed my cheek. I missed that, too.

'Let's go someplace like we used to do. Let's just get up and go,' she said, watching my eyes for enthusiasm. It was a major step forward, coming over so spontaneously, and must have taken some courage. 'Or . . . you already had plans,' she said, grinning.

'I need to go somewhere.'

'Last night you said you had to go to Reeder, Oregon and the trail of Willard Piser posing as Dainsto Runney?'

'It's even more of a horse race now to see whether it's Bohler or Marilyn's killer that gets me tagged for Marilyn's murder. Bohler followed me after I left your place.'

'Oooh,' she said, 'your plans fit so nicely with my plans.' She told me exactly how.

'No,' I said.

'You'll fly coach,' she said, and linked her arm in mine.

We walked up the hill to the street and she laughed her good laugh at the sight of the Jeep. 'Your Jeep . . .'

'Elegant, yes?'

'Santa will retire his reindeer, for sure,' she said. 'A green top on a red Jeep.'

I could only preen.

THIRTY-SIX

Sergeant Bohler was not at the county impound garage. Neither was Sniffy the wonder dog, whose nostrils had imploded from whiffing too many Burger King wrappers. Their absence – the sergeant's more than the dog's – simplified the lies I needed to get away with.

'I'm dropping off my Jeep,' I said to the young officer sitting at Bohler's desk.

'Huh?'

'Sergeant Bohler thinks I'm a murderer and she impounded my Jeep.'

'I remember.'

'She's desperate to prove it was used to destroy evidence and will want new noses, canine and otherwise, to examine it.' I did not add that Bohler might want the opportunity to install a new tracking device.

The young cop started to nod at the nonsense before he caught himself and stopped. 'You're nuts,' he offered reasonably.

'Perhaps, but new meds are being developed every day. May I have a receipt?'

'Sergeant Bohler wouldn't want this. Suspects don't bring in evidence.'

'She's got a nose for thoroughness,' I said cleverly. 'She won't turn down a redo.'

The young cop shrugged, grabbed a pad from Bohler's office and followed me outside.

He laughed when he saw the top. 'It's green.'

'You'll be envious, come Christmas,' I said.

His smile disappeared. 'And that?' the cop asked, pointing at the yellowish bit impaled on the braided wires protruding from the dash.

'More interesting than an ordinary air freshener, don't you think?' I said of the Cheese Whopper wrapper. It was the second-to-last touch of my inspiration, a restoration of the scent that had driven poor Sniffy mad.

The cop gave me a receipt and I walked away as though headed for the train station.

Amanda was waiting around the corner in her Toyota. 'You're sure that was wise, poking so arrogantly at them?' she asked.

'I don't want to leave the Jeep outside the turret if I'm not around, for fear of a new deposit. I won't leave it at Leo's, for fear I'll link him to this mess.'

'What about my building? Best guarded garage in town.'

'You don't need cops hanging around your condo.'

'We'll see who I want hanging around my condo,' she said,

and pointed her comfortably clattering old Toyota toward the airport.

Instead of continuing down 55th Street to the long-term regular parking garage, she turned south on Central Avenue and pulled beneath the portico of Signature Flight Support.

'Support?' I asked.

'For the rich,' she said. She held out her hand, palm up.

As we agreed before we left the turret, I gave her the $482 my coach seat would have cost to fly Southwest Airlines round trip to Portland, Oregon. It was a pittance and absolutely necessary.

'I'll have my secretary email you a receipt,' she said.

We walked into the lobby. A center cluster of black vinyl and chrome lounge chairs faced a big-screen television. Another row faced windows that looked out onto the ritzier runways of Midway Airport. Amanda stopped at the main desk to hand a woman her car keys and we went outside onto the cement bordering the closest runway.

We walked past a Rolls-Royce pulled up to the closest jet and down fifty yards to where two pilots in white shirts, dark ties and black trousers were standing next to a sleek, small white jet trimmed in burgundy and gold. They smiled as Amanda introduced me. A door with stairs was dropped on the left side of the fuselage and we stepped up into the cabin.

It was close enough to opulent to reinforce my belief that I would never feel comfortable in such a craft. Two tan leather seats faced each other on the door side, along with a single seat that faced the door. Two pairs of seats faced each other across the narrow aisle. Most of the hard surfaces were tan, textured plastic, trimmed in narrow, gold-colored metal. Amanda and I sat opposite each other in the larger seating group.

The pilots came on board a minute later. The captain slipped onto the left-hand seat in the cockpit and the first officer came back to give us the same instructions about emergency evacuation, oxygen masks and flotation cushions that I ignored on commercial flights. Pointing to a cabinet, he told us there was an assortment of booze, Coke and snacks, and for us to help ourselves.

'I asked them to stock Twinkies and Peeps,' Amanda said.

'You did all that this morning?'

'Crack of dawn,' she said.

'You were pretty cocky, assuming I'd prefer this over the press of mankind in the main terminal,' I said.

'I hedged my bet by stocking the Twinkies and Peeps. I knew you wouldn't refuse those.'

'The Peeps, they're fresh?'

'Wealthy people don't risk cracking teeth.'

We were off, then, and in no time we were above the clouds.

'Seductive, isn't it? No lines, no TSA screening, no waiting of any sort?' she asked.

'What if your shareholders find out you're using this for personal reasons?'

'This was my father's plane, not the company's,' she said. 'He used it for business, of course, but also for fishing and hunting trips with his buddies. I'll need it once in a while but not as often, so I've let it out for charter. I expect to make money on it.'

She got up, grabbed two Diet Cokes and asked what specifically I expected to find in Reeder, Oregon.

'The reason why someone isn't there,' I said.

THIRTY-SEVEN

Four hours, one Twinkie and two Peeps later, we landed at a bright and shiny small airport along the west coast of Oregon. Sounding not so bright and shiny was Sergeant Bohler, who had left eight messages on my cell phone. I called her back.

'What are you up to, Elstrom?' she asked, by way of an enthusiastic greeting.

'Yielding to the herd of folks giving you tips about my murderous ways. Leaving my Jeep with you makes it more efficient for them to plant evidence. You just have to walk outside to collect it.'

'We were done with your Jeep.'

'What about the most recent evidence?'

'What new evidence?'

'The green top, of course. Surely you knew about that.' I stopped short of asking her how long she'd watched Booster's garage from her fat-tired, black pickup truck.

'Pick up your Jeep, Elstrom.'

I hung up on her. It was no risk. Our relationship was already damaged.

Reeder was tiny, a meeting of two side roads along the Oregon coast set in tall pines so dense they cast everything in shade. The intersection held a mini-mart gas station, a long-abandoned ice house and two thickly wooded lots that had resisted development since the dawn of mankind.

The clerk at the mini-mart pointed to the steeple a hundred yards down the one road. 'That's Dainsto's church, though he took off.'

'You call him Dainsto? Not Pastor Runney or Reverend Runney?'

'He tried preaching for about a year but the man was mostly interested in money.'

Amanda and I agreed to split up. She'd park the rental at the ice house, where a man as old as the building was perched at the top of the steep stairs. I headed down to the church on foot.

The Church of the Reawakened Spirit was small, more of a chapel than a full church. Its white paint was faded and peeling but still stark against the dark green backdrop of the enormous pines. Two cars were parked on the gravel lot in front. One was a new four-door sedan and the other was an old hatchback, faded like the church. Two men came out as I walked up, each carrying a cardboard box filled with hardware. They got in the hatchback and drove away.

Large cartons of miscellaneous cooking utensils, printed church envelopes and office supplies were set out on folding tables inside. Plastic chairs, more folding tables and boxes of mismatched dishes were laid out on the floor against a side wall. The pews had been unbolted and pushed against another wall. Everything was affixed with a price on a yellow Post-It.

A woman at the far end, where an altar might once have been, noticed me and walked up. She was about forty years old, well dressed in a matching gray sweater and pair of slacks. 'No reasonable offer will be refused,' she said, waving a hand at the stuff for sale. She might have been the woman I'd talked to when I'd phoned from the motel in Laguna Beach, before I knew Marilyn Paul was dead.

'Is Dainsto Runney in?'

'Long gone,' she said. 'We're recouping.'

'You're with the bank that holds the mortgage?'

'I conduct their foreclosure sales.'

I handed her a card.

'This is about insurance?' she asked.

'An old friend of Runney's named Willard Piser,' I said.

'I don't know his friends.' She made a smile but there was resignation behind it. 'Look, I suspect Dainsto Runney is too broke and owes too many people to ever show his face in Reeder again. He disappeared in the night.'

'Suddenly?'

She nodded.

'When did he leave?'

'We think the week before last, though no one's quite sure. He didn't have any friends left to say goodbye to. He threw his clothes and some food into his car and took off, though some say he won't get far.'

'Why's that?'

'Apparently he drives an old white police Crown Victoria he got at an auction, back when he was trying to sell used cars. It was the only car he had left, some say, because it barely runs.' She put my card in the pocket of her slacks. 'If you do find him, tell him he'd make things a whole lot easier on us if he'd just sign some papers.'

I walked back down to the intersection. Amanda sat at the top of the ice-house stairs, laughing with the old man we spotted driving in. His clothes were worn but clean. He had a full gray beard, combed gray hair and looked like he'd been adorning those steps ever since ice boxes were common a hundred years earlier.

'Dek,' she called down, 'this gentleman has been telling me fascinating stories about Dainsto Runney.'

The man looked doubtfully at Amanda, then down at me. 'She finds that fool interesting. I was just telling her about his arm.'

'His arm?'

'I been telling your gorgeous associate here about Dainsto when he first came to town, and the backside of the church.'

He gestured for me to climb up and sit down. Likely the man didn't enjoy much company, perched as he was so high on the ice-house steps, and the story was going to be told his way, with every detail he deemed necessary.

'Dainsto blew into town twenty years ago, maybe intending good works,' he began. 'He bought the church and began holding services.'

'I thought preachers were hired by a board of church parishioners.'

'Nobody thought Dainsto was much of a preacher at all, him being so young, but there was no question he was rich, paying cash for a church that had sat empty all those years. He gave sermons but they were rambling affairs and attendance dwindled soon enough. Folks around here couldn't put much in the collection plate anyway, so he quit that altogether after a few months. When spring came he began fixing the place up, probably to sell, and that included a new paint job. It's peeling now but it was quite nice when he got it almost done.'

'He never finished painting it?' I asked, like I was really interested.

'Never did the backside. If you walk around you'll see the wood back there is raw. It ain't seen paint for fifty years, and that brings us to Dainsto's arm.'

'I'm not following.'

'The damned fool fell off a ladder and broke his arm. It was crooked ever since.' He turned to Amanda. 'Why is all this so interesting?'

'I thought if he was looking to sell the place he could have hired someone to finish painting that last wall,' she said.

'No; I meant why do you good-looking women find Dainsto so interesting all of a sudden?'

'I don't understand,' Amanda said.

'There was this other babe, said she was a reporter from San Francisco. Built like a brick sh—' He stopped, moved his eyes away from Amanda.

'Outhouse?' Amanda said, laughing, offering the more acceptable word.

He nodded, relieved. 'She was asking the same exact things you're wondering on.'

'Television reporter?' Amanda asked and turned exaggeratedly raised eyebrows toward me.

'Could have been,' he said. 'We don't get San Francisco stations up here.'

'What did Dainsto do after he quit preaching and painting?' I asked.

'He was a hustler, that Dainsto. Chock-full of schemes. After he quit the sermonizing business he got the idea to build a pee-wee golf course, but he lost a pile on that and ended up stiffing more than one lumber yard for the wood he bought on credit. He mortgaged the church some more to try buying and selling used cars, then switched over to selling them on consignment, right there in the church parking lot, but he was stiffing folks there, too, never giving the old owners money for their cars after he sold them.' He laughed. 'That Dainsto, he tried a hundred schemes, lost money on every one and screwed everybody in the process. No wonder he slunk off in the middle of the night. I'm going to miss him. Pure entertainment, that man.'

'I heard he left town in a heap,' I said.

'Clapped-out old cop car,' the man agreed. 'White Crown Vicky with black doors that he painted over with aerosol cans of white paint that didn't match and puttied up holes in the roof where the bubble light bar was. Been sitting at the back of the church for three or four years.'

'Nobody knows where he went?'

'Plenty of people want to,' he said, 'but I don't guess they'll ever see him again.'

It wasn't a guess to know he was right.

THIRTY-EIGHT

I had an inspiration as we drove out of Reeder, so we switched places and Amanda drove while I called Lieutenant Beech. 'There's a problem with the body found at Arlin's house?' I asked.

'Arlin's insurance medicals?'

'When are you telling the reporters about the problem?'

'We welcome visitors, including the press. We're right on the ocean. Our sunsets are spectacular.'

'What's wrong with the corpse?'

'I'm working until midnight, every night this week.'

'What about that red-haired fellow hanging around Arlin's house the night before the explosion?'

'Do drop by with medical records,' he said, and hung up.

'He wants the pleasure of my company,' I told Amanda.

'To arrest you for withholding evidence?'

'I might have leverage to keep him from doing any such thing.'

I asked her to pull over. I wanted her to call the Laguna Beach Police so whoever answered wouldn't recognize my voice calling back. She put it on speaker.

'Laguna Beach Police,' the woman who answered said.

'A friend borrowed my car,' Amanda said. 'She left it in a no-parking zone and it got towed. Where's the city impound lot?'

'No city lot. We use Ajax Towing. Here's their number.'

I made the call to Ajax. 'You've got my white Crown Victoria, Oregon plates?'

The man at the other end put the phone down for a moment, then came back to say, 'Sixty-five a day brings it to seven hundred and eighty. Cash only.'

Ajax's deal with the city was to tow for free. They made their money on storage charges. Or not, if the owner never came back to claim a car.

I did the backward math based on the impound charges. Runney's Crown Victoria was towed the day after Arlin's house blew up.

Amanda read my face like a page printed large and smiled. 'Two hundred extra for a dog leg on the way back to Chicago?'

'Done,' I said, peeling off four fifties.

She dialed a new number and said, 'I'd like you to file a new flight plan.'

THIRTY-NINE

I checked for voice and text messages during the short flight to Laguna Beach, and then handed my cell phone to Amanda.

'Dear Mr Elstrom,' she read aloud from the small screen. 'Regarding your note, I possess no answers to the questions you raised. Sincerely, Theresa Wade.'

She handed me back my phone. 'Congratulations. You got a

response from the famously reclusive Theresa Wade, hot from her address on Tim's campaign website.'

'My note to her said simply that she and I had a mutual interest in a matter for which I was being framed. I didn't mention that someone had disguised herself to look like her, nor did I write anything about Marilyn Paul. If Theresa Wade is totally clueless, as she claims, either she would have tossed my note away without responding, like she must do with the hundreds of others she receives from cranks, or she would have asked what our mutual interest was. She didn't do either. She knows something.'

'Dek, I've come to know these people—'

'Not her,' I interrupted.

'No one knows her. But I do know Tim. He's a good man. He does a lot of good.'

'That never comes up. Unusual for a politician.'

'He's reluctant to brag. He stays totally focused on the future.'

'And his sister facilitates that?'

'She administers everything, to help him keep that focus.'

'He's still the fourth musketeer,' I said.

'Happenstance,' she said.

But she said it tentatively.

'Damn, Elstrom, I didn't expect to see you so quickly,' Lieutenant Beech said. He was all grins, coming into the tiny interview room. He turned to Amanda. 'And you are?'

'A very wealthy woman who employs lots of lawyers who report to lots of lawyers who report to her,' she said, calmly enough.

I think I must have stared, as shocked as Beech at the arrogance of her opening salvo. She was looking out for me, telling the cop that hell would pay if he tried to arrest me. This, most certainly, was not the Amanda I'd married and would love forever. This one possessed interesting, though intimidating, new possibilities that I was very much likely to love forever.

The lieutenant sighed, accepting. He was used to confrontations with the rich.

He turned to me. 'So, what's this about the sheriff liking you for dumping that woman in the river?'

'You found Bohler.'

'It took me some time to find someone interested in you. Are things so messed up in Chicago, budget-wise, that a deputy who runs an impound garage heads up a murder investigation?' he asked.

'For some reason, an anonymous tipster called her to blame me. Must be that every other cop thought it was ridiculous.' I smiled at Amanda. 'And dear Miss Phelps' lawyers will keep me out of jail.'

'OK, I get it – you're both crazy,' he said. 'For now, we'll try to get along, if no one tries lying.'

'You're having trouble identifying the body found in Arlin's house?' I asked.

'I don't know how you found that out, but yes. Arlin was a tennis player, like so many around here. He sought treatment for an arthritic condition last winter. The doctor took X-rays.'

'Which showed there was no break in his arm?'

Beech leaned across the table. 'Who are you, Elstrom, and what do you know?'

'I was hired by a heavily disguised woman to look in on Arlin here, and Dainsto Runney, an erstwhile preacher and hustler, up in Reeder, Oregon. She didn't say why. It took no time on the Internet to learn Arlin had just died in a house explosion, which must have triggered her hiring me. Runney left his church in Oregon a day or two before Arlin's house blew up.'

'You think he came here?'

'He broke his arm painting that church, years ago.'

'Lots of people break their arms.'

'But not David Arlin, according to his X-rays?'

He shrugged.

'A white Crown Victoria with Oregon plates is impounded here at Ajax Towing. If I'm right, it's Runney's and the DNA inside will belong to your corpse.'

He leaned back, rubbed his eyes and said, 'Runney drove here and Arlin killed him to take his place?'

'Have you identified the cause of the explosion?'

'Loose gas fitting, like with a wrench.'

'Arlin's car was blown up in the explosion?'

Beech nodded.

'Then Arlin left town some other way. Did you ever follow up on that red-headed man?' I asked.

'Arlin's neighbor is elderly. People stop all the time, asking for directions. Or he could have been delivering a pizza.'

'Maybe he wasn't asking for directions. Maybe he wanted to be noticed asking for the directions.'

'You think it was Arlin in a red wig, dragging a herring across the road to confuse us dogs?'

'Perhaps, or perhaps it was someone else – a real redhead,' I said.

'Who?'

'I have no idea,' I lied.

He sighed. 'Your client might know, but you're sure she's no longer available?'

'That's all I'm sure of,' I said.

FORTY

'**Y**ou omitted a lot back there,' Amanda said as we sped through the California night to the airport.

'He might share with Bohler and she'll just get in my way.'

'Of your messing with a future United States senator?'

'And, potentially, a president of the United States,' I said.

'Don't joke. Mixing the Wades in with whoever killed Marilyn Paul ups the threat to you tenfold. They're powerful people and all you've got are vague suspicions that they know things they won't tell you.'

'I have suspicions because Marilyn Paul had suspicions. It's why she planted those bones and the little axe, and someone killed her for it.'

'Fair enough, but right now the case is stuck with a junior-grade cop supervising an impound garage,' she said. 'A woman who is trying to blame you for the murder. How quickly can you prove enough to get real police detectives involved who can make you safe?'

'Things might firm up if Laguna Beach PD identifies Runney as the corpse in Arlin's rubble.'

'Arlin killed him to escape his own money woes and start a new life?'

'If it was Arlin.'

'You really think it could have been that red-headed man that asked for directions?'

'I don't know. Halvorson is the most mysterious of the musketeers. He's stayed under the radar for twenty years. He could have been in on the plan with Arlin.'

'Whatever the plan is,' she said.

'There is that confusion, yes,' I said.

'Want to go to Tucson?' she asked.

I did. I wanted to go there badly, to put my hands around Halvorson's landlord's neck and shake everything he knew about his tenant from his head. But more than that, I wanted to get Amanda home, safely away from me. She'd been right. I was messing with a future senator. Guys like him employed people who didn't smile much.

'Halvorson's long gone from Tucson,' I said.

'The grims are waiting,' Amanda said. She pointed to the two men waiting outside Signature Flight Support at Chicago's Midway Airport as we taxied up. It was four in the morning. 'No doubt they're displeased I gave them the slip.'

'They watch you closely?'

'When I called work, saying I wouldn't be coming in, they would have checked with security at my condo, found out I'd left and begun tracking me.'

'You can't play hookey?'

'Sure I can, so long as they can come along. Remember, my father was murdered not that long ago. Today they had to make sure I wasn't abducted for ransom.'

'Again,' I said. Amanda had been abducted for ransom when her father was still alive.

'I was wrong to blow off the day on the sly. I was wasteful of their time and that's company money. I should have notified them.'

'Have they been waiting here all day and all night?'

She laughed. 'No. They knew when I'd be landing. There's a website, free and accessible to all, that tracks all flights by aircraft tail number. They plugged in mine first thing this morning, saw that we were in the air to Oregon then tracked us flying to John Wayne Airport outside Laguna Beach. It was only when they saw us airborne back to Midway that they began to breathe easily.'

'Why didn't they call your cell?'

She grinned. 'I left it in the Toyota.'

I was amazed and appalled. 'Cat and mouse? That's really your life now?'

She gazed out at the lights of the runways. 'I'm wealthy; I'm a target. I felt confined and needed to rebel, like a young schoolgirl. But it was wrong.'

The co-pilot dropped the cabin door and we climbed down into the chill of a predawn, late October Chicago. 'We'll drop you in Rivertown,' she said.

'I'll get a cab.'

'Take my Toyota, at least.' It had been pulled up behind a black stretch Escalade.

'Cabbing is easier. Call me tomorrow?'

'If I'm allowed a call from my gilded prison,' she said.

I looked out the lobby window as I called a cab. One of her guards got behind the wheel of the Escalade; the other held the rear door open for her and then got in front next to the driver. A third guard followed in the Toyota. Her gilded prison was thickly walled, indeed.

She'd surely traveled a long distance since we'd first met in that small art gallery on Michigan Avenue in Chicago. Watching her taillights disappear into the last of the night, I wondered if it would prove to be too far, or whether I'd simply not traveled far enough.

FORTY-ONE

'Booster Liss?' I asked Leo the next morning as I climbed aboard his sparkling silver Dodge Ram van. It smelled strongly of chlorine.

'Full cleanse,' he said, grimacing. 'All those naked old people . . .'

'I understand.'

'I don't,' said Leo, the most optimistic of men. 'They said they wanted to do field trips to the zoo, the Arboretum, Chicago Botanic, Ma and her lady friends, even that guy—'

'The one I saw in the pool – the one without his suit?' I asked, unable to resist. 'The guy who I then saw exiting this very vehicle, again without his—?'

He groaned. 'I'd only stepped out into the hall for a minute, to take a call, when up walked the lizard that runs the health center. He's with two sour-looking fellows. I smiled nicely, thinking the sour guys were considering membership. They walked into the pool area and I went back to talking on the phone. Next thing, I heard shouting. I ran back into the pool area. What did I see? It isn't Ma who's doing the yelling, or her lady friends, or even the old gent whose applesauce I suspect they're dosing with Viagra. No, it was the sour guys. They were going ballistic, yelling, pointing at Ma and her friends in the pool. They pushed me aside in a panic to get out. One of them was on the phone, calling the cops. Turns out the two sours were from the government agency that approves funding for senior rehabilitation facilities.'

'Ma and her friends: they were, ah . . .?' There really was no delicate way to probe.

Leo nodded. 'Buck naked, the lot of them. Especially the old guy in all his chemically re-erected glory. Ah, jeez.'

'I still can't believe the cops busted them.'

'Public lewdness. They said they had to because those two sours were federal representatives.'

'Now what?'

'I hired the Barracuda. He fixed it.'

Jerry Lopes, the Barracuda, was one of Cook County's most flamboyant lawyers. He'd gotten rich representing Rivertown's lizards, though he rarely entered a courtroom. He worked the dimmer parts at the backs of the courthouses, passing cash.

'How much?'

'Five grand because there were multiple defendants, but he got the case dismissed.' Then he asked, 'You don't think leaving your Jeep at the sheriff's garage is provoking them unnecessarily?'

'Amanda's worried about that, too.'

His face relaxed into a smile for the first time. 'Spending more time together, are we?'

'We flew out to Reeder and Laguna Beach yesterday,' I said, sidestepping his nose. 'I needed to leave the Jeep where nobody could plant something inside.'

'Baloney. You're taunting that Sergeant Bohler. And when she arrests you I'll have to get you a lawyer.'

'Call the Bohemian, not Jerry Lopes, though I don't think either will be necessary. Remember, Booster did a cleanse for me, too.'

He raised his nose to sniff his own chlorine-scented air and nodded knowingly. 'What else is Amanda worried about?'

'Timothy Wade.'

'Just because he was the fourth musketeer?'

'She genuinely likes the guy. Plus, she thinks I'm poking at a very powerful future presidential candidate, someone with resources to hit back hard.'

'I'm with her. I don't know Wade but I like him.'

'I think Marilyn Paul suspected him of something. She planted the bones and the axe in the silo.'

'Jeez!'

'That was Amanda's reaction, too.'

We turned the last corner and headed to the impound garage down the street.

'Actually, it's Halvorson who bothers me the most,' I said. 'I can't get a lead to where he's been for the past twenty years.'

'If Bohler asks I'll vouch that you have trouble figuring things out,' he said, trying for light.

He slowed. 'My God. The Jeep. The top has gone green. And look what's on the bumper.'

It was Sergeant Bohler on the back bumper, sitting, waiting. She knew we were coming.

'I didn't think to look for a tail behind us,' I said as Leo pulled to a stop.

'Would it have changed anything?'

'No.'

Bohler scuffed the cement with the heel of her sensible cop shoe and stood as I walked up. 'My cop friend in Laguna Beach says I should play along for now,' she said, reaching into her jacket pocket, 'but first, a DNA sample.' She pulled out a small kit sealed in plastic and a pair of thin latex gloves.

'You got usable DNA off Marilyn Paul, even though she'd been banged around, submerged, at the dam?'

She took a long cotton swab from the kit. 'Don't forget, she scratched at you before she died. Lucky for us, you were nice enough to put the poor woman in a really thick, big plastic bag. The bag stayed watertight and preserved her fingernails. God bless thick plastic, and God bless you, Elstrom, for being such an idiot.'

I'd squinted at enough police dramas on my four-inch television screen to know the procedure. She swabbed the inside of my mouth and put the swab inside a long plastic container. Everything then went in a plastic bag and back in her pocket.

She gestured at the Jeep. 'Cute, you leaving the insult of a Cheese Whopper wrapper stuffed in the dash,' she said, 'along with two entire Whoppers, though cheese-less, under the front seats.'

'Ah, jeez,' Leo muttered from a couple of feet behind me.

'I knew I forgot to eat something,' I said to Bohler. It was a lie; I've never forgotten to eat anything. Along with the wrapper, I'd left the burgers to foul the noses of any interested dogs, though my confidence in Booster Liss's cleansing protocol was supreme.

'You might be able to fool one of our dogs but not us two-legged cops, not forever,' she said. 'Anyway, in the spirit of friendship, I repositioned your Jeep several times while you were gone, to keep your burgers warm under the fullest force of the sun. Everyone likes hot, festering burgers, right?' She offered up a smile. 'Especially raccoons, those nocturnal foragers who can slip into cars if their doors have been carelessly left open by someone like me. Nothing's ever wrong with raccoon noses, that's for sure.'

I opened the driver's door and released the stench of the sergeant's vengeance. Raccoons had found the hamburgers. Worse, they'd lingered long enough to complete their full digestive processes before leaving.

'As for me, Elstrom,' she went on, smiling, 'from now on, I'll have to keep an eye on you from afar. The Paul murder was trans-ferred, officially, to our detectives.' She started toward the door of the garage.

'Time for the grown-ups to investigate?' I called after her.

'Damn it, Dek!' Leo whispered, moving up right behind me. 'She'll arrest you just on the basis of your attitude.'

Bohler stopped and turned around. She'd heard. 'Tell your friend not yet,' she said. 'In fact, I didn't tell our dicks anything about you, because I'm reserving the honor of arresting you for myself.'

She turned back around and went into the garage.

FORTY-TWO

I needed links.

After an hour spent removing the Jeep's seats and carpets, hosing it out and reinstalling everything to pre-raccoon freshness, I sat at my computer, as I did so ever-increasingly.

Election Day for Delman Bean was November 8, 1994. That meant that three of the four musketeers – Shea, Piser and Halvorson – had left Chicago sometime right after the first of November, seemingly to take good-paying jobs.

It took less than four minutes to find the right county database to confirm what the old man told us in Reeder. Willard Piser, as Dainsto Runney, had paid cash for his church. He'd paid fifty-eight-thousand dollars for it on December 5, about a month after he quit the Bean congressional campaign. It meant Willard Piser had come up with a significant amount of money in less than a month.

I called Lieutenant Beech. 'Your pal Bohler is off the case. It got transferred to real sheriff's detectives.'

'Don't relax. That firecracker will hound you until she learns what you know about that Marilyn Paul, even if it means arresting you.'

'You don't think I'm a killer?'

'She does. Me, I just think you're withholding a ton of information.'

'When did Arlin arrive in Laguna Beach?'

'Early to mid-November, 1994.'

'Did he come with cash?'

'I doubt it. He went to work selling kitchen and bath hardware on straight commission and lived in a tiny apartment miles from the water.'

'Straight commission means no advance for living expenses up front?'

'I suppose he could have arrived with money and just didn't flash it around . . .' He paused, thinking. 'Three years later, he had enough to buy out the distributorship.'

'For cash?'

'There's no way to trace purchase details back that far. The owner is dead. Arlin is dead . . . I mean, Arlin is supposed to be dead.' He stopped to consider what I wasn't saying. 'Why are you asking about cash? And if Arlin came here with cash, why would he bide his time before spending any of it? What was he hiding? And where did he get the cash?'

'I don't know, yet. You found that Crown Victoria?'

'Right where you said, in Ajax's lot and registered to Dainsto Runney. It's too soon to compare DNA from the car to the corpse but our medical examiner just got something almost as good. He located a doctor in Oregon where Runney went with a broken arm. The doctor is a genuine small-town practitioner, a few miles from Reeder. He still had Runney's X-rays. They show a break that matches the one in our corpse. Who is Dainsto Runney, Elstrom?'

'A man who showed up in Oregon about the same time Arlin arrived in Laguna Beach. Runney paid fifty-eight-thousand dollars in cash for a church. He tried passing himself off as a preacher, holding services before spending the next twenty years chasing other ways of making a buck, like a mini-golf course and selling used cars. Nothing worked. He mortgaged his church and borrowed from everybody else he could tap. He slunk out of Reeder, dead broke and owing everybody, a few days before Arlin's house blew up.'

'You're thinking his money trouble links him to Arlin?'

'I think if you check out Runney you'll find out he has no past, just like Arlin. And both of them were in financial distress at the time Arlin's house exploded.'

'You're convinced it was Arlin who blew up Runney?'

'Him or that red-headed man you refuse to look for.'

'We've gone door-to-door in Arlin's neighborhood. No one other than that old lady saw the red-headed man but she backed up what you're suspecting. He lingered.'

'Lingered, I think, to be remembered.'

'So you said last time.'

'Or, the man might have been Gary Halvorson, an old pal of Arlin's and Runney's from Chicago. His friends called him Red. Or . . .'

'This Halvorson, he doesn't have a past either?'

'Just the opposite. He's got a past but no visible present, at least not for twenty years. He probably arrived in Tucson about the same

time Runney hit Reeder and Arlin landed in Laguna Beach.' I gave
him Halvorson's address. 'You should make a friend in the Tucson
police department.'

'I still don't get the connection.'

'I don't either,' I said, and hung up.

FORTY-THREE

'**D**ear Ms Theresa Wade,' I emailed again to the campaign's
website. 'Thank you for responding to my previous
inquiry. I'm confident that you and your brother know
much about John Shea, Willard Piser, and Gary "Red" Halvorson.
Let's meet before the story appears in the television news.'

I hit 'Send' and fired my note into cyberspace, hoping it was a
rocket and not another dud.

My phone rang two hours later.

'Mr Elstrom?' a pleasant voice asked. It was a voice I'd heard
on television.

I admitted it.

'This is Tim Wade. You wrote the magic words.'

'Shea, Piser and Halvorson?'

'No.' He laughed. '"Television news." Those are magic words,
especially to my sister.'

'You're avoiding the media.'

'Absolutely,' he said. 'How about stopping by for a drink?'

FORTY-FOUR

'**Y**ou're back,' the guard at Wade's driveway said through the
gate. And with little enthusiasm.

'And drier,' I said, waiting for admiring words about
my new green top, clear plastic windows and even the little green,

pine-tree-shaped air fresheners I'd hung festively from the exposed wiring to kill the lingering reminders of the raccoons that had done dinner and more inside my Jeep.

Smothering his enthusiasm, the guard noted the time on a clip-board. And that gave me a better look at the gold watch I'd noticed him wearing the last time. It was a gold Rolex Day Date like the one my former father-in-law had worn at the moment he'd been murdered. A watch like that went for at least ten thousand dollars and must have been a gift from the Wades, brother and sister, maybe at Christmas. Ten-thousand-dollar Rolexes make excellent stocking stuffers from the rich.

The guard stepped back into the shack and pushed a button. The gate slid back and I drove up the circular drive to the house.

The front door opened before I came to a complete stop. Tim Wade himself, and not some servant or butler, was coming down the steps to greet me.

'Mr Elstrom, it's a pleasure,' he said as I got out.

'Likewise,' I said, surprising myself by really meaning it. The guy had an air of non-pretension about him as well as the grace to not stare at a Jeep sporting a green on its top that surely clashed with the color of his carefully tended yews.

He led me inside and down a short hall, past stairs with a chairlift mounted on the wall. Oddly, a retaining bolt at the bottom had worked itself out from the base molding.

We went into a living room comfortably furnished in cloth-upholstered furniture, mostly beiges and pale greens, and sat opposite each other on settees in front of a properly-sized fireplace burning real logs. My own fireplaces, one on each of the five floors of the turret, were preposterously larger, big enough to burn whole chunks of trees. And once again, for an instant, I wondered what my lunatic bootlegging grandfather had been thinking.

On the table in front of us was a bottle of whiskey, a small glass bucket of ice and two plain water glasses no fancier than those average people had in their average kitchens.

'As you might know, my family is reverential toward Canadian whiskey,' Wade said, grinning.

'My grandfather was in the trade, too,' I offered up. 'Beer, brewed in garages.'

He nodded like that would bond us forever, and asked, 'Ice?'

'Sure,' I said. 'How did you get my cell-phone number?'

'Amanda Phelps, your ex-wife and very strong admirer, gave it to me.' He handed me my drink. 'My sister directs all potentially alarming emails to Jeffries, our security chief. He researched you and reported your relationship to Ms Phelps. I called her and asked her for your number. She was hesitant to give it to me but when I read her the contents of your email she relented. Though she acknowledged nothing, I got the feeling she shares your concerns.'

I turned to look out into the hall.

'There are no guards inside,' he said. 'We're alone except for my sister, who spends most of her time upstairs.' He smiled again. 'It was Theresa who thought it best if we spoke face-to-face.'

'Because I threatened to go to the media?'

'That, of course, but also we're worried about losing Ms Phelps' support. She's part of my Committee of Twenty-Four. Though a newcomer to my political world, her counsel is well received.' He paused to take a sip of his drink. 'Concerns on her part could become contagious, perhaps spread to other members of the committee, and that could affect all sorts of things. So, from a very practical point of view, you can ask me anything about John, Willard and Red, as long as my responses are kept confidential, for your ears only. Most especially, that includes not saying anything to Miss Jennifer Gale.'

'You saw that Internet photo of Jenny and me.' It had been taken at a television news awards banquet the year before.

'My sister found it, actually.'

'I can't control Jenny,' I said, 'but I'll respect your confidence. Let's start with that silo business.'

He winced. 'Not my finest hour.'

I nodded.

'The police believed it was just a prank. My sister thought otherwise. So did I, at least at first. We get all sorts of nasty surprises, though that was the first that actually had a weapon, such as it was.'

'That little axe.'

'That little *rubber* axe,' he said. 'We thought it a threat all the same. My sister put out the word that it was a security issue, which was truthful, at the time. Now we think it was simply a prank related to absolutely nothing, since nothing ever came of it.'

'Nothing to do with your old friends?'

'Will, Red and John, as you mentioned in your email to my

sister?' He shook his head. 'I haven't heard from Will and Red in years, though unfortunately I did hear from John, and very recently. He made several disturbing telephone calls to our campaign office, demanding to speak with me personally.'

'For what purpose?'

'Blackmail, I think.'

'You never spoke to him?'

'No. My campaign office manager, Marilyn Paul, did. We dismissed it. There is nothing in my past that's problematic.' He held up the whiskey bottle. 'You have to go back to my great granddad to catch the Wades doing something illegal.'

'Have you wondered if Shea murdered Marilyn Paul?'

'Impossible. She only intercepted his calls. And besides, John has since died, out in California.'

'As did Marilyn Paul, only she was killed here in Illinois.'

He stared at his whiskey for a long moment before looking back up. 'I don't understand your inference. I don't see a link between John and Marilyn.'

'You just said she intercepted his calls to you.'

'She intercepted many crank calls. His got passed to her as would any other. He'd used his personal number for the first one and she did a reverse look-up. She learned he was living under an assumed name – David Arlin – but recognized his picture on the Internet. She knew John from way back, as did I, of course. She confronted him, demanded to know what he was up to. He hung up on her.'

'Did you wonder if she planted the plastic bones and rubber hatchet?'

He looked genuinely shocked. 'For what end?'

'I'm hoping you'll tell me.'

'Marilyn wouldn't have done that thing with the bones. She had no reason. And anyway, those bones and that little axe meant nothing, as I said. They were just a prank that I overreacted to, which we then covered up.'

It was impossible not to like the man's straightforwardness. Yet something – his overwhelming earnestness, maybe – held me back from telling him it had been Marilyn who'd salted the silo with the bones.

'Maybe John said something on the phone,' he went on, 'that she never passed along to us. Perhaps she thought all three of the old gang were involved in shaking me down; I'm wealthy, I'm running for office. I'm vulnerable. Above all, Marilyn must have believed that we weren't taking John's vague threat seriously enough. And that says a lot about her, that she'd use her own funds to hire you to get to the bottom of a threat aimed at me. I'm going to miss her.'

He smiled at my lack of a response and went on: 'No, Marilyn did not tell me she'd retained you but it's obvious from your two emails. First, you contacted my sister saying you and she have a mutual interest in something for which you are being framed. After we learned you live just up the river from where Marilyn's body was found, it was simple to assume you were being framed for her murder. Then you wrote, demanding to know what we know about John, Willard and Red. That connects you to her because Marilyn had those same concerns, or at least about John. I'm guessing now she was concerned about all three of them, since you're concerned about all three.'

He held up the bottle, offering to freshen my drink. I shook my head. I'd taken only one sip.

Wade leaned back. 'We were the Four Musketeers: John, Willard, Red and me. I don't remember who tagged us as such but the name stuck. We worked on the Delman Bean campaign years ago and we had fun. We were young, single, liked to drink and liked to laugh. They were good times. And then it was over. John and Willard and Red got great jobs with some oil company in California.'

'They quit so suddenly.'

'Who could blame them? They had lousy jobs here and they saw a great opportunity.'

'It was so sudden that not even you, their fourth musketeer, had any inkling they were about to take off?'

'They never said a word, and for a long time I was a little hurt by that. Now I realize they didn't think I'd understand because our economic circumstances were so different.'

'They gave you no hint, whatsoever, that last night you were together?'

'Beers as usual. I was shocked all to hell when John called me the next morning.' He looked out the window for a moment. 'It sure screwed Delman Bean. We were depending on them to chauffeur voters to the polls. Bean lost by just a few votes.'

'You never heard from any of them again? Not a word, not a card?'

'Not until John called my campaign office a couple of weeks ago.'

'Only John Shea?'

'Red sends a Christmas card every year but it's a preprinted, impersonal thing – something a mailing service could do.' He picked up a cell phone from the lamp table beside him, made a call and asked for the security man he'd mentioned, Jeffries. 'I'd like to send someone over to talk to you,' he said to whoever answered. 'Tell him about Marilyn and John Shea. Hold nothing – repeat, nothing – back.' He listened for a moment, and then clicked off.

'I don't expect you to take my word for anything, Mr Elstrom,' he said.

FORTY-FIVE

A dour-looking, heavy-set man was standing on the sidewalk when I pulled up to Wade's campaign headquarters on Chicago's near west side. 'Name's Jeffries,' the security man said, eyeballing my khakis for anything weapon-like.

We went inside. 'Lousiest-looking campaign shop in the Democratic Party,' he said, sounding proud, as we walked past stained fabric panels enclosing young people staring at computer screens and talking into telephone headsets.

'Yet your candidate is rich,' I said.

'He never acts it. He's just a regular guy.' We went into a small conference room. A young woman, about nineteen, was sitting at the table reading a dog-eared copy of *Time* magazine.

'Earlene,' he said, 'tell Mr Elstrom everything you told me about those calls you and Marilyn took.'

'About two weeks ago,' the young girl began, 'I took a call from a man who sounded drunk. He said he wanted to get a message to Mr Wade. I said I could take down the message because that's what we're supposed to say, even though the only people who call here wanting to talk to the candidate are nut jobs. This man says to tell Tim – that's what he called him, "Tim" – to leave his private number with us here for when he calls back. I said I most certainly would, and then I asked him his name. He said never mind and asked me my name. I said it was Mindy, which was a name I made up just for him. He hung up. I thought he was just another wacko and forgot about him. But then the next night, one of the other girls stood up above her partition and asked if any of us knew anyone working here named Mindy. Nobody said anything for a second, and then I remembered the call from the previous night. I said it was me and took the call, more curious than anything. It was the same guy, except he didn't sound drunk this time. He asked if I'd passed along his message. I said not yet. He said to tell Tim that if he wanted to keep the hatchet buried Tim better give me a private contact number I could pass on. That sounded a little more serious so I got up and told Marilyn about it, because she was my boss and that was procedure.'

She looked at Jeffries, who said, 'Go on.'

She looked back at me. 'Marilyn said we ought to write it up since the guy called twice, and came back with me to my cubicle. We have computer histories of all the incomings and we were able to figure out which were the two calls from this guy, though they came from two different numbers. Marilyn wrote them both down and told me to alert her if the guy called again. Which he did, the very next night, again asking for Mindy. I told him what Marilyn told me to say, that I was transferring the call to my supervisor who could better assist him. I switched him over to Marilyn and that was the end of it for me.'

Tears had formed in the girl's eyes. Jeffries thanked her and she left.

'She feels responsible for turning the calls over to Marilyn,' he said, 'though I told her that was procedure, just as she said, and in any case those calls had nothing to do with Marilyn's death.'

'You're sure?'

'If course I'm sure, damn it.' He took a breath and went on more calmly: 'Or almost sure. Marilyn had decided to do a little investigating on her own before reporting the calls to me. She was like that: always had a strong faith in her ability to handle every damned thing, bullheaded to the extreme. So she did a reverse lookup on both numbers and hit pay dirt on the first one, the call he'd placed when he was tipsy. It was from his own number out in California. Turned out she knew the guy from way back. When the guy called again she told him a few things about himself that he probably didn't like to hear, namely that she knew he was an old buddy of Mr Wade's.'

'John Shea of Laguna Beach.'

'Calling himself David Arlin. When Marilyn looked up Arlin on the Internet she saw Shea's face, someone both she and Mr Wade knew from long ago.'

'Blackmail, that business about keeping the hatchet buried?'

'Some sort of shakedown of Mr Wade, it seemed. I told him about it but he wasn't concerned. Whatever this Shea-Arlin fellow had, it couldn't have been much. Mr Wade told me to forget about it.'

'What about that silo? You think it was coincidence, Shea mentioning a hatchet and that rubber axe business?'

'It crossed my mind that they were related, but "bury the hatchet" meant the same thing as "let's forget about our disagreement," and probably nothing more.'

'So you did nothing about Shea?'

'Marilyn wasn't happy about that, but like I said, Mr Wade said to drop it. I told her there was nothing I could do until the guy presented himself as a problem, here in Chicago. That's when she mentioned you.'

'She mentioned me by name?'

'Nothing so direct. She said she knew of a private investigator she could hire cheap, and that if I didn't get off my dead ass she'd hire the fellow herself. Which,' he said, shaking his head, 'she obviously did.'

'She told you this before Shea got blown up?'

He stared at me, surprised. 'What the hell, man? There'd be no need for an investigator after the explosion, right? I mean, the threat was gone when Shea got killed.'

'Of course,' I said, but he had it wrong. She'd hired me right after she thought Shea got killed.

'And then she got murdered,' he said. Something in his eyes had changed. He had cops' eyes, hungry for what I knew that he didn't.

'That got you worrying?'

'You bet. If her murder hadn't resulted from something else entirely, it meant Shea had an accomplice who killed Marilyn to destroy any evidence that might link back to him.'

'Or the accomplice was set to pick up where Shea left off,' I said.

He nodded. 'Sure, except nothing's happened since. No phone calls, no threats, nothing at all. It's over, Mr Elstrom.'

'You never thought to tip the cops?'

'I had nothing to give them except speculation,' he said, which meant it was campaign season and he didn't want anything nasty sticking to Timothy Wade.

'You're sure the accomplice hasn't contacted Wade without you knowing?'

'Mr Wade's got plenty to lose. He would have gotten me involved right away.'

'You've been with the Democrats a long time?' I asked.

'More years than I like to think.' He made a point of raising his arm to check his watch, an ordinary rubber Casio quite unlike the multi-thousand-dollar gold timepieces Wade's personal guards wore.

'I'd stay on guard,' I said.

He dropped his arm. 'What do you mean?'

'Call the cops in Laguna Beach and check on their investigation of the Arlin explosion.'

'There's something new?'

'Marilyn Paul's killer is still loose in Chicago. That's new enough.'

FORTY-SIX

'Such is the fear you engender in politicians,' I said on the phone. I was standing by a second-floor window, looking out into the night. No one appeared to be lurking.

'The power of my father's purse,' Amanda said. 'Was Tim helpful?'

'Everything he said sounded reasonable.'

'But . . .?' She'd caught the hesitation in my voice.

'He sounded too reasonable. He admitted being friends with the other musketeers, back in the day. And both he and his security chief believe Shea initiated some sort of blackmail scheme but that it blew up with Shea, out in Laguna Beach.'

'You didn't tell them it wasn't Shea who got killed?'

'I told the security man, Jeffries, to call the Laguna Beach Police Department directly. I don't think he will. He doesn't want to see past the Democratic campaign office.'

'What did they say about Marilyn Paul?'

'That's what's most puzzling. Wade and his sister are sharp. They figured out she'd hired me but neither Timothy nor his security man, Jeffries, pressed me much about it. They took her to be a busybody, someone best forgotten.'

'Did you tell them Marilyn planted the rubber axe and the bones?'

'I suggested it as a possibility to Wade. He acted appropriately shocked.'

'So they're seeing no link between John Shea and Marilyn Paul's murder?'

'No, despite the fact that both Wades surmised Marilyn hired me to look in on all three of the old musketeers.'

'Maybe Tim's got other, more pressing things on his mind, like getting elected to the United States Senate.'

'I admit that's very likely.'

'Have you stopped?'

'Merely awaiting inspiration,' I said.

Leo Brumsky's girlfriend, Endora, was almost a foot taller than he was but they shared the same high IQ. She'd made a pile as a fashion model, bought a condominium with a view of Lake Michigan and quit modeling for a low-paying research job at the Newberry, Chicago's quirkiest private library.

I called her cell phone an hour after I hung up with Amanda. 'That fellow who helped me find the Confessors' Club, Mickey . . .' I'd forgotten the man's last name.

'It's Dek,' she said to someone nearby.

'Hang up on him,' Leo told her from a distance. Likely, they were at Endora's place.

'Mickey Rosen,' she said to me. 'He knows everything about Chicago history.'

'Does he like to drink?'

'What a strange question.'

'I'm looking for the names and locations of bars that were in Chicago twenty years ago.'

'That's a tall order for a drinking town like ours.'

'Hang up on him,' Leo said again.

'I can narrow the search area to a three-block radius of a specific address,' I said.

'Mickey's your man,' she said.

I gave her the address of the campaign headquarters where the four musketeers had worked with Marilyn.

'Hang up on him,' Leo said for the third time.

She laughed, and did.

FORTY-SEVEN

'**M**ickey said there were nine bars within three blocks of your address,' Endora said at ten the next morning. She read off the list.

'Now I'll bet there are twenty,' I said, because the neighborhood had been yupped up in recent years. I thanked her and called Lena Jankowski, the used-to-be Democratic volunteer who'd worked with the musketeers.

'I was wondering if I'd hear from you again,' she said.

'I'm like termites,' I said. 'Almost impossible to eradicate.'

'Or understand completely,' she said.

'I'm going to read you a list of bars, or lounges, or small restaurants. I want you to give me any memory or association that comes to mind.'

'We're playing games?'

'I hope not. First name: Tony's.'

'None.'

'Willadean's Whistle.'

She laughed. 'We went there, back in the Delman Bean days.'

'You, John Shea, Willard Piser, Red Halvorson and Tim Wade?'

'And others,' she said.

'Marilyn Paul?'

'I told you, she didn't hang with us after hours. She was all business, that woman.'

'Anything else about Willadean's Whistle?'

'It was a real dump. Too bright, fluorescent lighting, sticky red tile floor. They were still serving Harvey Wallbangers twenty years after the last young person in Chicago ordered one.'

She had no memory of the next two names I read off.

'Harley's,' I said.

'Motorcycle-themed,' she said. 'Spicy chicken wings. We went there once in a while.'

'Anything else?'

'Despite the biker name, a nice place. Clean.'

'Lakota Nation,' I read out.

Dead silence. I couldn't even hear her breathe.

'Lakota Nation?' I repeated. It was the name of an American Indian tribe that moved around the Midwest.

'Sorry; remembering that place set off a lot of memories,' she said finally. 'We went there the most because they had cheap pizza and good-enough beer. It was American Indian warrior-themed, can you believe it? No one worried about political correctness back then. Chicago still has its Blackhawks hockey team, but so many of the other Indian themes are gone from here . . .' Her voice drifted away for a moment, and then she said, 'That was the place, I'm sure of it.'

'Sure of what?'

'That was our last good time. I remember because we got as drunk as coots and some of us got thrown out.'

'The musketeers?'

She laughed. 'Probably. They always got drunker than the rest of us.'

A queasy thought flitted in my mind. 'Tell me about the decor,' I said.

'Why?'

'I might have been there, long ago,' I lied. My gut was already sure.

'What you'd imagine,' she said. 'Dark wood booths, American Indian stuff on the walls – fake feather headdresses, bows and arrows.'

My mind replayed the television video of the bones falling out of the silo. 'Tomahawks, too, I seem to remember,' I said, trying to keep my voice steady. 'There were tomahawks on the walls.'

'Those little Indian axes you used to see in old Westerns?'

'The very same.'

'They were everywhere,' she said. 'There must have been a hundred of them stuck on the walls – cheap little plastic ones so much smaller than the other junk. You know, Mr Elstrom . . .' Her voice trailed away.

'Yes?'

'The sad part was how it ended. We had so much fun working on that campaign. And then John, Willard and Red walked out of that place and out of our lives without so much as a goodbye and the rest of us had to get crazy busy trying to cover their jobs. We couldn't do it, not on such short notice. We lost the election.'

'They said nothing about leaving, you're sure?'

'Not one damned word. The next morning they were gone and we were stuck. We couldn't get all our voters to the polls. And worst of all? Not even after the election, after the candidate we'd worked so hard for lost by so few votes, did one of those guys think to send a note of apology for leaving us in such a lurch. We would have understood. Good jobs were tough to get, then as now.'

'Just Christmas cards, every December, from Halvorson?'

She sighed. 'After that, we grew up.'

I read her the last of Mickey Rosen's names but she had few memories of them. That was fine. I'd gotten more than I'd phoned for. The cryptic threat that John Shea, living as David Arlin, wanted passed to Timothy Wade had nothing to do with American Indians, or headdresses, or bows or arrows.

'If he wants to keep the hatchet buried,' Shea had threatened, playing off an old cliché. He'd been cryptic, so that only Timothy Wade would understand.

Marilyn Paul hadn't understood but she suspected enough to set a rubber axe and some plastic bones tumbling from a silo. Likely, she'd merely intended to nudge Wade just a little into dealing with what Marilyn saw as a real threat. But Wade had overreacted and gone into hiding. And then the man who she thought was John Shea got blown up. It set all her alarm bells ringing. She tried to locate Red Halvorson and Willard Piser because they were both musketeers and might know something about Shea's blackmail plot, and because they'd fled town twenty years earlier, along with Shea.

Both had disappeared. One very recently, the other perhaps years before.

She hired me to see if I could learn more, on the cheap. But someone was watching her, someone who needed to kill her before she could ever know that Shea's cryptic message had nothing to do with a hatchet, or even a tomahawk.

It had been about a bar.

FORTY-EIGHT

B y now my gut was sure that Shea, Piser and Halvorson had not left Chicago to take oil rig jobs together in California. They'd fled Chicago abruptly, split up and scattered to Laguna Beach, Reeder and Tucson. They'd quit on a lie. What my gut didn't know was what triggered it.

I went to Chicago's online newspaper archives for mentions of the Lakota Nation bar, seemingly the last place the four musketeers had been together. There was only one, and that was when the place was gutted to become an Italian restaurant, several years after the Delman Bean campaign.

I went into the kitchen and nuked a purple Peep. As I watched it collapse into a marshmallow smear I wondered if Shea's message to Timothy Wade had nothing to do with the bar itself but was a more cryptic reference to their whole last evening together.

I left scraping the microwave for later and went back to my computer to print out a ten-square block map of the area surrounding the Democratic campaign headquarters. I then searched the Internet for mentions of the five streets surrounding it, adding the words, 'crime, accident, disturbance and police' and finished up by qualifying the search to include only events that happened during the four days that were likely the trio's last in Chicago.

I got seven newspaper hits. A purse was snatched one block from the campaign headquarters; a window was smashed by two kids throwing a chip of terracotta that had fallen from a century-old building; a shoplifter was arrested in a women's store, another in a Walgreen's and a third in an office supply shop.

There was also a killing. The remaining two mentions reported the murder of a convenience store clerk two blocks from the campaign office and one block from the Lakota Nation.

The first, on November 6, reported the crime:

MOTIVE A MYSTERY IN CONVENIENCE
STORE MURDER

At 12:48 this morning, November 5, a silent alarm summoned police to the Super Convenience Mart on West Willoughby Street, where the body of Anwar Farrug was found bludgeoned to death behind the counter. The cash register was full and a fifty-dollar bill lay on the counter, leading police to rule out a robbery. The silent alarm button, three feet away from Mr Farrug's body, did not contain traces of the dead man's blood, though both his hands had been bloodied. Police believe someone else pressed the silent alarm. The clerk's gun was found dropped behind the counter. One bullet had been fired. Police are investigating.

The second mention of the case came two days later, in smaller type on a back page:

POLICE ASK FOR PUBLIC'S HELP
IN CONVENIENCE STORE KILLING

Chicago police today requested help from anyone knowing the circumstances surrounding the mysterious murder of Anwar Farrug, a convenience store clerk found bludgeoned to death two days ago behind the counter of the Super Convenience Mart. Gunshot residue found on his hand and blood evidence found on the floor near the front door suggest that Mr Farrug fired one shot at his assailant, striking him, but likely not fatally, since the perpetrator managed to escape out the front door. Blood evidence of the same type was found leading away from the store to a spot on the street where presumably the perpetrator managed to get into his car. Unexplained are the fifty-dollar bill found lying on the counter and the absence of Mr Farrug's blood on the silent alarm button, despite the fact that both his hands were bloodied, probably from cradling his head after he was struck. Anyone familiar with this crime is asked to contact their local police precinct.

I rootled more in the newspapers' archives but found no further mention of the convenience store killing. Nowadays, shootings had become almost commonplace in Chicago as the city morphed into a major distribution hub for drugs moving through the United States, but I'd expected that, twenty years earlier, a convenience murder would have been more newsworthy. I took the absence of follow-up reports meant that no progress had been made on the case.

I leaned back and considered all the cops I was friendly enough with to call for more information. There were none. I called Bohler.

'Ready to confess to killing Marilyn Paul, Elstrom?' she asked, right off.

'It could be a few lifetimes before I'm ready to admit to something I didn't do,' I said, taking no offense.

'Why are you tormenting me with your call?'

'I'd like you to research an old killing. Twenty years ago, a convenience store clerk got gunned down a little after midnight. Someone else's blood was also found at the scene. I'd like to know what was learned.'

'And you thought of me?'

'I thought of no one else,' I said, truthfully.

'How is your inquiry relevant to anything in my life?'

'I have no idea, but when I do, you'll be one of the first to know.'

'I'll go along, but I expect a full explanation when I come to arrest you for Marilyn Paul's murder.'

'Maybe even sooner,' I said.

Or so I hoped.

FORTY-NINE

I ate the Peep scrapings from the microwave, vowing to set down a paper towel next time, and called Lieutenant Beech in Laguna Beach. 'What did you learn from Tucson?'

'I just got off the phone with Sergeant Bohler. You've got a big cheek, Elstrom, asking her to check on an old case without telling her why.'

'Did you tell her she should help me out?'

'I told her you asked me to help you out without telling me why and that she should go along so I wouldn't be the only fool.'

'So, what did you learn from Tucson?'

'Tucson cops have no record of a Gary Halvorson at the address you gave me. As a favor, they drove by the place, called the number on the For Sale sign and spent some quality minutes with the property owner. He said Halvorson was a nut job, a recluse, but as far as the landlord was concerned, an ideal renter. He traveled a lot and didn't cause any wear and tear on the house, paid the rent early, demanded nothing in the way of maintenance or upkeep and didn't bother the neighbors.'

'So why is the landlord selling the place now?'

'A break-in spooked him and the house had tripled in value in the last twenty years. The landlord is approaching retirement. He got to thinking that a tenant who was always gone wasn't good protection for his investment. So, for all kinds of reasons, he decided to cash in.'

'Did he say anything about having to scrub the place?'

'He said Halvorson left a mess but that it was a small price for twenty years of prompt rent. He also said he was getting freaked about the attention he was receiving. Some newswoman from San Francisco paid him a visit, asking the same sorts of things an insurance guy was inquiring about. I'm thinking the woman from San Francisco was the same one that pestered me and I'm thinking the insurance guy was you, Elstrom. I'm also thinking you two know each other, and both of you know a lot more about Halvorson than the Tucson cops or I do. Also, I just got a call from a security guy working for the Democrat party in Chicago. He asked whether we were sure of the identity of the man that got killed in a house explosion out here. I said we were working on it and then I asked him if he knew you. He hung up. Everything stinks of you, Elstrom. What do you know?'

'Arlin's real name is John Shea. I think Halvorson was involved with him in something.'

'Involved in what?'

'I don't know.'

'Dainsto Runney was involved, too?'

'Probably. His real name is Willard Piser.'

'Where would they be now? Not Runney, we know he's here; in fact, he's all over Arlin's neighborhood – the street, the yards, everywhere.' He chuckled but there was no mirth behind it. 'We matched DNA from the car to the corpse, by the way, so we know he drove here. So, this Halvorson fellow, what's he been up to all these years when Shea was here and Runney up in Oregon? And how does all of this fit with the explosion in my town?'

'Halvorson is red-headed.'

'That's all you can offer me?'

'It's significant that a red-headed man asked that neighbor to make sure of Arlin's residence the night before the house exploded.'

'He didn't want to blow the wrong house?'

'Or, as I've suggested, it was Arlin himself, wanting to be noticed as someone else.'

'As Halvorson?' he asked.

'As Halvorson,' I said, as though I understood what that might mean.

I called Jenny's cell phone and got routed to voicemail. I asked what she'd learned in Reeder and Tucson without sounding petulant at not having been kept informed. I then called her extension in her newsroom, got sent to voicemail and left the same carefully controlled words.

Last, I called the newsroom's general number and asked to speak to Jennifer Gale's producer.

'Miss Gale is not in at the moment,' he said. 'You can leave information on our tip line and we'll get back to you.'

'My name's Elstrom. Jenny and I are friends. I need to talk to her.'

'You say you're a friend?'

'From Chicago.'

'Hold.' He came back on the line a moment later. 'She still uses a Rolodex, believe it or not, and you're in it: Elstrom, Dek, of Rivertown, Illinois, wherever the hell that is.'

'It's a beach town along the sun-drenched banks of Illinois' most pristine river.'

'She's doing a little traveling,' he said.

'Oregon and Arizona I know about. Now where?'

'She called from Chicago, three days ago, saying she needed personal time and nothing more. I assumed it has something to do with her mother, but as far as Oregon and Arizona go you probably know more than I do. Jenny's like so many reporters – secretive, paranoid even, about getting scooped within her own newsroom. I don't know what she's up to. And we're worried because she's not answering her phone. It's not like her to not check in. Can you help?'

'I didn't know that she's here,' I said, but I should have.

I'd mentioned Timothy Wade's name.

FIFTY

G alecki's was like a thousand restaurants in Chicago. A two-room place of plastic, fake wood-grained tables with their glosses scrubbed off, worn green vinyl benches and chairs and wallpaper yellowed by decades of frying food, it drew bus drivers, real estate and insurance people for breakfasts, cops and shop folks for lunch, and families for the blue-plate specials at dinner. And me, that day. I got there at one, just past the lunch rush.

Mrs Galecki, Jenny's mother, watched every plate that was served and every nickel that paid for it. But that afternoon, as I walked up to her perch at the cash register, she didn't see me.

It was a relief. She was dodging.

I continued on into the side room and sat at the booth farthest in the back. They never sat customers at that booth because its back cushion was below the shelves that stored the ketchup. It was a highly trafficked spot. Galecki's customers loved ketchup.

A waitress brought me a glass of ice water, pointed to the menu in the wire holder against the wall and said she'd be back in a minute.

She wasn't. Thirty minutes passed. By then, the side room had emptied of everyone, including any sign of a waitress. By two o'clock, the main dining room had quieted into low conversations and gently clattering dishes. I supposed the waitresses were having their own lunches, for there was no noise coming from the cash register, nor was the usually voluble Mrs Galecki yelling at anyone in English or Polish or a mixture of both, as was her custom when the place was busy.

I sipped my water, ate the crackers in the little straw basket and read the newspapers that had been left in the next booth. And I thought about the time Jenny and I had eaten in that same booth when we'd been wary and new to each other, and hopeful, perhaps, of the distances that might come to grow between ourselves and our ghosts.

My waitress finally returned. Or more likely, she'd been dispatched to dispatch me. 'We had to close the kitchen,' she said.

'I'm fine with the crackers,' I said. 'The water, by the way, is delicious.'

She stared at me like she was witnessing true idiocy for the first time, which might have been the case, given her young age. She turned and walked away.

Ten more minutes passed, and then another ten. Finally Mrs Galecki stomped up, squeezed her short bulk into the seat opposite me and fixed me with a steely glare.

And said nothing.

'I'm learning how to cook Peeps,' I said, after the silence got too irritating.

'Peeps?' she asked, elongating the word with several more letters 'e.'

'Bunnies. Rabbits.'

'You cook rabbit?' She wrinkled her nose but what she was really trying to crumple was my optimism. She wanted me gone.

I shook my head. 'Not real rabbit. Bunnies. Marshmallow. Marshmallow bunnies.'

'Eets not Easter.'

'Peeps are for always and forever.'

'How you cook such theengs?'

'Until they form a puddle. It takes a while but I'm a patient man. I can wait and wait.'

She squeezed out, grabbed a handful of Saltines from another booth and dropped them in front of me. 'You stay,' she said, and left.

Twenty-five minutes passed. The delivery bell rang at the back door. Mrs Galecki returned and pulled open the door. A huge bearded man in a bulky windbreaker came in carrying a case of ketchup, set it on my table and took a long minute to look around. The windbreaker was not bulky enough to conceal the semi-automatic tucked in his belt. He motioned for me to follow him outside.

A van was squeezed between two cars, backed tight against the service door. Its rear doors were open wide, almost touching the back of the building. No one would be seen going in the back of the van. He told me to get inside and sit on one of the dozen boxes of canned goods. He climbed in beside me, pulled the doors shut, slid down the lock and sat on another of the boxes. A driver started the engine and we pulled away.

The van wasn't like Leo's. It had no windows, so I couldn't see where we were heading. By the number of turns the driver took I would have gotten lost anyway. We zigged and zagged and seemed to turn down every cratered side street in Chicago's old Polish, Scandinavian and Bohemian enclaves.

We pulled to a stop after twenty minutes and the driver cut the engine. His door opened and closed. Three quick knocks sounded on the back doors and the man who'd ridden silently beside me reached to unlock them from inside.

The man who opened the van's door from outside was also big and bearded, and he, too, had a semi-automatic, though his was in his jacket pocket. He could have been my fellow passenger's twin.

I stepped down. We were in an alley behind a brown brick three-flat. The outside man, who I assumed was the driver, motioned for me to follow him up the exposed back stairs to the third floor, my fellow rider following close behind. The man in front knocked twice on the door and twice again. The door was opened by yet another bearded fellow that could have been a third brother of the other two men, and we stepped into a kitchen. The third man kept his semi-automatic in a leather holster on his belt. My driver and my fellow passenger went to the refrigerator, took out beers and sat at the small table.

I followed the third man down a short hall. He knocked on a bedroom door at the end, then opened it and stepped aside so I could go in.

A television, tuned to a cable news channel, was playing in the corner. The sound was set low.

A nurse, sitting beside it, had a newspaper on her lap. Her hand rested on a revolver next to a plate of cookies on a tiny table. The third man nodded. She pulled her hand back and picked up the newspaper.

Only then did I turn to look at the other person in the room. She was sitting on a beige vinyl recliner with her two legs extended on the footrest. Her right leg was in a brace that ran from her foot up to her mid-calf. Her face was black and blue everywhere. One eye was almost swollen shut and her lips were swollen.

'Hiya, Dek,' Jenny said.

FIFTY-ONE

'So, what's new?' I asked smartly, sitting on the edge of the made-up bed.

'I'm being held incommunicado, a prisoner,' she said, not quite managing a smile. 'Mama grabbed my cell phone and I haven't seen it since I was brought here.'

She pointed to the man who'd led me down the hall. 'That's my cousin Bernie,' she said. 'His brother Stanley is the one who drove you here. Their other brother is Frank; he rode beside you in the back, ready to snap your neck if you began acting suspiciously. And the nurse with the gun here is Eloise, Stan's wife's sister.' She looked past me, toward the door. 'And of course, you remember Jimbo, my old cameraman from Channel Eight?'

I turned around. Yet another bearded fellow, this one wearing a red Chicago Blues Fest T-shirt, had followed me in and was leaning on one crutch against the door jamb. I smiled; this man I remembered. He'd come with Jenny to Rivertown to report the arrest of

Elvis Derbil, the town's zoning czar, for switching out stale-dated labels on a truckload of salad dressing.

I turned back around. 'Who did this?' I asked her.

'Two dark shapes, in balaclavas and camo jackets, in the woods across the street from Timothy Wade's house.'

'Wade's guards?'

'I don't know, because I don't know why we were attacked. We were trespassing on someone else's property, not Wade's. I didn't hear Jimbo going down before they came for me.'

'I got knocked down, felt my leg being twisted,' Jimbo said behind me. 'No break, just torn ligaments. They were done with me in a second.'

'Professionals? They could have killed you but didn't?' I asked Jenny.

'It's always risky to kill a reporter. They wanted me sidelined and scared, not dead.'

'You chased information down to Laguna Beach, up to Oregon and out to Tucson before coming here. What exactly led you here, to the woods across from Wade's estate?'

'You said Wade is the fourth musketeer, and the only one who is accessible.'

'I meant, what caused you to drop everything in California and come back to Chicago?'

'I wanted to see my mother.'

'Liar.'

'Well . . . I thought as long as I was back visiting Mama I'd have a preliminary look around, in advance of all the information you promised to give to me.'

'And that's why you didn't let me know you were coming.'

'You were on my call list. First, I phoned for Wade at his campaign headquarters but got dusted off, of course. Then I emailed Theresa Wade at that campaign office but never heard back from her either.'

'What did you write to Theresa?'

'That I was looking into her brother's association with three men who came to bad ends out west.'

'That was certainly subtle.'

'I was hoping to jar her enough to reply. When she didn't, I came up with the brilliant idea of finding others who might talk to me about Timothy Wade. I contacted Jimbo and we set up cameras across from Wade's place. I assumed Wade had day help, people coming in to cook or to clean. If we could capture their license plate numbers, I could trace them and ask about Wade. Brilliant, huh?'

'Are the cameras still there?'

'Retrieving them was what got us into trouble. Jimbo had already taken down the one from the north side and put it in his car. He was taking down the center camera when we got jumped, so that camera got seized. The third, at the south edge, is still in the woods, though by now its battery will have run down.'

She pointed to a laptop computer on a dresser. 'We're about halfway through watching the footage from the first camera. So far, nobody came and nobody went.'

'No day help at all?'

'One grocery delivery left at the gate, which a guard took up to the front door, but nothing else for the two days we recorded.'

I looked at Jimbo. 'You were able to drive yourselves away from there?'

He pointed at Jenny.

'This is my story to tell, not my story to be,' she said. 'If I'd called cops or EMTs I'd have become the story, and that would tip the competition. I got us a mile away and pulled in at a gas station. I needed a safe place to recuperate and regroup. I called Frank. Frank called Stan. They brought us here, to Eloise.'

'You could have called me,' I said. 'Matter of fact, that could have been your opportunity to alert me you were in Chicago.'

'Yeah, and you would have said I got clobbered because I didn't listen to you, and that I should stay away from the story, that it wasn't ready yet, that you didn't know what was going on, and I shouldn't risk—'

'Stop!' I said, holding up my hand. 'I understand.'

She smiled.

'I don't understand why you were a threat, even with cameras,' I said. 'Wade seemed almost too cooperative with me.'

She tried to lean forward but dropped back in pain. 'You talked with him?' she asked in a whisper.

'He invited me to the house. I met with him. He was affable and accommodating. He became my best, sincerest buddy in just a few moments.'

'Truthful?'

'Seemingly. He said he thought Shea wanted to blackmail him, though he couldn't imagine with what. He sent me to talk with the campaign's security chief, a man named Jeffries, who told me Marilyn Paul intercepted Shea's demand to speak to Wade. Marilyn confronted Shea, telling him she remembered him from the old Delman Bean campaign. Jeffries said everything ended when Shea got blown up. Case closed.'

'Except judging by the confusion out in Laguna Beach, it wasn't Shea who got blown up.'

'It was Dainsto Runney, late of Reeder, as you've already guessed. You made quite an impression on the man by the ice house.'

'A darling old man,' she said. 'You told Jeffries about Runney?'

'I told him to call out to Laguna Beach, that there might be more to the blackmail story.'

'How interested was Jeffries in Marilyn Paul's killing?'

'He doesn't see any connection but he's learned to look the other way. His job is to focus on the candidate. Still, Beech did tell me Jeffries called out there, though I think Beech shut him down and didn't tell him anything.'

'Since Shea's still alive, he's likely here in Chicago,' she said, 'continuing on with his blackmail plot?'

'Maybe Halvorson's here, too, but Jeffries insisted whatever blackmail attempt existed, it's now over. No accomplice has come at them for blackmail.'

'Unless the Wades aren't being forthcoming with Jeffries.' Then she said, 'Speaking of other things, I also took blood scrapings in Halvorson's Tucson house.'

'They're worthless. Red Halvorson's sister-in-law said that other than her husband there were no other blood relatives. That means you have nothing to compare your scrapings to.'

'Rats,' she said, a half smile forming on her face.

'Rats, indeed,' I agreed.

'I didn't know there were no blood relatives when I flew to Tucson, obviously. I called the landlord and arranged to meet him at Halvorson's house. He got there fast, thinking I was a buyer. He led me inside to look over the place. I remembered that you'd taken scrapings. I wanted some of my own. I'd come prepared with plastic bags and a small pen knife and headed straight for the kitchen. As soon as I knelt to take my samples, the owner started sputtering. I showed him my press pass and used my phone to bring up a video of me, on TV. I told him I was going to put him on the San Francisco news if he wasn't cooperative, and that would get back to Tucson and jeopardize his ability to sell his house. He got talkative and told me interesting things about Gary Halvorson. Such as he'd never once set eyes on the man. Twenty years ago, Halvorson called, saying he'd driven past the place, seen the For Rent sign and wanted to take it, inside unseen. He said he'd send three months' security deposit and two months' rent upfront. The landlord asked what would happen if he didn't like the place. The prospective tenant said he'd call back, but in any case the landlord was free to keep what was the equivalent of five months' rent.'

'This was about the same time Shea arrived in Laguna Beach and Runney showed up in Reeder?' I asked.

'Yes. And so it went with rent, for twenty years, without one word from the tenant, ever.' Her smile had turned quizzical, perhaps taunting. 'I told the landlord I'd heard he was secretive in removing garbage.'

'Effective sleuthing on my part,' I said.

She sighed. 'Rats,' she said again, watching my eyes.

'Rats,' I said, though suddenly I felt like I was looking clearly into a new, bright room. I understood.

'You see, don't you?' she said anyway.

'Halvorson never moved in,' I said. 'Only rats did, free to breed, because the house remained unoccupied for so many years.'

'Generations and generations of them, the landlord admitted. Mice, too, but they weren't survivors like the rats. That's why the landlord didn't leave the garbage bags around for anyone to poke through. He didn't want a neighbor to tell a prospective buyer the house had been full of rats, rats he'd caught in traps that he must have set everywhere.'

'And that's why he scrubbed everything down with bleach. Rat waste.'

'Enough to kill a sale, for sure,' she said.

Eloise got up to stand between Jenny and me. 'Visiting hours are over.'

'You do see why I came to see the Wades in Chicago?' Jenny asked me.

'All those rats point to someone who had enough money to rent a house as a ruse for over twenty years,' I said.

'Oh, you're so smart,' she said.

'Out,' Eloise said, clearly not as impressed with my intellect.

I touched Jenny's lovely cheek. 'And also, someone with enough money to pay for new lives for Shea and Piser out west,' I said.

'And Halvorson somewhere else?' Jenny asked.

Or nowhere else, I thought.

FIFTY-TWO

Stanley walked me back down the outside staircase and held open the back doors of the van. Neither of his two brothers joined me in the back. He walked around to the driver's seat, started us up and we pulled away. Again, we took turn after turn. He was disorienting me, making sure I'd never be able to determine where Jenny was recuperating.

Twenty minutes later, he pulled to the curb and let me out. 'You know where you are?'

We were at a bus stop but there were no street signs at the corner. 'No.'

'Three miles straight north of Galecki's. The bus will stop right across the street.' He got back in the van and drove away.

I checked my cell phone for messages while I waited for the bus. I'd gotten only one call. It was from Jeffries, the security chief at the Wade campaign headquarters. I called him.

He started off politely. 'I emailed Miss Wade asking whether I ought to look into Marilyn's murder,' he said, 'to make sure nothing might rise up and bite the campaign. She emailed back saying that I should forget about that. She said you should forget about it, too.'

'Was that before or after you called out to Laguna Beach?' I said.

He clicked me away.

I got back to Rivertown at seven o'clock, furious that Jenny was hurt yet relieved that she wasn't hurt worse. And tired, too tired to want to deal with the black Impala that looked like a cop car parked on the short street that led from Thompson Avenue to mine.

I drove my fatigue right past it but the car was an insult. My anger insisted I back up. I threw the Jeep in reverse and shot backward until I was abreast of the car.

I jumped out and walked around to the driver's window. Sergeant Bohler powered down her window and looked out at me impassively as though she was studying a museum oddity.

'Why the half-stab at surreptitiousness?' I asked. 'Why not pull right up in front of the turret?'

She nodded. 'Makes sense. I'll follow.'

I got back in the Jeep, took the turn too fast and slammed on the brakes in a most infantile manner. I stormed into the turret, slammed the door and left the outside light off so she could savor my petulance in full darkness.

Going up the wrought-iron stairs, I reconsidered, turned on the lamp on the first floor and went back outside.

'You can spy on me more efficiently inside,' I called out, holding the door open.

'Anybody ever tell you you're crazy, Elstrom?' she asked, walking up.

'Depends on the doctor,' I said, closing the door after her.

'What the hell is that?' she asked of the lamp-lit grouping on the first floor.

'Two plastic lawn chairs, an uninstalled furnace and a lamp to draw attention to it all.'

'There's no lampshade.'

'I haven't found the perfect one.'

'The right doctor might help you with that as well.'

I led her up the wrought-iron stairs and told her to take a folding chair at the temporary, plywood kitchen table.

'I'll get us some hors d'oevres and coffee,' I said.

I set a paper napkin in the microwave, set in my last two purple Peeps and switched it on. I'd just picked up the carafe of the morning's blend when the light surged brighter in the microwave – always a bad sign.

'Don't you—'

She stopped when the Peeps emitted a loud, gaseous sigh and began to ooze out beneath the bottom of the poorly fitting microwave door.

'Pardon me?' I poured coffee into two mugs, pretending not to notice the purple puddle hardening on the counter.

Visibly struggling to look anywhere but at the counter, she said, 'I was about to ask why you don't warm up your coffee.'

I picked up my plastic spatula and began to scrape the purple Peep particles from the counter, adding them to the by-now rock-hard puddle that had remained on the paper towel. 'In this microwave?'

'Too risky?' she asked.

'Scalding coffee can be lethal when airborne,' I said. I set the paper towel of reshaped Peeps onto the plywood, grabbed the mugs and set them and myself down.

'Cold coffee and warm, uh . . .'

'Peeps,' I said.

'Even if this is no act, you being certifiably crazy won't stop me from coming at you, Elstrom.'

'You said the Marilyn Paul case got kicked to your detectives. They've not called. Did you finally tell them about me?'

She shrugged. 'Nothing. They kicked the case, too.' She picked up a particle of Peep and put it on her tongue.

'Good, right?' I inquired.

'Surprisingly,' she said, peeling a larger piece from the napkin.

'Where was it kicked?'

'Chicago PD.'

'Marilyn Paul was discovered beyond the outskirts of Chicago.'

'I know, but the sheriff argued the murder probably happened in the city and the body traveled downriver. It's weak reasoning but the sheriff didn't want the case. There are no leads, except to you.' She licked her fingers. 'Really, really good, Elstrom.'

'Then there are no leads at all.'

She studied me for a moment and said, 'Want to know where Chicago PD kicked the case?'

'They kicked it, too?'

She nodded.

'Where?' I asked.

'Into the trash.'

'They give you a reason?'

'They're overworked, understaffed. They have no leads. Anyway, I'm not giving up and that's why I'm here. You know things, Elstrom.

Things you haven't told Lieutenant Beech; things you haven't told me. Things that will help me find Marilyn Paul's killer.'

'For that I need a peek at that old file I asked you about.'

'Why?'

'To make me sure.'

FIFTY-THREE

'Are your teeth chattering?' Amanda asked when she called at eight the next morning.

'I'm on the roof.' I'd been huddled in my pea coat up there since before dawn.

'Why are you on the roof?'

I could have said I was keeping watch for the murderer, red-headed or otherwise, that wanted me blamed for killing Marilyn Paul. Or, I could have told her I was hoping the cold autumn air would help me understand why he'd seemingly given up, or maybe brace me into seeing symmetry in the facts and events that swirled inside my head, unconnected, like confetti blown wild by a wind machine. But the truth was I'd simply awakened too early and too nervous to stay confined indoors.

So I said, 'I'm not sure why I'm on the roof.'

'I have an ulterior, conflicted reason to have dinner with you tonight.'

'You don't need an ulterior motive to suggest dinner. And as for conflicted, we're working through the mess I made in our past. All is becoming good again,' I said.

'You talked to Tim.'

'I already told you about that.'

'But, did he help?'

'He's an engaging, bright, rich guy. He'll fit fine in the senate. He read me like a book, or to term it more accurately in these wonder-fully modern times, he read me like a digital mobile device. As I said, he knew I wouldn't take his word alone so he sent me to meet with his security chief, who seemed to tell me a lot.'

'Not so truthfully?'

'We discussed all this. Why are you pressing me on it?'

'I'm so close to his campaign.'

Voices sounded in her background. She spoke to them. Then to me, she said, 'I'm already late for my third meeting in what's to be a full day of them. The Italian Village tonight, say at seven?'

'It's noisy and crowded,' I said. We'd rarely gone there before our divorce, simply because it was noisy and crowded. That mattered more now. We might be noticed there by one or more of her new, well-heeled associates. My nuzzling into the life of another big-timer, Timothy Wade, might blow up in my face, and in hers.

'Noisy and crowded and delicious food,' she said. 'We'll see you at seven.'

'We're being joined by others?'

She laughed. 'My security duo, the guys who waited for my plane the other night, will be there. I owe them. They absolutely love the Italian Village.'

FIFTY-FOUR

Bohler showed up at the turret that afternoon. She brought along a Chicago cop that looked like a Chicago cop. His gray hair was cut close and the skin around his eyes was deeply wrinkled from decades of squinting at people who weren't cops. His tag said he was named Gibbs.

'I brought the file you wanted,' she said.

I didn't see a file and she carried no bag or purse. 'Great,' I said.

I invited them in, offered them the two white plastic chairs set beside the new furnace and pulled up the orange can of tar I'd emptied before I could afford a new roof. I kept the can because it was a good reminder of my life's progress, and also because it doubled nicely as unpretentious, supplemental seating.

'You're not going to offer hors d'oevres?' Bohler asked with what I thought was a smirk.

'I ran out.'

She nodded, perhaps gravely, and turned to the man who'd still not said a word. 'This is Benjamin Gibbs. I called around this morning and got mostly nowhere, until I was given Ben's name. He knows the case you're asking about.'

'One car responded initially to the alarm in that convenience store,' Gibbs said. 'They called in more of us when they saw the Egyptian, Anwar Farrug. There was fear that some sort of rampage was going on, that other late-night places might be hit.'

'Farrug – the Egyptian – was already dead?'

'Head caved in along the side.' He pointed to the right side of his head, behind the ear.

'Blunt trauma?'

'The bluntest,' he said.

'The weapon was never found, according to the papers.'

'Maybe, or maybe it was consumed.'

'A bottle, pulled from the shelves?'

'The indent was narrower. The medical examiner thought the Egyptian was clubbed with a sixer of beer, never found.'

'Unusual weapon.'

'Spur of the moment, grabbed from a floor display,' he said. 'Not premeditated.'

'There were traces of someone else's blood at the scene?'

'That was baloney fed to the press. There were more than traces. There was plenty on the floor a few feet from the counter and a solid dribble going out the front door. More was found on the street in the next block, by the curb. There was an awful lot of blood there.'

'Too much to lose and live?'

'That was the word in the department.'

'What happened to the case?'

He shrugged. 'No clues, no leads. It got dropped. A couple of months later I got transferred to traffic, where I've been ever since.'

He looked at his watch. He had nothing more. I walked them out.

'When will you be sharing, Elstrom?' Bohler asked me.

'Soon, very soon.'

'You might not have much time,' she said.

'Oh, are my DNA results back?' I asked.

'My request has become a non-priority now that the case got kicked to Chicago, but I remain hopeful you'll be convicted. I expect to hear from you soon, Elstrom, with the complete truth.'

FIFTY-FIVE

I took the train downtown that evening because I didn't want to fight traffic and because I figured that I'd be going no place after dinner except home, alone.

Amanda was already at the Italian Village, upstairs and in front, where everyone passing by would notice her. Her two security guards loomed at the table across the aisle. They had napkins tucked into collars where necks should have been and wore excited smiles on their faces. I gave them a nod as I sat down across from Amanda.

'You're making a statement?' I asked, gesturing vaguely at the crush of diners surrounding us.

'We don't need to slink around.'

'With your business prominence and ties to Wade, slinking when with me might be wise.'

'Tell me again about your meeting with Tim.'

'Why are you so persistent about this, Amanda?'

'Tell me.'

'As I said, he seemed straightforward. He admitted to being good pals with Shea, Piser and Halvorson twenty years ago, and claims he was shocked when all three suddenly quit the Bean campaign. He said that other than a preprinted card every Christmas from Halvorson, he'd heard from none of them until Marilyn Paul intercepted a shakedown call from Shea. She told the campaign's security man about it, who told Wade. Wade said he had no idea what Shea supposedly had on him, and so neither of them ever responded to Shea. The security man backed Wade on everything, saying as far as they were concerned the matter ended when Shea, passing as Arlin, got blown up in Laguna Beach. The security man called me later on, said he'd asked Theresa Wade if perhaps he shouldn't look into the Marilyn Paul killing a little more, just to make sure there was nothing that could adversely affect the campaign. She told him to drop it, and for him to tell me to drop it, too.'

'Theresa Wade,' she said, almost to herself. 'You're sure you didn't tell Jeffries that it wasn't Shea in the rubble?'

'No, only to call Laguna Beach. Beech confirmed that he had.

I don't know what they discussed. Now there's a new problem. Jenny Galecki.'

Her face tightened.

'As we learned in Reeder, she's chasing this story—'

'Because you told her about it in San Francisco,' she interrupted.

'And later, when I told her of a possible connection to Timothy Wade. She flew to Tucson and talked to Halvorson's landlord. She found no trace of Halvorson ever having lived there. The landlord said Halvorson rented the place over the phone, sent in a generous check to secure the deal and didn't bother the landlord for twenty years.'

'The ideal tenant.'

'Or a beard.'

'Someone else rented the place to establish a presence?'

'Someone wealthy enough to maintain the ruse for twenty years,' I said.

The waitress came. Amanda told her to take the two guards' orders first, and then she ordered spaghetti with marinara. I ordered lasagna. Both of us needed time to think, so we hid behind talk of the electric utility she'd inherited. Our food came and we kept talking about electricity, with occasional glances at the guards across the narrow aisle. They'd ordered a platter large enough to feed an extended Italian family of first, second and third cousins, and were attacking it with a speed and ferocity that suggested they were worried an army was about to charge up with big spoons.

Amanda was never a big eater, but that night she didn't even touch her meal. When I'd finished eating – the guards finished ahead of me by several minutes – she signaled our waitress to take her spaghetti and wrap it up, along with a couple of extra meatballs.

'I've upset you,' I said.

'Everything I've heard so far is circumstantial.'

'After Tucson, Jenny came here. She and her old cameraman from Channel Eight set up surveillance cameras in the woods across from Wade's place. When they went back to retrieve them they got beaten, badly. No broken bones but plenty of damage inflicted by professionals.'

'My God! Because of Tim Wade?'

'That's my guess.'

She sat for a moment, stunned. Then she said, 'About my ulterior motive for this dinner . . .?'

'The one you mentioned earlier today.'

'Theresa Wade emailed, asking me to be their deputy campaign manager.'

'The election is in only a few days,' I said, instantly regretting the demeaning sound of my words. I was stunned, and appalled, at the Wades.

'You don't think I can handle it?' She grinned as though she was teasing, but she was dead serious.

'You can handle anything, as your recent entry into big business attests. It's just, just . . .'

I was stammering, babbling.

She held up her hand for me to stop. 'Of course, I understand that it's just titular, a ploy,' she said. 'They don't want my advice, especially since the campaign is essentially over and Tim's election is a sure thing. So why, Dek? Why offer me such a title?'

She was baiting me, wanting me to say the obvious: that the Wades were playing her like a harp to get me to back off.

The waitress walked up with Amanda's dinner in a white plastic bag and set it on the table, along with the check.

I grabbed the tab before the billionairess could. 'My treat, gents,' I said across the aisle.

Both bodyguards smiled. They were still sweating.

Amanda shook her head, grinning again. 'Tim and Theresa quietly pull strings to get good things done,' she said. 'Things you never hear of. Hospital funding, school additions, personal medical assistance – they do it all without one word of self-aggrandizement. So what you're inferring makes no sense to me. They're good people.'

I suspected both Wades to be nothing for certain at all, so I said nothing.

'Come on, there must be dozens of words circling in that brain of yours,' she prompted after a moment. 'You can't summon up one?'

There were more than dozens. There were hundreds, mostly variations of the words, 'Run like hell,' encircled in a cartoon balloon above the beaten, swollen face of Jenny Galecki.

I set down cash for the bill. She stood up. I stood up. Amazingly, the two guards stood up, and lightly despite the family platter they'd just knocked down.

She handed her spaghetti to me. 'Not one word, Dek?'

I found one for those cunning siblings, the Wades.

'Pre-emptive,' I said.

FIFTY-SIX

Pre-emptive.

Absolutely pre-emptive, I thought, looking out the train window into the darkness. By enfolding Amanda tightly into their campaign, the Wades hoped I'd stop investigating and threatening it.

I couldn't imagine what it was that the Wades thought I knew. Worse, I couldn't guess why they'd had Jenny and her cameraman beaten. Jenny said the footage they'd gotten from the one camera showed nothing sinister.

I got home at eleven o'clock that night; still early enough to sit at my computer to see what the satellites saw of the woods across from the Wade estate. Waiting for the picture to come up, I half-remembered an ancient prophecy that foresaw a rain of locusts hurtling down upon the earth. I wondered if the spirit, if not the specifics, of that prophecy might soon come to pass, though I imagined it might not be locusts, or even satellites, that would darken the skies, but rather swarms of drones with video cameras, set loose by drooling, pimpled peepers to crash into one another, tall buildings and airplanes. Then it would be no ordinary pestilence raining down on some dark day but rather harder hails of plastic, solder, microchips *and* people.

The woods across from Wade's estate looked ordinary enough, just acres of trees and nothing else. I dragged the cursor back across the road, to the wide house, broad lawns and circular driveway, all encircled by the tall wrought-iron fence that ran along the road, tucked back along the sides, and crossed to meet at the rear of the house. From there, the ground sloped sharply down to the road that ran along the shore of Lake Michigan. Like the woods across the road in front, the woods in back were thick with trees.

A long green rectangle stood out stark down that slope, about fifty yards up from the back road. It was devoid of trees but dense with low vegetation, like a carefully tended garden plot, except that no garden could function in such thick woods. A faint pair of parallel ruts, probably only recognizable from the air, ran from the road up the fifty yards to the plot.

That rectangle, so far down from the house, and those ruts up to it made no sense. And though the night wasn't young, my worries were thick. It would be hours before I could sleep. I grabbed my pea coat and headed out the door.

There was little traffic. It took less than forty minutes to get to Winnetka and the back road that ran along the lake. I pulled off to the side a few hundred feet before where I guessed the Wade estate would begin.

A quarter moon lit the sky, enough to see. I walked along the road and soon came to a rusted chain-link fence that marked the back of the Wade property. I stopped several times to look up through the trees, almost bare now of leaves, and finally I saw a house at the top of the slope, ablaze with lights. The Wades were pulling late nights, undoubtedly double and triple checking every last effort to ensure a flawless victory.

Strangely, I saw no guards nor heard dogs. I saw no motion-sensor security lights being tripped by animals running through the back woods. There seemed to be no security beyond the wrought-iron fence at the back of the house.

There was a break in the fence fifty yards down. The ruts I'd spotted in the satellite picture ran up through it. They were tire tracks, cut deeper into the soft ground than I'd imagined from looking at the photo. There was no fresh vegetation growing up along them; they'd been freshly tramped down by a vehicle.

I followed the tracks slowly up into the woods, tensed that with every step I might set off a security light. None came, and that brought a new certainty. The Wades wanted their house guarded at the front but not at the back, because they used a vehicle they kept back in those woods.

The rectangle I'd spotted on the satellite photo confirmed it. It wasn't a flat spot of ground as it had appeared from high up but a structure sunk deep into the hillside. Weeds grew, or had been planted, on its dirt roof. Only the front was exposed – two unpainted old doors hinged at the sides, weathered to almost the same brown as the trees surrounding them. Several small tree limbs had been leaned against them to further camouflage the structure.

I pushed the limbs off the rightmost door and turned the wood latch. The door opened noiselessly. Its hinges were kept well oiled.

I stepped in and immediately hit my knee against the rear bumper of a white SUV. I pulled the door closed behind me and switched on the pinpoint flashlight I'd brought. I'd seen that vehicle before. It was the Ford Explorer I'd chased before Sergeant Bohler had pulled me over.

The sunken building ran deep into the hill. Samuel Wade, Sr must have used it to store the whiskey he took off boats before transferring it to his construction trucks for delivery.

I eased along the side of the Explorer and came to another vehicle parked in front of it. It was an older Cadillac Eldorado convertible, filthy with dirt silting down from the slatted wood ceiling. Its top was down and a folded wheelchair stuck up from the back seat.

I recognized the car. Theresa and Timothy Wade had been photographed in it at a polo match, the month after Theresa graduated from Northwestern.

I shined my light onto the front seat. Like everything else on the old Cadillac, its cream-colored leather seats were filthy with dirt.

I ran the light forward to a crushed right front fender. The Cadillac was old, built when Detroit iron meant solid steel, but this car had suffered an impact hard enough to push its front headlamp back a full two feet. Yet the car had remained drivable enough to get it up the hill and into the hidden garage.

Beyond the Cadillac, a small workbench was mounted against the slats of the rear wall. Hand tools lay on top of the bench, an old-fashioned brace-and-bit drill, two saws and what looked like boxes of long screws. Dozens of short, cut ends of pine lay on the dirt floor around the bench. They were trimmings, the ends of planks, and all were the same eight-inch width.

I shined my light around one last time. There was nothing else to see. I went out, shut the door and stopped to look up the hill, to be sure of the line of sight. No camera of Jenny's from across the street could have captured the sunken garage I'd just searched. And I'd seen nothing inside that, at first glance, appeared troublesome.

Yet my gut told me I'd just seen something significant.

I hurried the few yards down the hill to where I'd parked the Jeep.

Even though I was alone, it was only after I'd gotten a solid mile from the Wade estate that I dared to speak to myself.

'I just got lucky,' I said. 'I think.'

FIFTY-SEVEN

There were no Peeps left for breakfast the next morning, so I ate half of Amanda's spaghetti and one of the meatballs, then took the last of the previous day's coffee and all of the previous night's observations up to the roof.

It was chilly, but as always it promised to be my best place to mull and brood. I unfolded one of the two webbed lawn chairs and settled in to think about what I knew and what to do about what I couldn't yet prove.

After an hour, I called Sergeant Bohler at the county impound garage. 'Ask Officer Gibbs how much blood was in the street the night of that convenience store killing, and where it was found.'

'Anything else I can do, Elstrom? Wash your windows, gas up your Jeep, help you toss bodies into your river?'

'I'm all set to advance your career, Bohler. I'm edging toward the truth.'

'Do hurry,' she said. 'I'm broke.'

Next, I called Galecki's restaurant and asked to speak to Mrs Galecki. When she came on, I got all the way through saying 'Dek,' before she hung up. I redialed, told the woman who answered I was calling only to talk about the cameraman, and that Mrs Galecki would know what I meant.

She came on the line, warily. 'What?'

'I want to talk to Jimbo, and only Jimbo,' I said.

There was a pause, one long enough to make me think she'd hung up. But then she said, 'Why?'

'Everyone will be safer.'

I gave her my cell-phone number and hung up faster than she could hang up on me.

I started for the trap door, to head back down the ladders and the stairs, when my cell phone rang. Mrs Galecki had worked fast.

It was Jenny. 'You called my mom, wanting to speak to Jimbo?'

'Feeling better?'

'I hurt like hell, but mostly it's my eyes from squinting at the footage we got.'

'Did you see anything?'

'That first camera was aimed at the left side of the estate, the grounds alongside and not quite half of the house. We didn't capture the guard shack, drive or the front door. So far, we've seen nobody coming into view from the left. Still, we'll double-check every frame to be sure.'

'Maybe the help lives in?'

'I thought about that. I don't know.'

'Whoever attacked you seized the second camera?'

'Jimbo had just taken it down when they were on him. That was the most important one. It was aimed dead center at the guard shack, driveway and the front door.'

'How about the third camera?'

'The one we left behind?'

'It would have kept recording, right?'

'You're thinking it might show our attackers at least moving toward us?' she asked.

'The thought crossed my mind.'

'That third camera was farthest down and pointed at the right side of the house and the grounds next to it. I doubt the attackers came from there.'

'Can you show me exactly where that third camera is, anyway?'

'You mean if the guards haven't found it?'

'Marking a zoomed-in satellite photo would be perfect.'

'You can't go there. It's too dangerous. Besides, as I said, that third camera might be too far down and aimed at the wrong side of the house. Nowhere near the guard shack, gate or front door.'

'Mark a photo anyway,' I said.

At the time, I thought I was grasping at straws and didn't think it would lead to anything.

FIFTY-EIGHT

Jenny sent me the enlarged satellite photo fifteen minutes later. She'd marked a specific tree.

I called Leo. 'Feel like danger?' I asked.

'Not if it requires taking Ma and her friends swimming.'

'This could be worse.'

'Nothing could be worse.'

I told him what I had in mind. He told me it would take him three hours. I said I would be waiting.

Leo rolled up in his shiny silver van two hours and twenty minutes later. Always one to dress appropriately for any ludicrous endeavor, he wore bright red pants, a metallic blue shirt and the shiny, red-and-white striped vinyl vest he wore once a year to serve ice cream at Ma Brumsky's church. A yellow, fake straw hat, molded several sizes too large, wobbled low on his head like a yard urn dropped from space, upside down.

Ma Brumsky rode up front, alongside her son, and was fully dressed in one of her better floral housedresses, a black fleece pullover, and from what I could see from climbing in the sliding door behind her, fur-topped snow boots. Daring sartorial flair had always been a hallmark of all the Brumskys.

Mrs Roshiska slid over on the middle seat to make room, tugging her walker to rest between us. She wore a pink sweatshirt, pink sweatpants and plastic hair curlers that almost matched the rest of the ensemble.

The other five ladies sat on the two bench seats behind us. The only member of their group that was missing was the lone gent. I assumed he was at home, resting his parts.

'Ready, ladies?' Leo shouted.

'Ready, Leo!' they yelled back in unison.

He pushed a button, the radio began blasting polka music loud enough for even the deafest of them to sing along to, and we were off.

Fifty ear-ringing minutes later, Leo pulled us to a stop right where we'd planned, directly in between the guard shack and the tree Jenny had marked in the satellite photo. Jumping out, he grabbed a bullhorn I hadn't noticed, ran around to open the passenger and sliding doors and set out a wood step. I remained crouched down in the van as he helped Ma, and then her friends, down onto the stool and then to the pavement. Mrs Roshiska's wheeled walker exited second-to-last, followed by the lady in pink herself.

'This way, lovelies,' Leo announced through the bullhorn at about a hundred decibels. As instructed, Ma and her friends shuffled around to cluster in the middle of the road, smack between the van and the guard shack.

I didn't dare look out the window, but I could well imagine the shocked guard radioing his partner, patrolling elsewhere, to help him disburse Leo and the lovelies milling about in the center of their road.

I jumped out of the sliding door and ran, bent low, into the trees, hoping the van blocked me from the guard's sight.

'Behold the magnificent residence of the next senator from the Great State of Illinois,' Leo blasted through the bullhorn. On cue, the ladies hooted and stomped whatever they could lift to stomp.

I worked through the trees, following the line I'd memorized in the satellite photo. The tree Jenny had marked was clearly standing separate between two copses of several others, but things looked different on the ground. Distances, so clear from the air, were now blurred. There seemed to be a hundred lone trees set between denser clusters.

'Note the clever clipping of the bushes!' Leo announced from the road. 'Each one very round, except for some that are square.'

I ran from tree to tree, looking up. Jenny had told me that the camera was small, no larger than a standard digital reflex model. It was black, exactly the color of most of the tree trunks.

'The exquisite shutters, all of them glossy and immaculate!' Leo shouted. He was not at his best, ad-libbing.

I found a tree in a perfectly clear line with where I guessed was the right side of the house, obscured now by the van. There was a small black mass tight against its trunk, about seven feet up. I reached for it and touched a bird's nest. There was no camera. Either the guards had found it or I'd found the wrong tree.

'Notice the front walk and how smooth the cement is. And look! No bird poop here. I'll bet they power wash it every day,' Leo intoned from the other side of the van. His voice was getting weaker.

Another lone tree was four feet ahead, lined up in what might also have been another straight camera shot to the right side of the house. I ran to it and pulled down two lower branches so I could see. No camera.

'You can't be here!' a different male voice yelled, just as loud as Leo. Leo, ever right thinking, was keeping the button down on the bullhorn so I could hear what was going on.

'It's a public place!' a woman screamed, maybe Ma Brumsky or maybe one of her friends.

'Public place! Public place!' Leo shouted through the bullhorn. 'All together now: public place, public place!'

The ladies joined together to scream in unison, 'Public place, public place.' It must have been deafening to the guard's ear.

I ran to a new tree, and then another.

'Move the damned van!' the same guard yelled.

'Public place! Public place!' the ladies shouted.

And then it was there – the camera, fixed to the trunk of a tree. Quickly, I undid the notched strap, tugged the camera down and ran low, for the van.

'Out now!' the guard yelled.

'Public place! Public place!' the ladies screamed.

I jumped through the open sliding door, dropped to the floor and reached to tap the horn for one brief second. Incredibly, Leo and I had forgotten to arrange a way to signal when I got back to the van.

'Sing, lovelies, sing!' Leo shouted through the miracle of severe amplification, and broke into one of the polkas they'd sung, interminably, on the way up to Lake Forest.

The lovelies joined in, and sing they did, those septuagenarians and octogenarians, belting in Polish as they marched back around to the open sliding door, happy as children on a field trip.

I huddled lower behind the driver's seat as Leo opened the front passenger door and helped Ma crawl up onto the front passenger seat. Leo then came to the sliding door and stood as best he could to partially block the opening as the first of Ma's friends climbed in.

A guard came up along the right front fender to hurry Leo along. Leo stood firmly between him and the opening as he helped the second of the ladies up onto the wood step and into the van. I worried that if the guard nudged Leo back just a little he'd spot me crouched behind the driver's seat. I wasn't sure what might happen after that.

'Back off!' Leo shouted at the guard. 'We're hurrying; we're hurrying.'

'Hurry faster, damn it!' the guard yelled back, loud, just inches outside Ma Brumsky's window.

Ma's friends, no dummies, bunched up tight against one another at the side of the van, edging the guard back a foot. And they stayed tight as the third woman clambered up and in, followed by the fourth. None dared look directly at me, crouched tight behind the driver's seat, as they got in.

'You, driver, get yourself behind the wheel,' the guard said. 'I'll help the last ones.'

He muscled diminutive, 140-pound Leo aside. Suddenly, the sleeve of guard's uniform and the gold of his bright Rolex watch were inside the sliding door opening.

The second-to-last woman pushed up against him as she got up onto the step and pulled herself into the van. She stopped, to teeter, to stall, to block the guard's view until the last woman outside, the formidably wide Mrs Roshiska could press in closer to the van.

And press she did, in the next instant. Looming up sudden and large was the substantial pink bulk of Mrs Roshiska, shifting from side to side behind her walker as she pushed against the woman teetering in the opening.

'Move it, lady,' the guard shouted at the woman who had remained crouched resolutely just inside the van. Both she and Mrs Roshiska knew that when the woman moved to the back I'd be exposed in the seconds, maybe a full minute, before Mrs Roshiska, the heaviest of them all, could haul herself in.

Mrs Roshiska said something in Polish to the woman teetering just inside the van. The teetering woman laughed. As did the other ladies, including Ma Brumsky.

'Ho, boy!' Mrs Roshiska shouted in what might have been English. It was a signal. The teetering woman stepped toward the back as instantly the pink of Mrs Roshiska rose up on the wood step to fill the void. The gray sleeve of the guard's arm reached to grab Mrs Roshiska's elbow, to hurry her up into the van.

At which time I'd be exposed, if he looked in.

Mrs Roshiska froze at the guard's touch but only for a second before she raised one hand from her walker to slap the guard's hand away. 'Hands off, pervert!'

The shiny brightness of Leo's vinyl vest reappeared below the open sliding door. His hand grabbed Mrs Roshiska's walker, folded it and set it aside, ready to slide the door shut in a hurry.

Mrs Roshiska swayed on the wood step, one hand steady on the grab handle behind Ma Brumsky, the other on the leading edge of the sliding door, readying to lunge inside.

'Damn it, lady,' the guard screamed. He moved closer alongside her.

Mrs Roshiska let her left hand drop from the edge of the sliding door, but instead of using it to grab one of the outstretched hands reaching to help pull her in, she reached behind her to grab the elastic waistband of her pink sweatpants.

'Hurry, hurry!' the guard yelled, moving behind her to push her in.

'Ho, boy!' Mrs Roshiska shouted. I froze. As soon as she lumbered up and in, the guard would see me.

Steadying herself now with only the one hand on the grab handle, Mrs Roshiska stared straight at me, gave me a wink and tugged down hard with the hand behind her. 'Ho, boy!' she yelled as the left side of the pink sweats dropped a good twelve inches, presenting the guard with a close-up, authentically puckered Polish moon.

The guard jumped back as if he'd been Tasered and fled around to the front of the van. The other ladies whistled and clapped as Mrs Roshiska tugged her sweats back up and reached to be pulled in by welcoming hands. Leo threw her walker and the wood step in and slammed the sliding door.

Mrs Roshiska collapsed on the seat next to me. 'Ho boy!' she shouted.

'Ho, boy!' they all shouted as Leo jumped in behind the steering wheel and started the engine. Pulling away, he pushed a button on the dash to fill our ears with the screeching of a hundred discordant accordions and we sped, laughing, down the road.

After that, the last act of the day was anticlimactic.

I called Jenny from Leo's van. She yelled for me to speak up. I yelled back that I was in the middle of a concert. She said she could tell; she knew Polish songs, too.

She understood enough of what I'd shouted to have a guy who said his name was Ralph waiting when we rolled up to the turret, voices singing, ears ringing.

'I'm a friend of a friend,' he murmured, proving he was no slouch at mumbling the Chicago way. I handed him the camera and he was gone.

What I couldn't have guessed was that I'd just given him something no one could have foreseen.

FIFTY-NINE

'd just switched on my computer the next morning, braced for intimate messages from the usual alternative energy suppliers, orthopedic shoe peddlers and western wear clothiers – all of whom thought I had interest, and money – when the little computer dinger signaled a new bit of incoming email.

It was from Jenny, and it was short. 'This clip from third camera. Up all night squinting. No attackers, no day workers. Attached are two minutes Rick enhanced. Upper right window. Nothing, or something?'

I emailed back. 'Who's Rick?'

She answered instantly. 'Guy who picked up camera from you.'

'His name is Ralph,' I sent back.

'Goes by Rick, too. Paranoid about secrecy.'

I opened the attachment. It showed a close-up of the rightmost, second-floor bedroom window. I recognized the window and the curtains. It was the same window through which Theresa Wade had been purportedly photographed some months or years earlier, probably seated in her wheelchair, by a photographer using a long lens. Other than her big hair, none of her features had been recognizable.

There was movement behind the window. Someone with the same big hair, no doubt a woman, was moving behind those lace curtains now.

The person's head was too high for someone seated.

I emailed Jenny. 'Any new evidence that the Wades have live-in help?'

'No.'

I watched the clip again. The movement lasted only five seconds.

It wasn't Timothy Wade behind that window. The hair was wrong. It was too full. It seemed to be a woman's hair, a woman's head.

Yet I was sure the hair was too high for a woman in a wheelchair. A woman was walking behind those curtains.

A wheelchair-bound woman might well need live-in help – a nurse, a maid, a cook.

But my mind wanted to see only that dirt-dusted Cadillac hidden in the sunken garage at the back of the Wade estate. And to recall the wheelchair left upright in the back seat, just as dirty as the car. A wheelchair never retrieved, never needed. A wheelchair that had nagged at me since I'd first seen it.

A car horn tapped twice outside.

SIXTY

Sergeant Bohler stood at my door, holding up a brown shopping bag. She was out of uniform, wearing a thin multicolored knit hat and a red wool jacket.

Parked at the curb was a black pick-up truck with monstrous off-road tires mounted on huge chrome wheels. Thousand dollar wheels, Booster Liss had called them.

'Hey, is that the same truck someone reported lurking outside the Rivertown City Garage a few nights back, acting on a tip that a wrong color top was being put on a Jeep?' I asked.

'I was investigating the disappearance of a hundred-dollar GPS transmitter that suddenly went dead.' She slightly shook the contents inside the bag. 'We'll discuss things honestly?'

I nodded and she thrust the bag at me.

Inside were two large boxes of yellow Peeps – a color I'd not yet sampled – and a pound of gourmet coffee.

'The coffee is fresh but it's hard to find soft Peeps this long after Easter,' she said.

'That's no matter.' I led her upstairs, pointed to the kitchen and went across to the card table to get the street grid I'd printed that morning.

'Where are your coffee filters?' she asked when I came back. She was looking in the cabinet above the coffee-maker where there were none.

'I use the paper towels.'

'Good thinking. You get the lip-smacking taste of pulping chemicals that way.'

She threw out my last dregs of perfectly warmable coffee, folded a sheet of paper toweling into the basket and added grounds that smelled better than anything I got at the Discount Den. When the coffee was done, she filled the travel mug I'd left out on the counter, found a cup for herself in the cabinets and sat down to study the street grid.

'I'll do the Peeps,' I said, standing four of the little bunnies onto a paper towel.

She got up fast. 'I'll leave the room.' No doubt she remembered the power surge the last time, when molten Peeps oozed beneath my microwave door like lava from an angry volcano.

She waited past the wall, as dental assistants do when X-raying, though this time there was no power surge. The Peeps flattened properly onto the paper towel and I served them with the plastic knives I get from Burger King.

'I'm broke, Elstrom. How quickly am I going to get promoted out of the garage?' she asked when we sat down.

'How's my DNA?'

'Not back from the lab.'

I took a sip of the best coffee that had ever been brewed in the turret. 'I need to be sure about the location of the blood,' I said, pointing to the street grid. I'd marked it with the locations of the Democrat party headquarters and the convenience store, two blocks away.

She picked up the pencil I'd set down with the map and, as I expected, drew a dotted line from the store to a spot between my two marks. 'Officer Gibbs said the trail ended right here.'

'A big pool?'

'Too much to live without, he told us. Someone bled out.' She chipped off a piece of Peep, put it in her mouth and began chewing appreciatively.

'Then Red Halvorson died right there, that night,' I said, putting my index finger on the mark she'd just made. 'That's a convenient

parking spot for someone working at the Democratic headquarters.'
I moved my finger a little, to the campaign headquarters.

'The robbers worked at the Democratic headquarters?'

'A fifty-dollar bill was left on the counter, remember? There were
no robbers.'

'So, just Democrats?' she asked, laughing.

'Four young guys, volunteers. One was named Shea, one Piser
and one Halvorson. The fourth was destined to be a US senator.'

She stopped chewing, her voice weak, disbelieving. 'Timothy
Wade was one of them?'

I moved my finger a fraction of an inch again, a block up a side
street from the campaign office. It was where the Lakota Nation
bar had been.

'After volunteering at the campaign headquarters,' I said, 'Wade
and his three friends went here, where they drank too much. They
got thrown out. With the cunning of the truly drunk, they headed
off into the night, intent on finding more alcohol.'

I moved my finger the short distance to the convenience store.
'One of the four – I don't know who – grabbed a six-pack and
made for the counter. Someone else pulled out a fifty to pay—'

'Wade,' she interrupted, 'because he had lots of money.'

'For sure,' I agreed. 'But then one of them – they were drunk,
remember – did something that threatened the store clerk enough
to make him panic. He pulled out a revolver. Whether on purpose,
or accidentally, the gun went off, hitting Halvorson. One of the
other three young men picked up the six-pack and crashed it down
on the clerk's head, probably justifiably, to stop him from firing
again.'

'Everyone panicked,' she said.

'Especially Wade, who must have seen his future going down
the drain. He helped the mortally wounded Halvorson out the door,
telling Shea and Piser to get lost, that he'd keep them out of trouble,
saying he'd make sure Halvorson got to a hospital. Shea and Piser
were only too happy to run, and they took off.'

'Leaving Wade to help Halvorson to his car,' Bohler said.

'Except Halvorson died. Now Wade had to think of how things
could be hushed. I think he drove home—'

'With Halvorson dead in his car?'

'Absolutely. He had to get out of there and he'd be safest at his estate. He drove home and dumped the problem in his sister's lap. Brother and sister must have stayed up all night planning, finally deciding that Tim would tell Shea and Piser that he and Theresa had gotten a doctor privately and were going to nurse Halvorson back to life quietly at their home. Based on what Piser paid for his church in Oregon, and likely the cash Shea lived on for a while in California, I'm guessing Wade sweetened the deal by giving Shea and Piser at least sixty thousand dollars each to head west and change their names. It must have seemed like a lot of money to Shea and Piser, but even better, Wade was offering them a safe ticket away from a murder rap, because by now they'd learned from the news that the store clerk was dead. They took the money and ran – Shea to Laguna Beach, Piser to Reeder. Wade covered their tracks, and Halvorson's death, by saying all three had taken oil rig jobs on the west coast. Wade buried Halvorson secretly and rented a house in Tucson to create the ruse that Halvorson was alive and well out in Arizona.'

'Wade paid rent every month to maintain a ruse?' She shook her head, marveling.

'Until very recently, when the landlord put the place up for sale. But it was cheaper than jail time, cheaper than a future in politics ruined,' I said.

'What upset the apple cart?'

'John Shea. His serious financial difficulties got him to thinking about his rich old pal, Tim Wade, who was now running for the US Senate, and how Wade would pay serious money to keep Shea quiet about Wade's involvement, innocent though it must have been, in that convenience store killing. Shea called Wade's campaign office, mentioning something cryptic about a hatchet. Marilyn Paul intercepted the calls, identified the caller and confronted Shea. She reported the calls to Jeffries, their campaign security chief, expecting Jeffries to go after Shea. But Wade told Jeffries to drop it, that Shea couldn't have anything because Wade was clean.'

'Gutsy to ignore it,' Bohler said.

'Gutsy, or maybe Wade was thinking he should handle Shea without anyone else knowing.'

'Still gutsy,' Bohler said, chipping at more of the Peep stuck to the paper towel.

'Except that's when Marilyn Paul intervened, changed everything and brought hell down upon herself,' I said. 'Seeing no action from Jeffries, Marilyn set up that stunt at the silo as a little nudge to Wade to deal with Shea, never imagining the impact that little rubber hatchet would have.'

'But why do it at all?'

'I'm guessing Marilyn Paul was first and foremost a loyal Democrat. She didn't want anything to hurt her candidate's chances. She couldn't know, of course, that the little toy axe was a specific reference to the night of the convenience store killing.'

'That American Indian-themed Lakota Nation bar, where the musketeers had been just before,' Bohler said.

'Marilyn must have been as shocked as anyone when Wade went nuts in front of the television cameras. But Wade must have believed that Shea was closing in and was nearby, perhaps in the crowd at that farmyard. He saw no choice but to run.'

'Except Shea was not nearby. He was still in Laguna Beach.'

'And going nuts himself, believing someone else was intruding on his action with that silo stunt.'

'Quite naturally, he thought it was Piser?' She held up her hand. 'Nope, I'm not that smart to guess that. Lieutenant Beech out in California told me about him.'

'Or Shea thought it might have been Halvorson. Remember, neither Shea nor Piser knew Halvorson had died. They assumed Wade and his sister had nursed him back to health and sent him packing with sixty thousand dollars, like the Wades had done with them.'

'Shea couldn't find Halvorson, but he did contact Piser?'

'They must have stayed in loose touch, at least enough to know where the other had landed. Either Piser saw Wade's meltdown on TV and called Shea, fearing their involvement in the liquor store killing was about to become known, or Shea called Piser, suggesting the same, and maybe also suggesting there was big blackmail money to be had if Piser came to Laguna Beach to discuss it. But Shea wanted him for something else. Piser came and Shea blew him up because he needed a corpse to double as his own, at least long enough for him to slip out of California.'

'And come where? Here?' she asked.

I nodded.

'To kill Marilyn Paul?'

'For openers,' I said. 'Shea knew as soon as Piser arrived in Laguna Beach that he had nothing to do with the silo. That left only two other people who could have known enough to set up that stunt in the farmyard. One was Halvorson, who he didn't know how to get at. The other was Marilyn Paul, because she'd intercepted his threat about the hatchet. He must have guessed it was most likely her. For sure, she had to be gotten out of the way, because she could tie him to the blackmail threat against Wade.'

'With her gone, his way was clear to collect large from Wade,' she said.

'It's one scenario.'

'So Shea comes to Chicago, kills Marilyn Paul and then calls the sheriff, tipping us it was you?'

'He must have found out about me when he ransacked Marilyn's apartment, looking for anything that might lead to him.' I saw no need to tell her I was sure of it, since I'd searched Marilyn's apartment myself.

'Our tipster said her corpse was in your Jeep. How did it leave your Jeep and get into the water?'

'I would have no idea about that. What I'm sure of is that your tipster then called you to say I tossed a knife into the Willahock. Most interestingly, he's not called since then.'

'You think he collected from Wade and is now basking on some sunny beach in the Caribbean?' she asked.

I told her to come across the hall for movies.

SIXTY-ONE

She sat in the listing red vinyl chair and I stood behind her as we watched the short clip Jenny had sent me.

'I don't get it,' Bohler said, leaning back after squinting at the figure moving behind the curtains.

'I think your tipster, whoever it was—'

'Shea, right?' she interrupted. 'I mean, who else had need for us to think you killed Marilyn Paul? Not Wade; he wants no attention drawn to this case at all.'

I told her about my post-midnight trip to the back of Wade's property.

'Ah . . .' She shook her head hard. 'Criminal trespass onto his property, breaking and entering into his outbuilding?'

I nodded.

'And you're sure it was the same exact Ford Explorer parked in that sunken garage, the same exact one you were chasing the night I pulled you over?' The disbelief in her voice was clear. 'You're positive Timothy Wade, our next senator, risked his future, his enormous stature, everything, to come for you that night, to do you harm? But because you spotted him first and came charging out, you hero you, he got scared and took off? You really want me to believe that?'

'You were there. You saw it.'

'I was just pulling up when you shot past me and turned onto Thompson Avenue. I saw nothing except you driving crazy. I pulled you over before you killed someone.'

She pointed to the image frozen on the screen. 'And that's supposed to mean what?'

'That maybe it wasn't Timothy Wade who came at me that night.' I pointed to the screen. 'If I'm right, that's Theresa Wade and she's not paralyzed at all. She can move about freely.'

'Come on, Elstrom. So what if she's been able to walk a little, all this time? Maybe she can only go a few feet on crutches or with braces. So what if she's able to drive and came to your place? Maybe she's a little nuts. No crime there.'

'She could have killed Marilyn Paul. She could have driven the corpse over here, in that Ford Explorer, so her brother could be alibied elsewhere. No one would ever suspect a woman who is wheelchair-bound.'

'I need more coffee and you need less,' she said.

We went back to the kitchen to wind ourselves up with more of her excellent grounds.

'Do you know Jennifer Gale?' I asked.

'Television reporter. She left Chicago.'

'She's back. She got beaten when they went to retrieve surveillance cameras she'd placed across from the Wade estate.'

'Is she as crazy as you? Why would she place cameras across from Wade's house?'

'She's working on some sort of story, I suppose. Her attackers, who I think are Wade's guards, grabbed one camera but Jenny's cameraman had already gotten to another and I went back to grab the third.' I pointed across the hall. 'That video we just watched came from that third camera.'

'Ask yourself: how many cameras are aimed at the Wade place? It's only going to get worse after he's elected senator. You're crazy if you think the Wades hurt people for coming with cameras. Or do you think Jennifer Gale was assaulted because the Wades don't want it known Theresa can really walk? This is too weird, Elstrom.'

'I take your point: the Wades are used to people photographing their house. But I do think Wade's guards beat up Jenny and her cameraman to stop them from recording something else.'

'What?'

'A grave on Wade's property.'

'I was wondering when you'd get back to your notion that Timothy Wade drove Halvorson's body back to his estate. But Elstrom, get real. It's been twenty years. If Wade did bury Halvorson there, he threw him in a hole without embalming the corpse. There'd be nothing left. Besides, if that convenience store killing went down as you say, Wade didn't do anything wrong to begin with. He cleaned up the mess, is all, and that's a far lesser crime than murder, even if it could be proved.'

'Maybe there's more than one grave on Wade's land,' I said.

'You think because our tipster was really Shea, and that because he hasn't called in a while, it's because Wade killed him and buried him on his property?'

'Wade, or his guards.'

She leaned back and smiled. 'I know why you called earlier, suggesting this little chat. You think Wade's guards weren't worried about Jennifer Gale filming Halvorson's grave. You think they were worried about her finding fresh digging.'

I pushed the package of uncooked Peeps toward her. 'Have a reward for brilliant thinking.'

She grabbed a Peep, pushed it whole into her mouth and gave me a goofy yellow grin. 'What the hell, Elstrom?' It came out muffled through the marshmallow.

'Is it so hard to believe that Shea approached Wade, saying "I've proved I'm willing to kill both Willard Piser and Marilyn Paul. Pay me big and I go away, or I tell everybody about the convenience store"?'

'But Wade didn't buy it?' she asked.

'I wouldn't have, either. There was nothing to prevent Shea from coming back to the well time and again.'

'So Wade killed Shea.'

'Or his sister did.'

'Or his guards, right? There are all kinds of killers on that estate?'

'There's a lot to be learned there,' I said.

She studied my eyes for a moment, knowing what I was asking. Finally, she said, 'I don't think any judge, Democrat or rare Republican, would give me a warrant to dig up our next senator's estate based upon such a flimsy theory, even if I could get the case back from Chicago PD.'

'Have another Peep,' I said.

'Damn it, Elstrom.'

SIXTY-TWO

Bohler left, thanking me for the musings of a confused mind and not much else. Still, there was a chance she'd find a compliant judge and that she'd dig. And if she did, it would be bad for one and good for the other.

I called the one first.

'You sound tense,' Amanda said. 'I'll call you back in five minutes.'

'You're working on Sunday?'

'It's what tycoons do. Five minutes.'

I stewed for those five minutes, and then for the twenty more that followed, silently, after that. And then she called.

'I don't want you to be caught unprepared,' I said.

'Unprepared for what?'

I told her about my conversation with Sergeant Bohler, the grid map I'd printed out and the spot where all the blood had been found. And I told her what I'd asked Bohler to do.

'My God, Dek! What if you're wrong?'

'It probably won't get that far. Bohler doubts any judge would be crazy enough to give her a warrant to dig at Wade's estate even if she was crazy enough to ask for one.'

She exhaled softly against the phone. 'I emailed Theresa, saying that my becoming deputy campaign manager this close to the election would look like eyewash, a meaningless reward for a contribution. She was very understanding.'

'She won't be if men come with shovels. She'll blame you for me.'

'Imagining they'd be involved in secret burials seems . . . so unfair. No, it's nightmarish.'

'Murder is worse.'

'You've alerted Jennifer Gale?'

'I'll call her next. She's owed this story. She and her cameraman got beaten, badly, just across the street from Wade's place.'

'The election is in two days,' she said.

'I doubt Bohler can act that fast. If anything happens it will be long after Timothy Wade has been elected.'

'You and your Sergeant Bohler better be right, if she does decide to proceed. Otherwise, good people are going to get muddied. You, most of . . .' She didn't finish. She let it taper away.

'No, not me so much. You've got more to lose. That's why I called you.'

She paused for a long moment. 'Ah, hell, I'm a tycoon now. And I've weathered you before.' She clicked off.

I called Galecki's. 'Don't hang up,' I said to Mrs Galecki. 'Tell Jenny the story might break.'

Mrs Galecki hung up, but I hoped she'd done it after I got the words out.

I didn't have to hope long. Jenny called within a minute.

'Bohler might go for a warrant to dig up Wade's estate to look for graves,' I said.

'Now, like today?'

'Not today. Maybe not tomorrow, or in two months, or ever. Bohler is a cop in a Democratic county in a Democratic state. She has to decide whether messing in Wade's estate is worth the risk to her career. If she thinks it is, she still has to convince her superiors at the sheriff's department to get the case back from Chicago PD and then to assign it to her. Then she's got to convince a judge to give her a warrant. Then she's got to assemble—'

'Digging up Wade's estate on election day would be so perfect.' Her voice had risen, imagining video, imagining audio. She'd been only half-listening.

'Not for those who believe in elections.'

'And I'd have to figure out who'd air my report,' she said.

'That's probably a long way off—'

'Channel Eight, right here,' she said. 'My old station. They'll do it.'

'Make sure your team includes Bernie, Stanley, Frank, Eloise and any other tough cousins you've got.'

'The story could run simultaneously, here and in San Francisco, then break national.' She clicked me away.

What happened next happened quickly.

And happened wrong.

SIXTY-THREE

Nine o'clock, Monday, the morning before election day.

I balanced the last of Amanda's spaghetti, a cup of coffee made with Bohler's very excellent grounds, my tiny television and myself on my electric-blue recliner, expecting to see the usual numbing, last-minute pleas from candidates for the public's trust and, unspoken, the opportunity to pursue privately profitable shenanigans.

But that morning there was no numbing on television. The local stations were playing, and replaying, a short video just sent out by the Wade campaign.

A somber Timothy Wade sat in the living room where we'd met. The room was darkened, except for two lamps and the fire roaring in his reasonable fireplace. He was dressed in a medium-colored suit, a crisp white shirt and what I guessed was the obligatory red necktie. I could only guess at the color of the tie because my mini TV offered images only in black, white and mostly gray. He half-smiled with teeth as white as his shirt.

'As you know, we suspended active campaigning after we encountered what might have appeared to be a simple prank in a farmyard.

We knew otherwise. It was the latest in a series of threatening moves made by a troubled individual. My campaign manager, who you might have heard is my iron-willed, big sister . . .' he paused so the folks in the viewing world could laugh to themselves appreciatively, '. . . insisted I step back a bit until the threat was dealt with. That's now done. We will not reveal anything about this individual other than to say he's suffered a history of emotional issues. His family has retained excellent professional help for him and I've been asked to entrust the individual's future to their most capable hands, and to honor his family's request for privacy in this matter. I'm happy to comply.'

He cleared his throat and went on: 'Today, the day before the election, we are facing a new threat. Anonymous, unfounded accusations have been made against me and my sister concerning the disappearance of a person I knew long ago. Specifically, this fairy tale even has us burying his body in our back yard.'

He raised his hand, palm out, and managed a rueful half-smile for the camera. 'I know; I know. It's crazy. But the Cook County Sheriff's Police has decided to search our grounds nonetheless for this secret grave.' He sighed. 'Ah, politics. Crazy, aren't they?'

My cell phone rang. 'You watching the news, Elstrom?' Sergeant Bohler asked. There were vehicle noises in her background; she was in a car.

'I'll call you back.' I clicked her away.

'In the interest of putting this nonsense behind us immediately,' Wade was saying, 'my sister and I are inviting every accredited news department to come join us here at our home this morning to witness this instance of political dirty tricks run amok.' He reached down and brought up a plate of cookies. 'So, to you news folks, come on up. We'll be serving coffee and cookies.' He smiled and the video ended.

My screen shifted to a news commentator. I turned down the sound and called Bohler.

'What the hell is going on?' I asked.

'Those two Wades are incredible,' she said, sounding out of breath. 'At six-thirty this morning my boss gave me permission to call Chicago PD.'

'Doesn't he have to ask for the case to be assigned back himself?'

'Ordinarily, but this time he wants plausible deniability. He's afraid of the Wades so he left it to me to back-channel the request. If it goes wrong he'll claim he gave me no such permission.'

'According to what Wade said on the news, you got permission.'

'Faster than a fly can fly,' she said. 'The Chicago police gave me a verbal to take it back at seven o'clock.'

'Why so fast?'

'They're afraid of the Wades, too. I know a rare Republican judge. He hates Democrats because they control the courtroom assignments and they move him to a different one every month. He drools in anticipation of taking down any Democrat and was delighted to prepare the warrant himself. I got my search team assembled just an hour ago and now we're driving north to Winnetka.'

'One of them called the Wades?'

'As I said, faster than a fly can fly.'

'Maybe you shouldn't rush. Obviously the Wades know you're not going to find anything if they've summoned news organizations to witness your folly.'

'They're arrogant, those Wades. And it's too late. If I quit before I start, they'll say I knew it was a political trick to begin with. I have to play it through.'

'And get humiliated.'

'I want you there, Elstrom, right beside me, my shovels and my saliva-spattered warrant from a crackpot judge. You suggested this. I want you there.'

I owed her that. I told her I'd see her in Winnetka.

SIXTY-FOUR

I walked past three-dozen cars and four news vans on the road up to Wade's estate. Two sheriff's cars and two sheriff's vans were parked on the circular driveway, inside the gate.

The gate was open. The guard in the shack recognized me and pointed to the flagstone walk at the side of the house. 'The party is around back,' he said.

'Everyone's invited?'

'Mr Wade said not one damned fool is to be kept out.' He stared at me long enough to be sure I understood I fit in that category.

A bit of camouflage cloth was visible behind him, wedged behind a wastebasket. It could have been the sleeve of a jacket.

'Got a black balaclava to go with that camo jacket?' I asked what was certainly one of the bastards that had worn it, attacking Jenny.

He jabbed a thumb toward the side yard. 'Happy hunting.'

I followed the path around to the back. It was easy to see clear down the long slope to the road where I'd parked the night I'd snuck onto the property, and it was easy to see how the thick damp blanket of rotting leaves that lay on the ground would play hell for the cops trying to find a grave. Or two.

A long folding table had been set up on the brick patio behind the house. Two large silver urns of coffee were on it, along with huge trays of bagels, cream cheese and cookies. I recognized several of the television reporters milling abound, sipping coffee. The local stations had sent their big guns to report the circus.

Eight officers in tan shirts and brown pants moved in two ragged clusters down the hill. Two pairs of deputies in front pulled leaves back with wide plastic rakes so the two pairs of officers following could see to probe the ground with long, thin metal rods.

Thanks to me, they were wrecking Bohler's career. No grave would be soft enough to find with a probe after twenty years, and Wade's arrogant invitation to the press meant that Shea's grave, if he was even dead, was nowhere nearby.

Spotted everywhere down the slope were scores of reporters and cameramen. Jenny stood by a tree partway down the slope, away from everyone. I walked over.

'Gutsy counterattack,' I said.

'The Wades are forcing us to report there's nothing here.'

'You're looking better,' I said, though her face seemed more purpled than the last time I'd seen her. She hadn't covered any of it with makeup.

She didn't bother to answer the lie. 'That's Sergeant Bohler down there?' she asked, pointing.

There was no mistaking Bohler's bright yellow hair. 'She gambled a lot, thanks to me.'

'Gambled and lost?'

I nodded.

Jenny nodded toward the closest cluster of news people. 'Even as jaded as they've gotten, covering crooked Illinois, I don't think anyone believes that sainted Timothy Wade could have had anything to do with a secret burial, let alone a killing.'

'They don't know what you know.'

'They weren't knowledgeable enough to get beaten, you mean.'

'The guard out front was especially happy to point the way for me.' I told her about seeing a camouflage jacket in the guard shack.

She forced a smile. 'Oh, we must take his picture on the way out.'

'Did you bring your cousins for protection?'

'Just Jimbo, with his camera. We tagged along with the regular Channel Eight crew.'

'Play safe. Don't go near the guard shack.'

One of the groups of deputies had reached the bottom and was turning to probe a new swath up the hill. 'That's only their third trip. This is going to go on for an agonizingly long time.'

'I'm afraid it's all going to be over, today,' I said.

SIXTY-FIVE

I admired Bohler's tenacity. Despite the near certainty that nothing would be found on that slope, she urged her searchers on until every square foot had been probed. It wasn't until two o'clock that she scrambled up the hill for the last time, red-faced, sweaty and furious.

'There's not one damned soft spot on this whole hill,' she said.

I felt red-faced and sweaty, too. I'd been so wrong.

The rest of her team trudged up with the news crews and disappeared around the side of the house at the front.

'My boss wants me in his office at eight o'clock tomorrow morning,' she said. She held up a hand when I opened my mouth. 'It was me, too, Elstrom, not just you. I was too willing.'

She left without saying a word to Jenny, standing next to me. Perhaps she hadn't recognized her; her appearance was so changed.

Jimbo, lugging his camera, was the last to make his way up the hill. It took him longer because he was using a cane to favor his leg. He didn't look at Jenny and he didn't look at me as he headed to the front.

'You're a good man, Dek,' Jenny said. 'You attempted justice here today.'

'I guessed wrong.'

'You put yourself on the line for the killing of someone who was deceitful to you. That's to be admired.'

'It blew up in my face, and in Bohler's. And it will blow up in Amanda's face as well when word gets out I'm behind all this. Perhaps it landed hardest on your face, though I can't figure out why you were beaten. There's nothing here.'

'Maybe whoever attacked us got something wrong.' She touched my shoulder. 'I called my station in San Francisco. I'm heading back tomorrow. They're being generous, insisting I take a couple more weeks off, read books I've meant to read since college and let my bruises fade. Then it's back to the pumpkin patch.'

'The pumpkin patch?'

'Pumpkins, remember? That night in San Francisco when we met for dinner, I'd just aired a most unmemorable piece on pumpkins. Pumpkins are the reason why the Wade story was so important to me. I can't waste more time reporting on pumpkins.'

A quick glance at the set of her face told me she wasn't really thinking about pumpkins. She was thinking about her husband, who died reporting war.

I walked her to the front of the house and guided her with a firm elbow down the drive and past the guard in the shack. The Channel 8 van had pulled up, idling.

She stopped me a few yards away. 'That night, in San Francisco, we talked about our ghosts. Do you remember?'

'I remember everything about that night.'

'The way you talked about Amanda,' she said. 'You were nervous, remember? Not wanting to hurt me?'

I nodded.

'Our ghosts,' she said. 'My dead husband, your ex-wife. We must cherish them.'

She squeezed my hand and let it go. A cameraman helped her into the back seat. They drove away.

I turned to go the other way down the road, to where I'd parked the Jeep.

And almost ran into Timothy Wade.

SIXTY-SIX

'Care to chat for a moment, Mr Elstrom?' he asked.

I followed him back up the drive and around to the patio at the back of the house. We sat at a white iron table.

'Was that Jennifer Gale you were just speaking with?' he asked.

'I violated my promise of confidentiality to you, since she was so badly beaten.'

'I almost didn't recognize her, she was so horribly bruised.'

His calm, almost singsong manner signaled something more sinister to come. And he hadn't asked how Jenny had gotten beaten. I said nothing and waited.

'And how is Amanda?' he asked.

The back of my throat went dry. He wasn't asking; he was making a threat.

'Confident that I would kill anyone who harmed her,' I said.

He gestured at the trees sloping down the hill. 'Nice view, don't you think? Though I'm afraid the color on the trees is gone. Your color seems to be gone, too, Elstrom.'

'Nah.'

His face hardened. 'What the hell were you thinking? That foolish woman deputy, a sergeant . . .'

'A good cop,' I said, 'incensed at the murder of one of your most loyal campaign workers. And wondering, like me, why you're not furiously demanding a thorough investigation.'

'That stupid sergeant marched in to dig up my grounds, based on an anonymous tip, the day before the vote? I'll have her badge and the badges of everyone who came with her, but it won't be enough. I'd ruin you, too, Elstrom, but you've already been ruined.'

'You made sure the press was here.'

'That was my sister's genius, not mine.'

'I'd like to think you merely wanted to create sympathy for yourself,' I said. 'Maybe even boost your vote.'

'You don't know what the hell you're talking about.'

'But I think that, more importantly, you want to shut down any investigation of what happened twenty years ago.'

'Not a damned thing happened then.'

'Marilyn Paul tried to protect you from John Shea. She got her throat slashed.'

'What does that have to do with anything?'

'Shea could tell us. Where is he?'

'In fragments, in Laguna Beach.'

'That was Willard Piser.'

'Will Piser? You're seeing a conspiracy among all my old friends?'

'Don't forget Red Halvorson. Where has he been, all these years?'

'You're talking in riddles.'

'Shea played it clever, and stupid. He put on a red wig to leave a trail to Halvorson before he left Laguna Beach. He never knew Halvorson's trail went dead twenty years ago.'

He stood up. 'It's time for you to get off my property.' He was good, but good politicians are good. He hadn't batted an eye or twitched a carefully shaved cheek.

I stood up, too. 'It's good, us talking like this. I got your message. And I think you got mine.'

SIXTY-SEVEN

I called Amanda after I got home and went to sit by the river.

'So, how's your day?' I asked, watching the sun sparkle on the four empty windshield-washer fluid jugs snagged on the riverbank in front of me. For some reason, someone had tied them loosely together with very thick twine.

'Much calmer than yours, I think. I'm getting phone calls from my fellow tycoons, asking if I know what's going on with Tim.'

'What did you say?'

'I said I was shocked. And I'm going to stay publicly shocked until your name gets identified with the whole mess. Then I'll say that this was obviously not a political dirty trick because you're not a political hack, and because not even a neophyte would be loony enough to stage a body search the day before an election.'

'Thanks, I think.'

'You're welcome, I think.'

'Wade will tar you once the press links us.'

'No, he won't. I'm too rich and I'm too friendly with the others on his Committee of Twenty-Four. If the Wades are asked about my being married to you once, they'll simply cluck and murmur and say none of this is my fault. As for the press calling, one particularly disgusting creature already has, that jerk from the *Argus-Observer*.'

'Keller,' I said. Rarely troubling to get the facts of a story, he'd trashed me years earlier when I'd been played in the fake evidence scheme. 'Details to follow,' was his signature tag line, though his columns rarely carried any factual follow-ups.

'What did you tell him?'

'Details to follow,' she said.

I laughed a little, and she hung up.

I got up, pulled the tangle of washer jugs from the river and threw them in the back of the Jeep. I had to take such stuff to a recycling center across the city line in Chicago because the lizards that ran Rivertown didn't encourage the recycling of anything beyond parts stripped from newer cars.

News of the search at Wade's estate spread fast on the Internet. Timothy Wade was well-respected and a potentially superb future presidential candidate. Most of the reports accepted the lead that Wade offered up in his video – that the search was a clumsy political dirty trick and that one particular Cook County sheriff's deputy, a Sergeant Bohler, had been manipulated and played for a chump.

I wasn't mentioned anywhere, nor was Amanda. That would change the next morning, when Keller's column in the *Argus-Observer* came out. He'd report Amanda's link to Wade's campaign, my presence at the search site, and remind his readers that she and I were once married. Details to follow.

And from there, I would be oozed, much like the molten Peeps beneath my microwave door, into the news. Other reporters didn't like Keller's ethics but they respected the man's nose for stink.

They'd look past his innuendo and study the video recorded at the search. More than one of them would recognize me and remember my past involvement in the phony evidence scheme. And they'd recall that, as Keller said, I was once married to Amanda. Because of her new prominence in Chicago's business circles, they'd summon up what was old and stupid about me, and infer, reservedly, about what might be new and stupid about me. The story would be dropped into the business news like spoiled meat. Amanda's board of directors would go ballistic.

Amanda knew that. She'd simply been talking brave.

I keyed up the satellite photos again. Looking down at the sides of the Wade house and the long slope in back, searching it seemed ludicrous now. Too many trees had dropped too many leaves. Too many years had hardened the ground. And Timothy and Theresa Wade had always been too smart. Even as kids, they'd never have chanced burying Halvorson on their own land, just as now, as adults, they'd never risk planting John Shea there. If they'd even killed him at all.

And now the Wades, those smarties, had gotten me, Bohler, the press, and the whole Cook County Sheriff's Department to shut down any further investigation of the Wades' complicity in Marilyn Paul's murder. No cop would ever again risk a career-ending embarrassment of investigating the Wades.

I moved the cursor to the woods across from the Wade estate, trying again to imagine why Jenny and Jimbo had been attacked there. Nine sheriff's cops, including Bohler, had just combed the Wade estate. They'd found nothing troublesome at all, nothing that could have been caught by the surveillance cameras placed across the street.

Across the street.

The property across the road wasn't big, perhaps six acres spanning the same width as the Wade estate. The woods were surrounded on three sides by houses built on half-acre plots. The undeveloped woods had to be worth millions.

I clicked over to the Cook County Assessor's website. It showed that the property had been purchased in 1924 by an entity called 100 Partners. I did an Internet search on the name and came up with nothing. Whoever those hundred partners were, their heirs had been sitting on a small real estate fortune for almost a century.

I then looked to see what the assessor showed about the Wade estate. It had been owned by Timothy Wade and Theresa Wade since the deaths of their parents. Before that, ownership of the land and house had followed the expected progression, inherited down the generations by children from parents, going back to when the whiskey runner, Samuel Wade, Sr bought the land in 1924, the same year that the 100 Partners acquired the property across the street.

Both parcels had been purchased in the same year. That didn't necessarily mean anything, for the whole plat could have been subdivided for development and offered for sale for the first time that year.

Not sure of anything at all, except the need perhaps to apologize once again, I called Bohler's cell phone. 'I think the Wades might own the small woods across the street from their house.'

'Meaning what?'

'How far-reaching is your warrant?'

'It allows a search of all land and buildings owned or controlled by Timothy or Theresa Wade in Winnetka.'

'Check the ownership of that land across the street. You might find the Wades own it under a dummy name. Send your team back to Winnetka.'

'I'm meeting with my boss tomorrow morning, remember? By noon I'll be writing parking tickets with Officer Gibbs.'

'Blow off the meeting with your boss. Don't give him the chance to bust you down before you can search that ground.'

'Screw this,' she said, sounding almost hysterical.

'That land across from Wade's estate is worth a fortune yet it remains undeveloped. It was purchased by something called the One Hundred Partners the same year Wade's great grandfather bought his own land. I'll bet anything the Wades own that land.'

'Those purchase dates are probably just coincidence.'

'I'm going to check it out anyway.'

'Stay the hell away from that land, Elstrom,' she said, sounding frantic now. 'You're going to make things ten times worse for me.' She hung up.

I called Jenny. She picked up right away. 'All set to fly?' I asked.

'I'm not leaving without regret,' she said.

'And ghosts?'

'I'll probably be bringing two now,' she said with a small chuckle. Meaning, I supposed, that I'd become her newest ghost.

'Where exactly did you get assaulted?'

'I told you, already. Across the street from Wade's house.'

'I need to know exactly.' I asked her to go to the same satellite website we'd used before.

'See that cluster of three trees, sort of in the middle, the largest one being off to the right?' she asked after a moment.

'About fifty feet in from the road?'

'That's where Jimbo was standing. He'd mounted the second camera in that cluster because it gives an excellent sight of Wade's front door.'

'And an excellent sight from the guard shack, in reverse.'

'Where are you going with this?'

'How far were you from Jimbo?'

'About five yards farther south.' Then, 'What exactly are you up to?'

'I'll tell you after dusk,' I said.

'I'll be gone after dusk.'

'You might hate me if you are.'

'I could never . . .' Then, 'What's going on?'

'I'll call you after dusk.'

SIXTY-EIGHT

Even if John Shea was buried across the street, it was going to be a crap shoot. Internet satellite photos can be old, sometimes three or more years. The trees would have grown; the terrain would have changed.

I parked on the residential side street closest to the southern edge of the 100 Partners property. Most of the houses that abutted the woods across from Wade's estate had fences to keep deer out, but one dark house had a yard that ran back unobstructed to the tree line. I waited until the dusk was thick enough to move unseen but still light enough to check out the five likely spots I'd circled on the satellite photo. I estimated I had fifteen minutes, at the most, to scout for low growth or, even better, no growth at all.

I ran into the woods.

The closest spot was fifty feet in, a ragged clearing in a copse of seven trees. I'd brought a small shovel to jam into the ground. The dirt was hard. I ran on.

The second spot was in a direct line from the first, twenty yards closer to the road that ran in front of Wade's house. It, too, was nestled in a copse of trees but the clearing was larger.

My foot sank two inches into the dirt as soon as I ran up. The ground was spongy, as if loosened by the last rain.

I stabbed my shovel at the ground to be sure the boundaries were far enough apart. It only took a couple of minutes to find a rectangle of soft earth, six feet by three feet. Nature doesn't like straight lines but whoever had dug in this spot certainly had. It was enough.

By now, it was almost completely dark. I began to pick my way back through the thin woods, toward the row of house lights filtering through the leafless trees.

A twig snapped behind me. Before I could turn, he hit me square across the back, knocking me face down onto the ground.

And then he was on me, a fast blur in the dark, beating at the back of my neck with his fists. Raising my hands to cover my head, I raised my knees enough to buck him off. His hands grazed the soft skin of my neck as he fell away.

I pushed my heels hard into the ground, clawed at the ground ahead and found the handle of my shovel. Clutching it tight, I scrambled up to stand and swung into the dark. I hit something soft, like a belly or a neck.

He wheezed hard; I'd caught him but he was up, too. I swung again, hit nothing, threw the shovel where I hoped he was and ran for the house lights at the edge of the woods.

All I could think was that the Wades' guards had guns.

He came crashing loudly behind me; he was following the sound of my feet. But no flashlight lit the night. I was as invisible to him as he was to me.

I slammed hard into a wall, the rough cedar crisscross of a fence. I stabbed a toe into its thick lattice, climbed up a foot, and another. He was swearing loudly, only a few feet behind me.

I pulled myself onto the top of the fence, rolled over and fell onto a flowerbed. A patio was ahead, lit with little lights.

He crashed into the other side of the fence, bending it toward me. I scrambled up and ran toward the little lights.

I tripped a motion detector and a high-wattage security bulb flooded the entire yard with bright light. I didn't dare look back. I was lit up now, easy enough to shoot.

Twenty feet ahead, a woman stood looking out her kitchen window, lifting a telephone. Cops would come. Cops would be good now. Cops would be very good.

Other security lights tripped on ahead, and from the house next door. I ran between them, past the sidewalk and out onto the street. The Jeep was several houses farther down. I heard no one pounding behind me. I pulled out my ignition key. Fifty feet, twenty feet and I was there.

I jumped in, twisted the key and sped to the main intersection. Two cars were approaching from the direction of the Wade estate. I slowed, to be normal. Oh, please, I begged the night, let them be cops.

I turned the other way and drove slow enough to watch in my rearview mirror, coming up fast. They got to the intersection.

They turned in, lit up for an instant by the street lamp, before disappearing into the housing development. They were cops, running without their bubble lights.

Coming for me, but now I was gone.

SIXTY-NINE

My breathing had calmed enough by the time I got to the outskirts of Winnetka to pull over and call Bohler with the good news. 'Your career is saved. We got the wrong woods. There's soft ground the size of a fresh grave across the street.'

'I'm done,' she said.

'I'm telling you, the ground is soft.'

'Damn it, I told you to stay away from there.' She was speaking fast. 'If the Wades own that land their ownership will be impossible to trace. I wouldn't be able to use any warrant, even if I could get one, for years. They're powerful people, those Wades. If they find out you've been poking around across the street they might sue you and me for harassment. Stay the hell away, Elstrom.' She hung up on me, maybe for good.

I stayed at the side of the road, thinking hard. The way she saw it made sense. I hadn't tossed her a lifeline for her career; I'd offered up a chance to get in even more trouble. But the longer I sat, the louder the empty plastic jugs I'd fished from the river, tied with thick twine, beat in time with the idling engine, and against each other at the back of the Jeep.

Beating, too, with the beginnings of an inspiration.

I called Jenny. 'Still in town?'

'Until tomorrow.'

'There's a soft rectangle in the woods across from Wade's place.' I told her of the 100 Partners, my shovel and the guard who chased me. And I told her of Bohler's refusal to take a chance on resurrecting her reputation.

'You can't blame her, Dek. And she's right about the ownership of those woods. It could take years to untangle it and probably longer to find another judge willing to issue a new warrant.'

'You once told me Jimbo stays up nights, listening to his police radio scanner.'

'He says he gets the best stuff in the middle of the night when the crazies come out to play,' she said. 'Why do you ask?'

'You shouldn't leave tomorrow,' I said.

'Why not?'

'Tomorrow is election day.'

SEVENTY

Jenny called me at five-fifteen in the morning. I was awake.

'What the heck . . .' Her voice disappeared into the sirens blaring in her background. 'I can't believe this!' she yelled. Her voice vanished into sirens again.

'Shout loud, Jenny,' I said in a normal voice.

'Dek?' she screamed. 'The woods across from Timothy Wade's house are on fire!'

I expressed appropriate amazement.

'Can you believe it, but then . . .?' she asked, and then oddly, she laughed. 'Luckily, it's contained to a small patch. Someone phoned in an anonymous tip before it could spread.'

Her voice faded away. She was talking to someone there with her.

I picked up my travel mug and took another sip of Bohler's excellent coffee. I was pleased to wait.

'Anyway,' she said, coming back to me, 'Jimbo was listening to his police scanner. He was tuned to the North Shore, hoping for something new about the fuss yesterday, when the fire department radioed the Winnetka police, saying there was a fire across from Wade's.'

'I'll meet you up there,' I said.

'Oh, and Dek? I called the cell number you'd given me for Sergeant Bohler, figuring at least she'd be interested in the fire. She wasn't, not at all. She sounded afraid, just as you said a few hours ago. Gotta go. Bye.'

I already had my pea coat on. I took a last sip of coffee, put a Peep in my mouth to keep from whistling and walked out to the Jeep.

The flames were out by the time I got there, of course. I doubted they'd ever been big.

The road was blocked off. I parked behind the police tape and walked up. The gate to Wade's driveway was closed. Strangely, I saw no guards. Jenny and Jimbo stood beside a fire truck a hundred yards ahead, talking to a young fire department lieutenant. Two Winnetka police cars were parked a little farther on.

'Good morning,' I said.

'Who might you be?' the lieutenant asked.

'Insurance investigator and a friend of these folks,' I said, smiling at Jenny and Jimbo. 'I was supposed to meet with Miss Gale on another matter this morning but she called to cancel because of this. I thought I'd swing by.'

'Nothing to see here,' the lieutenant said.

'Ah, but there is, isn't there?' Jenny asked him. She turned to me. 'They say there's a scorched shovel next to an odd patch of soft ground that might have been freshly dug, right at the point where the fire was set.'

'Set? It was arson, perhaps to cover up strange digging?'

'They think gasoline was carried in plastic jugs, though they're all melted. They think the fire was reported by the arsonist almost immediately after it was set.'

'He used thick twine, probably soaked in gasoline, as a fuse to buy him enough time to get away and phone in the fire,' Jimbo added.

Jenny was watching my eyes. 'To make sure the fire didn't spread to the houses,' she said.

'Unusual for an arsonist,' the young fire department lieutenant said. 'Usually they want a big blaze.'

'Any idea where he called from?' I asked, because it was expected.

'The pay phone outside the library. It's only a half a mile down the road, easily visible to anyone driving here.'

'Surveillance camera?' I asked, because I really didn't know.

He nodded. 'A police officer just checked it. All we got was a blurry image of a man in a short dark coat with a wool hat pulled down over his eyes.' He took a long look at my pea coat, one of what I was sure were many thousands in Illinois, and shrugged it off.

Jenny was studying my coat, too, but only for an instant. She looked up. The smallest of smiles had started on her lovely mouth.

'How about Wade?' I asked her. 'I didn't see him when I walked up.'

'It's election day, remember?' she said. 'A car came for him right after I called you. He got in and was whisked away without so much as a wave. Maybe it was too small a fire to elicit his attention. Jimbo shot video of him anyway, looking studiously uninterested.'

'Election day for sure,' I said.

'I told the lieutenant here that we'd been in the woods behind Wade's house, just yesterday,' Jenny said.

'Everyone in Illinois seemed to be in the woods behind Wade's house yesterday,' the lieutenant said. 'What a waste of time.'

A police officer wearing plastic gloves came out of the trees carrying my shovel by the point of its blade, upside down. It was scorched almost beyond recognition, as though it had been drenched with accelerant.

'Have your guys move your truck,' he called to the fire

department lieutenant. 'The fire's been out for a long time and we've got a crime scene in those woods.'

'You mean worse than arson?' Jenny asked the cop.

The cop didn't answer. He opened the rear door of his car and set the shovel on the seat.

'I'd better leave,' I said.

'Not me,' Jenny said. 'We've got news happening here.'

I started back to the Jeep, but passing the guardhouse I noticed it was still empty. Someone should have been inside, defending the fortress against firemen, cops and the two or three neighbors milling about on the road.

I pushed at the gate. It slid open easily. It had not been left locked.

I walked up the drive and rang the bell. Though Timothy Wade had left, someone else was surely at home. Someone who was not paralyzed. Someone who could walk.

I peeked through the sidelight. The house was dark inside. I rang the bell again. More minutes passed.

The knob turned easily. Wade might have accidentally left the door unlocked or perhaps he figured it was unnecessary to lock it since a guard was expected to be in the shack.

Jenny was just across the road but I thought it better to call.

'I thought you'd left,' she said.

'About Wade being driven away this morning . . .?'

She laughed, happy on the cusp of a developing major story. 'I remember like it was just this morning.'

'The car that came to get him – did it have to wait for the gate to be opened?'

She thought for a moment, then said, 'No. It waited on the road. Wade walked out through the gate.'

'He opened it?'

'Slid it back just enough to get out. As I told you, I figured he would say a few words before he got in the car, about the fire, about election day, about anything. He didn't. He just got in and was driven away.'

'And the gate stayed closed behind him?'

'He'd only opened it a little. These are strange questions, Dek.'

'Do you remember seeing a guard in the shack?'

'What are you thinking?'

'I haven't seen a night-shift guard.'

'I don't remember what the gate did,' she said. 'And speaking of pea coats . . .'

'There are thousands of them in Illinois,' I said, and clicked off. I opened Wade's front door all the way.

'Hello?' I called in, inventively.

After a minute of silence, I called in again. No one responded.

I stepped inside. 'Miss Wade?' I shouted, and then strained to listen, but no one called back.

I walked to the base of the stairs and knelt to the chairlift screw that had worked its way out from the track mounted to the wall. That loose screw had bothered me the first time I saw it, and it bothered me even more once I'd found a long-unneeded wheelchair left in the back seat of the Cadillac parked in the sunken garage. A spider had spun a small web around the loose screw. Dust, maybe several years' worth, had been caught in the web.

I turned the screw. It turned too easily. I pushed it with my thumb. It slipped easily into the wall. It had worked its way out of the wall, from long use. But now it was useless. A thicker, longer screw was needed to safely snug the chairlift track to the wall.

No one had used the lift in a long time and that made no sense. For surely it had been needed once, starting with Theresa Wade's trampoline accident, when she was ten years old.

'So what if she can walk?' Sergeant Bohler had asked as she watched the video of the figure moving behind an upstairs window. There was no crime in pretending to be paralyzed, she'd said.

That made no sense either.

'Miss Wade?' I shouted up the stairs.

Again, there was no response.

I started up the stairs.

SEVENTY-ONE

I t was barely the middle of the day. There'd been nothing on the radio, or television, or the Internet about the fire. I was tired but I couldn't sleep. I tried to work on my ductwork but my hands were as nervous as my head. They wanted to call Jenny and ask what had been found in the ground. My head told them to be patient.

My phone finally rang at two o'clock. I got it on the first ring but it was Amanda. 'It was just on the news that there was a fire across from Tim's.'

'So I understand.' I hated to be vague but I wanted to explain in person.

'Crime-scene analysts were called in. They set up a tent. The search yesterday was merely conducted in the wrong place?'

'I hope that's why there's a tent.' A different worry then rose up. 'I forgot to check Keller's column in the *Argus-Observer* this morning.'

'Your past history is inexplicably expressing itself in a new vendetta against our future senator, Tim Wade,' she recited. 'Because we were once married, it's going to send my company into bankruptcy. Details to follow.'

'What's your press office saying?'

'Not what I wanted, which was that Keller's meds are failing. Not to worry; our stock is up five points this morning.' Then she said, 'I'll bet you're dying to tell me much more about what's going on, right?'

'As soon as I see you,' I said, relieved.

'That will be tonight. We'll do something really exciting.'

'Your jet to Tahiti? It'll only take a minute to pack my Peeps.'

'I'm expected to attend Tim Wade's victory celebration at the Palmer House. I can bring a date.'

'You're crazy.'

'They'll have cocktail wienies and little squares of hard cheese.' She knew I was a sucker for high cuisine. And confrontation.

She said Wade was set to declare victory at ten so I should meet her at the hotel at nine-thirty. She hung up before I could tell her that she was nuts.

And that I loved her.

I listened to radio news all afternoon but nothing beyond a routine-sounding arson investigation was being reported. The lid on the case was tight.

Jenny called at three-thirty. 'I'm doing a breaking news leader for the four o'clock on Channel Eight.'

'Reporting what?'

'Only what the cops will let me confirm. John Shea was discovered buried in the woods. His wallet was in his jeans. The Winnetka police chief said he might have something bigger for me later if I play along. They're still in the woods.'

'They found Halvorson's grave, too?'

'I don't know.'

'Shea's cause of death?'

'Gunshots, recent, twice to the chest, but I can't say that until the medical examiner confirms it. I can't even say he was found buried. For now, I'm going along, about to mislead the public by inferring he died in the fire in the hope they'll give me more.'

'I'm going to Wade's victory celebration tonight.'

'You?' She laughed. 'They'll never let you in.'

'I'm going with Amanda. Wade's going to speak at ten.'

'At ten? You're sure? At ten?'

'What's raging in your mind?'

'Election day,' she said.

SEVENTY-TWO

In the eight decades since the latest incarnation of the Palmer House was built, it had hosted all of the city's ruling elite at one gathering or another. I loved the venerable old place for its architecture, history and proximity to Millenium Park, the lakefront and the chicken pot pie served in the Walnut Room of what used to be Marshall Field's before it was darkened cheaply into a Macy's. Mostly, though, I loved Palmer House for my memories of when Amanda taught and curated at the nearby Art Institute and we used to meet for a drink beneath Bertha Palmer's exquisite ceiling frescoes. They still serve good booze there, but earnest business creatures with laptop squints have sucked the levity out of the first floor, so lately I've retreated to the seclusion of the alcoves on the balcony to wait for the day when a grander parade passes by.

That night came close. Finely attired folks I recognized from the newspapers and local television marched up the marble steps to the ballroom to be seen applauding Timothy Wade.

Amanda arrived promptly at half past nine, lovely in a black dress and the garnet earrings I'd bought her because they caught the fire in her eyes. She sat on the other chair in the alcove. 'You wore a tie,' she said.

'Not just any tie. The yellow bow model you gave me not so long ago.'

'And you remembered how to tie it?'

'With instructional help from a high-school boy in an online video,' I said, giving a modest, two-handed tug to the ends of the bows. 'Still, even wearing such a splendid tie, I'm not sure my attendance will be welcome.'

'If Tim's innocent, he won't mind. If he's not, you're the least of his worries.'

'You watched the news?'

'Jennifer Gale's report at four o'clock and again at six. She didn't report much, other than it was John Shea who was found buried in a wood in Winnetka. She mentioned, but didn't emphasize, that the site was across the street from Tim's house. Will John Shea's link to Tim and Marilyn Paul come out?'

'She's going to do a follow-up on the ten o'clock news.'

Amanda's forehead tightened, always a sign of concern.

'I told her that's when Wade is scheduled to speak,' I said.

'I'd better be prepared for anything. Let's go in and drink.'

We got up and headed for the stairs to the grand ballroom.

SEVENTY-THREE

Amanda showed her engraved invitation to a black-suited man at the door and we entered the grand ballroom. A waiter came up with flutes of champagne and we took two. A moment later, a sweet young thing offered a silver tray of interesting-looking breaded things. Amanda, of course, declined.

When I declined, too, she said, 'Whoa.'

'I'm waiting for Peeps,' I said.

'You're nervous,' she said. She looked at her watch. 'Let's stay here at the back, where there's less chance of being photographed looking unhappy.'

It was true. The still and video photographers were setting up along the walls, closer to the stage.

A gray-haired man stopped to say hello to Amanda. She introduced me, though the man seemed more interested in my yellow bowtie than in anything that might come out of my mouth. I looked around while they talked.

My eye stopped on a man leaning on a cane, standing in front of a panel of multicolored lights half-concealed by a curtain at the right rear corner of the ballroom. Something about him was familiar; he had the burly bulk of someone I knew. Yet this man was clean-shaven and wore a brown plaid sport coat, white button-down shirt and pressed, tan slacks. There was no scruffy beard, no Chicago event T-shirt. And this man's hair was neatly trimmed, not at all the wild tangle of the person that I knew.

But this man was looking straight at me and shaking his head slightly, as if beseeching me to look away. I knew him then, in that instant. He was Jimbo, Jenny's cameraman from Channel 8, so changed in appearance as to be almost unrecognizable.

I looked away and tried to think. It was no mystery how he'd gotten in. As a member of the working press he had the credentials of a television cameraman. A puzzle was why he'd shaved, gotten a haircut and put on conservative clothes, but I was more interested in why he was lurking by the panel of colored lights that likely controlled the electronics in the room.

I snuck another look back at him. He was looking up at the huge television screens hanging high above the stage at the other end of the room. There was one for each of Chicago's five major television stations, each displaying its own stable of analytical geniuses discussing the day's election returns. I wondered how Jimbo had managed to switch places with the person in charge of monitoring the network feeds. And I wondered whether Jenny had set up something to rock the evening.

Amanda noticed me staring across the room. 'Dek?' she whispered as the gray-haired man left.

'Under no circumstances get near the candidate tonight,' I said.

'Why?'

'Toxicity.'

'Here, tonight?'

I nodded, trying hard to not sneak another backward glance at Jimbo.

A waiter came by with more champagne. I gave him my empty and Amanda's almost full flute and took two fresh ones. And then a matronly woman wearing an impressive amount of brocade, or maybe it was simply sofa upholstery, came up to Amanda. Amanda introduced us, but I would have bet the woman forgot my name as quickly as I forgot hers. For sure, she expressed no interest in my bowtie.

I was relieved. I didn't want to talk. I wanted to see what Jimbo was up to. I snuck another look at the back corner of the ballroom. The curtain had been closed across the panel of colored lights. And presumably, Jimbo.

The upholstered woman went away and Amanda and I chatted about nothing relevant. Too many ears were too close.

At exactly ten o'clock big red letters flashed across the silenced feed from CBS Channel 2. To no one's surprise, their statistical prognosticators were calling the senatorial election for the Democrat, Timothy Wade. Everyone in the room cheered. Almost. I didn't cheer. Amanda clapped because it was expected, but it was faint. She was preoccupied, watching me. I snuck another backward look. The curtain was still closed.

The crowd cheered louder as Timothy Wade strode up to the podium and looked up at the big, silent screens. He was dressed somberly in a navy suit and white shirt, but he'd slipped on a festive tie in a yellow similar to mine.

Channels 5, 7 and 9 followed Channel 2 within thirty seconds, flashing their own projections that Wade would win an unprecedented sixty-five percent of the Illinois vote. The room roared. People stomped their feet.

Channel 8's screen, which had been showing a panel of four politically wise people talking noiselessly, suddenly switched to a fire blazing in a dark woods. The room fell silent. Everyone supposed the fire to be a conflagration that had just raged up, serious enough to push aside the night's election coverage.

I knew better. It was footage from early that morning. Jenny and Jimbo had been the only news people to record the fire.

The crowd gasped as the other four screens were switched to Channel 8 and Jenny's voice boomed loud from the big speakers spotted throughout the room.

I looked back. The curtain was partially open. Jimbo had moved down along the side wall and was aiming a video camera toward the podium.

Jennifer Gale, always known as a great beauty to television viewers throughout northern Illinois, came into view, live on all five screens. She stood in presumably the same woods, the small, extinguished clearing behind her lit harshly in the night by portable floodlights.

This Jennifer Gale was not beautiful; this Jennifer Gale was as Wade's guards had left her. One of her eyes was swollen almost shut and her lips were puffy from being hit repeatedly. Big spots of purple, blue and brown covered her face and neck and she looked shrunken in too-large blue jeans and the plain white button-down shirt she wore beneath a blue jeans jacket. Her good eye was narrowed. It was clear she was in pain.

'Good evening. I'm Jennifer Gale, reporting live tonight from Winnetka.' She winced as she turned to briefly survey the blackened ground behind her. 'Setting off what might become one of the most remarkable stories ever to unfold in Chicagoland, this small, otherwise unimportant patch of woods began burning mysteriously shortly after four o'clock this morning. Summoned by an anonymous tip, fire department personnel quickly put it out.' She paused, obviously trying to summon strength, and said, 'They believe the blaze was deliberately set.'

She turned to face the lens. 'Why is this remarkable? Because of what was discovered after the fire was put out.' She pointed to her left and the camera zoomed in on two rectangular holes dug in the burned ground. 'The fire exposed a sunken, rectangular section of soft earth where investigators discovered the body of a very recently buried, middle-aged man. Based on information in his pockets they believe him to be John Shea, a former Democratic volunteer worker who left Chicago abruptly over twenty years ago.'

The camera panned slightly to the second hole. 'The fire also burned away a section of undergrowth where a second grave was found. It contained the corpse of a male presumed to have been buried decades earlier. It might be weeks before identification is made, if ever.'

Jenny turned and the camera followed her as she took five more steps to her left. 'And then there is this.' She pointed down to the ground. 'A third grave, containing the remains of another body. This one, though, was carefully interred in a well-constructed, solid pine coffin.'

My mind flashed back to the scraps of wood I'd seen in Wade's sunken garage. He'd taken time with that pine coffin, to make it right.

'Based on brief examination,' Jenny went on, 'it's believed the third person died of some sudden blunt force trauma.'

Killed in the wreck of a Cadillac Eldorado convertible, I could have said, that's been hidden ever since in a sunken garage, along with a wheelchair that would never again be needed.

Jenny turned almost halfway around and her cameraman turned with her. Behind her now, recognizable to almost everyone in the room, was Timothy Wade's white frame house, lit up bright in the night. Many gasped. More began to murmur. There was no mistaking the inference.

'One forensics team member speculated, and cautioned me to clearly call it as such, that the body recovered in the pine coffin might belong to a young woman in her early twenties, perhaps someone who lived nearby.'

'Oh, no,' Amanda murmured.

'Today's gruesome discovery of three bodies,' Jenny went on, as her cameraman resolutely kept the Wade house in her background, 'comes on the heels of yesterday's search of the estate of Timothy Wade, tonight's presumptive winner in the race for the US Senate. Though the two locations are across the street from one another, authorities have not indicated that the two investigations are in any way linked.'

Jenny signed off, all five screens defaulted back to the Channel 8 studio and the ballroom fell into a hushed silence. Only the panelists on television were speaking, though they were doing so in hushed tones, having heard the news, too.

Everyone in the ballroom looked to the man at the podium.

As ashen-faced as he'd been when the hatchet and bones came tumbling at him, Wade had stepped out from behind the podium and was flapping his arms crazily at two young aides who were standing below the stage. No one in the ballroom had to guess what he wanted; he wanted the televisions shut off. They nodded and began pushing their way through the crowd, heading toward the curtain at the back. In just seconds, the screens went silent and dark.

Wade suddenly became aware that everyone was watching him. He straightened up, his face a strange contortion of fury and fear. He walked slowly back to the lectern, for there was no place now to run. For a long moment, he looked out at the crowd that had come to cheer his stunning success, a crowd now as silent as mourners at a burial, staring back at him. The horror on their faces told him there could be no words.

I looked to the side of the room where Jimbo stood pressed against the wall, still recording. Jeffries, Wade's campaign security chief, was walking quickly toward him. I tensed, thinking I might have to run over to pull the security man off Jimbo.

Jeffries slowed and gave Jimbo a nod that might have meant nothing or might have meant everything. And then, without a backward glance at his candidate at the lectern, Jeffries walked out of the room.

I turned to look back at Wade. He still stood stiffly behind the lectern. Only his eyes moved, restlessly. He was looking for someone.

He stopped. His eyes had found mine.

His lips tightened and, for a moment, I thought he was going to scream.

I heard myself speak the four syllables slowly, conversationally. They carried easily across the hushed room.

'Marilyn Paul,' I said.

SEVENTY-FOUR

My cell phone rang at two-thirty in the morning. It was no matter. I was awake and cold and alone at the turret.

'You ditched me at the Palmer House,' Amanda said. 'I looked around and you were gone.'

I'd taken off right after I blurted out Marilyn's name, hoping Amanda might escape being photographed with me.

'That's why you're calling at two-thirty in the morning?' I asked.

'You're up anyway,' she said.

'How could you know that?'

'You've been to the window more than a dozen times. Are you waiting for the press to storm the turret, demanding to know why you called out Marilyn Paul's name or, like Leo, are you worried about the car parked down your street?'

It was true enough; I was troubled by the car but I didn't understand her question. 'What does Leo have to do with it?'

'That car down the street belongs to one of my people.'

'You put security on me?'

'I'm confused about Tim Wade but clear about the look he gave you at the Palmer House. I'm having you watched because I'm guessing you need it, and because I can afford it.'

'It's no worry. All of Wade's guards have taken off. The daytime thugs and, according to Jenny when she called right after her newscast, the night shift, too. I'm hoping he doesn't own anyone else.'

'Tell that to Leo. He must have seen your star turn on television calling out Marilyn Paul's name and was worried it would spell trouble. He's been watching my man watch your turret. That made my man edgy enough to run his plates. I thought Leo drove a Porsche, not a big van.'

'It's a long story.'

'Then tell me a shorter one. I saw your face when Jennifer Gale reported that one of the corpses might belong to a young woman. You were the only one in the ballroom who didn't appear surprised.'

'Almost the only one in the room,' I corrected.

'Tim wasn't surprised?'

'Remember I told you Wade's guard shack was empty when I got to Winnetka this morning? I thought that was odd, given all the strangers that were milling about. But it wasn't until I was leaving that I realized the guards had taken off. Wade had been paying them very well – in money and in Rolexes – to do more than simply guard his estate, but obviously they decided it wasn't enough to hang around and get arrested for assault and maybe even murder.'

'They killed Shea and Marilyn Paul?'

'I'm hoping a DNA analysis of Shea's body will tell us exactly who killed her.'

'And the young woman in the woods?'

'I didn't know about her when Wade left his house early this morning, I thought I might catch an unguarded—'

She groaned at the wordplay.

'An unguarded moment to speak with Theresa Wade,' I went on. 'I knocked on the front door and when the supposed invalid didn't come down to answer it, I stepped inside.'

'You expected her to answer the door herself?'

'I hoped to provoke a moment of candor. Don't forget, Jenny's short video captured a woman walking in Theresa's bedroom, something that was borne out by a chairlift that hadn't been used in a very long time.'

'It should have been in constant use ever since the girl was little.'

'I wasn't sure what to think when I stepped inside. I called out Theresa's name from the base of the stairs several times.'

'And when she didn't answer you ignored any thought that she might have been asleep or in the bathroom, and took it upon yourself to go up?'

'I kept calling out at almost every step.'

'And when you got upstairs?'

'There are four bedrooms. One had obviously belonged to Tim's parents. One had been turned into a small study. The third was Tim's. The fourth was Theresa's.'

'What did you say when you barged into her room?'

'She wasn't there. The bed was made and the room was recently dusted.'

'You tossed her bedroom?'

'I peeked in discreetly and saw a gray wig on one of those Styrofoam heads on the dresser, a wig that likely wouldn't be needed by a woman who never let anyone see her.'

'So, a wig to fool, like the wig Marilyn Paul had worn to fool you?'

'Maybe not identical, but the intent was the same, except the wig in the Wade house was worn by a man.'

'A man mortified that he'd accidentally killed his sister,' she said.

'A man who needed to convince the world that she was still alive.'

'Tragedy had struck him again,' she said.

'No. Theresa was the first. She disappeared from the newspapers right after she graduated from college. That was well before Halvorson got killed.'

'What a nightmare that must have been for him, looking out his front window every day for the past twenty years knowing two secret graves were across the street.'

Neither of us said anything for a moment; we just listened to each other think. And then she said, 'Give me Leo's cell number. I'll tell him I've got the turret covered and that he should go home and sleep. You should sleep, too.'

I gave her Leo's number and went to bed, sure I was in for the first of many restless nights, mulling over the tragedies of Timothy Wade. But I was wrong. Those were for the future. I fell asleep in a minute.

SEVENTY-FIVE

S ergeant Bohler stopped by a week later. Her eyes were puffy and her cheeks seemed sunken. She looked like she hadn't slept in a month. That didn't surprise me.

Her uniform was different, too. That didn't surprise me, either.

'You can't return my phone calls?' she asked in a rasp.

'I'm racing to get my furnace working before winter.' She'd been calling twice a day. I wasn't ready to talk; there was still so much thinking to do.

Her eyes narrowed, recognizing the lie. 'Got any of my coffee left?'

'Plus newer, old yellow Peeps,' I said. I'd bought more like the ones she'd brought over, hoping their sunny color would bring cheer. They hadn't, though I was optimistic about a report yet to come.

She sat heavily at the plywood table as I put the last of her grounds in the coffee-maker. 'You haven't been in the news since that first day,' she said.

'They only pestered me about calling out Marilyn Paul's name. I told them she'd worked for the Democrats, was murdered and no one seemed to be investigating the case. They accepted that's all there was to it and left me alone.'

'Wade was on the news last night, first time since he went underground after that mess in the ballroom. He's saying he and Theresa buried the Jane Doe in their family plot because everybody deserves a proper interment.'

'He's got connections everywhere, including the medical examiner's office. No one else would want the body so the ME let him have her the moment he was done.'

'Where she can never be examined again?'

I could only shrug at that. 'Next, Wade will say that Theresa's health is getting dangerously worse. Then, after another month or two, he'll announce that she passed away. He'll have a friendly mortician bury a weighted coffin next to Jane Doe, and that problem will be put in the ground.'

'Officially dead at last.'

'He's tidying up, Bohler.'

I put four Peeps onto a paper towel in the microwave. Such was her weariness, she made no move to get up and flee when I turned it on.

'They'll never identify Halvorson's body either?' she asked.

'Even if the cops did suspect it was Halvorson, there's no one to compare his DNA to. Red's sister-in-law told me her husband had no other blood kin, so short of digging him up for comparison, the young man in the woods will remain a dead end John Doe.'

'Chicago PD might still have blood evidence taken at the convenience store.'

'Worthless as well, even if they knew to compare it to the young man's body in the woods. A match would prove nothing, unless an eyewitness came forward to say the person shot was Halvorson.'

'And that could only be Wade, and he'll admit no such thing.'

I nodded.

'So there's nothing to tie Wade to the convenience store killings?'

I nodded again.

'And proving Wade owns the land across the street won't tie him to the bodies there either,' she said, speaking faster now. She was coming at Wade from every direction, testing his vulnerability.

'Even if it can be proved he owns it, he'll just say the bodies were buried there without his knowledge.'

'Case closed, for sure,' she said.

I turned suddenly from the counter, for she'd spoken almost gaily.

'I meant, that's too bad,' she said quickly.

I slid the towel of collapsed Peeps out from the microwave, added some scrapings of the bit that had seeped out from beneath the door and brought it with coffee to the table.

'There's still that DNA recovered from Marilyn Paul that you threatened me with, remember?' I said.

'I never did submit that to the lab, you know,' she said, smiling outright now.

'I know,' I said.

'How?'

'I have a friend at that lab,' I said. It was a lie. It was Jenny who knew someone in the Cook County Medical Examiner's Office.

'There was a recycling cart full of empty soda cans in Wade's guard shack but I heard that none matched Marilyn,' I added.

'So, Wade's in the clear?' she asked. It was the big question, the reason she'd been calling, the reason she'd driven out after I hadn't returned her calls. She was desperate to know, desperate to sleep.

I shrugged that away, too, and asked, 'New uniform?'

'I'm on loan to the forest preserve police. I chase out neckers at dusk and chain gates.' She took a sip of the coffee and grimaced. I'd made it too strong, suddenly anxious to use it all up. 'My boss wanted me gone for the stir I created at Wade's back slope.'

'He's wrong to want that. Bodies were found. They were just across the street, instead of down Wade's back yard.'

'Doesn't matter,' she said.

'Wade complained?' I remembered his threat to have her badge, but now I suspected he was merely bluffing, creating another ruse.

'He probably complained just enough to make himself look innocent.' She fingered a Peep but left it on the paper towel. 'Woods are everywhere in this thing, right? I mean, Wade's back slope, the trees across the street and now my non-future as a forest preserve cop?' She forced a laugh at the symmetry. 'I'm going to quit. I'm going back to private security. I used to work it sometimes as a second job.'

'I know,' I said.

That startled her. 'How?' she asked.

'I asked Jeffries, the Democrats' security chief. He remembered you from a few years back.'

She nodded absently. She saw no threat.

'Is this almost over?' she asked.

'Wade is tidying up,' I said.

She left visibly happier than when she arrived, despite not having had a taste of Peep, or even asking what I'd meant.

SEVENTY-SIX

Two mornings later, Jenny attached a DNA report to her email. 'I can't use this at present because it's unsigned and unofficial. Cheers. Jenny.'

I took it up to the roof. I stayed there for two hours and then I emailed it to Amanda.

She called twenty minutes later. 'You've sent me a bomb.'

'I'm thinking about Wade's Committee of Twenty-Four,' I said.

'Me, too.'

'How many of them do you know well?'

She didn't hesitate. 'I'll start with the two who were closest to my father. If they get on board I'll let them decide how far we should ripple out. We won't need all twenty-three.'

I told her, then, exactly what I wanted. 'My concern is with speed, to get him quickly off the stage.'

'And Jennifer Gale?'

'She'll report only what can be doubly confirmed as fact. That will play hell in her reporting for quite some time.'

It took Amanda the rest of the work day. By five o'clock it had been decided, by fourteen of the twenty-four. The most senior of them, an insurance magnate, would make the phone call that evening.

In Cook County, Illinois, sharks swim faster than other fish.

The biggest sharks swim fastest of all.

SEVENTY-SEVEN

We met in the side room at Galecki's at eleven that evening, after the restaurant had closed and once Bohler's shift patrolling the forest preserves was over. And after the phone call had been made.

I told Jenny I'd pay for the Polish cabbage rolls and beer later if her cousins managed to keep things under control. Stanley, Bernie, Frank and Eloise sat toward the front at a table big enough for the large platters and their handguns, set out in full view. The blinds had been closed against the night.

We sat farther back, at a table in the middle. Jenny wore tailored jeans and a finely woven yellow sweater. Bohler wore a beige holiday sweater that had a Thanksgiving turkey on the front and enough double-knots to suggest it had been someone's introduction to knitting. It was a little too tight and showed the outline of the small revolver, perhaps a .22, holstered at her waist. I wore what I had: khakis, a blue button-collared shirt and my best sweatshirt.

Mrs Galecki was our waitress and the only other person in the restaurant. She wore black slacks, a white blouse and a meat cleaver in the pocket of her faded yellow apron. She hadn't smiled when she let me in. I'd brought trouble to her daughter, and by the looks on the faces of the cousins and the guns they'd set on the table, I was bringing more.

She took our order for drinks. Jenny asked for a dirty martini and Bohler an upscale Pilsner Urquell. I ordered a Pilsner Urquell, too, since I'm almost never out, socially. Mrs Galecki set down their drinks as ordered, in glass and stein, and slammed down a Miller Lite in a bottle for me.

'So, what's the urgent news?' Bohler asked me. She'd seen the guns on the table in front and had chosen to sit facing the cousins.

'Marilyn Paul's killer shared some DNA markers with the Jane Doe found in the pine coffin,' I said.

Bohler inhaled sharply; she'd understood in a hard heartbeat. 'You told me Wade buried the girl without them doing any tests,' she managed, almost whispering. She was wonderfully frightened.

I could have said I hadn't known of the testing but I was done lying. I was after some measure of satisfaction now.

'Timothy Wade has been told he's going to resign tomorrow,' I said. 'He's going to say he has to take care of his sister, whose health is deteriorating.'

'We talked about that sister story,' she snapped. 'Why resign over it?'

'Wade's being given no choice if he wants to avoid prosecution.'

'We decided there's no way to prosecute Wade.'

'There's no way he'll even be swabbed for DNA,' I said, 'just as that DNA analysis done on the girl will likely never see the light of day. The samples will be destroyed, the report will get lost. Wade's DNA will never be linked to his sister, Jane Doe, or through her to Marilyn Paul. In Illinois, Democrats and Republicans are vultures of a feather. They work together to avoid embarrassments, so Wade must go quietly.'

Bohler relaxed back in her chair and smiled a little. 'Wade gets off scot-free.'

I smiled, too. 'He can look forward to spending the rest of his life in philanthropy and having people marvel at what a generous, upstanding person he is.'

'Almost,' Jenny said, right on cue.

Bohler shot her a fast look. 'Almost?'

'Almost,' I said, leaning closer to her face. 'Wade will realize he still has to worry about the accomplice he paid to frame somebody for murdering Marilyn Paul, to keep him aware of what was being learned by that same troublesome private investigator and, later, to set up a failed search of his back yard to shut down any further investigation. He won't want to spend his life worrying that she might spill all of that to some overzealous, do-good prosecutor who won't be stopped by crooked politicians.'

'Wade won't want that,' Jenny said.

'He'll have to tidy up,' I said.

Jenny touched Bohler's wrist and spoke soothingly, as though to a child. 'Wade kills people who can hurt him. Marilyn Paul. John Shea.'

'Why would Wade leave a loose end that could come back to haunt him?' I added.

'A big loose end,' Jenny said, patting Bohler's wrist hard now.

'A blonde loose end,' I said, unable to control myself.

Jenny squeezed Bohler's wrist. 'Dead for sure.'

Bohler, frantic, began looking back and forth between Jenny and me.

'You know what bothered me right off?' I said, making a show of asking them both. 'How did an impound garage cop catch the Marilyn Paul case in the first place? Lieutenant Beech out in California questioned that right away.' I shook my head. 'I let it go, figuring that with all the cutbacks and such, sheriff's deputies must be doing more than their normally assigned duties. Stupid, stupid me.'

'Stupid, stupid you, Dek.' Still squeezing Bohler's wrist, Jenny shook her own head as if in sympathetic confusion.

I turned to Bohler. 'Of course, I know now that you didn't catch the case. Real detectives caught it but they move slow and they let you in because you said you got a call about a corpse in my Jeep. You didn't get tipped; you got told, directly, by Wade, who put it there. The problem was I was out of town, and you needed me in Rivertown to arrest me while in possession of the body. But then, the body disappeared, right out from under your nose. I can only imagine Wade's fury when you told him about that. Still, he had a back-up plan. He had you search for the murder knife he planted in my Jeep.'

Bohler shifted in her chair slightly, carefully. I slammed my hand down on her other wrist before she could pull away from Jenny's grasp and grab her gun.

'This time you were leaving nothing to chance,' I went on as conversationally as I could. 'You planted the knife and then hung around after phoning for a flatbed and a dog. But again your luck went bad. The knife got found before your dog arrived. Still, you figured you'd recover residual evidence, but the dried blood traces got trapped by a top layer of Burger King wrappers that went away with the knife.'

Bohler's eyes narrowed. She was looking at the cousins sitting at the table in front, no doubt calculating her odds of escaping if she could tug free from Jenny and me.

I nodded to the cousins, who'd been watching us, for such was the price of the cabbage, and later, beer. They grabbed their guns, kicked back their chairs and hurried up to our table.

Jenny and I let go. 'Waistband, right side,' I said.

Eloise took the revolver from beneath Bohler's sweater and motioned for her to stand up. She patted her down, found no other weapon and looked to me.

'No extra bullets in her pocket?' I asked.

Eloise shook her head.

'If you could please remove the bullets from her gun and give it to me?' I asked.

Eloise snapped open the cylinder, removed the bullets and handed me the revolver. I put the small gun in my pants pocket and told the cousins they could go back to their table.

'If things go well you can have your gun back,' I said to Bohler.

'I didn't kill anybody,' she said.

'For an expensive truck, Bohler?' I asked, remembering Booster Liss's assessment that the truck's wheels alone cost a thousand dollars each. 'You tried to frame me, just for money for a damned new truck?'

'I was only supposed to discover the body. Then I was only supposed to leave the knife, come back with my partner, have him find it and impound your Jeep. That was all.'

'How about the night Wade came to my place? You came along as back-up. What was he going to do, shoot me?'

'He was crazy that night, paranoid about what you might have learned. He called me at the garage, told me I'd damned well better meet him at your place. I didn't know what he was going to do. Whatever, he chickened out.'

'You pulled me over before I could see who it was.'

'That doesn't connect me to anything.'

'Remember, Jeffries remembers you from ten or fifteen years ago, working private security for a couple of Democratic events. He connects you to Wade.'

She pushed her chair back and got up. 'This is crap.'

'Wade won't do time and he won't forget that you're the only one who can get him prosecuted. He'll hire killers. They'll find you.'

I handed over the small revolver. 'Keep it handy, Bohler.'

She made for the door. I signaled to the cousins to let her go.

'How far will she get?' Jenny asked.

'The meanest part of me wants her to run for the rest of her life, to be always looking over her shoulder. That same mean part wants Wade to be hunting her for forever, too, to always be sweating a day when Bohler tells all.' I tried to summon up a smile. 'For Marilyn Paul, I wish long lives for the both of them.'

'What finally convinced you she was in Wade's pocket?'

'When I told her I was going to search the woods across the street. She tipped Wade that I was coming because that's the only reason a guard could have been waiting so close. He heard me, found me and would have killed me if I hadn't outrun him. When I got away, he and the other night man took off. They must have called the day shift boys to stay away as well. None of them had signed on to be questioned about the fresh grave across the street.'

'They were gone by the time we arrived at that fire,' she said.

'I got lucky. If they'd hung around they would have put it out and no cops would ever have come to discover those graves.'

'No, Dek. You wouldn't have given up. You would have set another fire.'

I gave that a nod.

'Explain something,' she said. 'Why didn't Wade simply call the police when Theresa died in that crash? It would have been ruled an accident.'

'He must have been in deep shock, and in denial. They were close, those two Wades. But part of him must have been lucid enough to fear what the crash would do to his future. He drove the Cadillac up into that sunken garage, closed the doors and built her a fine pine casket. He buried her across the road, on a property no one would ever think he owned. And he grieved. He must have grieved deeply.'

'And then along came Red Halvorson, not that long afterward?'

'Another horror not of his conscious making,' I said. 'I can almost pity the person Wade became, buffeted by such tragedies.'

'So many years passed, living with such guilt.'

'Years of doing many good things,' I said. 'And then along came John Shea and Marilyn Paul, threatening to stop all the good he still intended to do.'

'Marilyn Paul, a nosy pest who could upend his entire career,' she said. 'And John Shea, a blackmailer and a murderer. Both had to be gotten rid of.'

'As I had to be gotten rid of, though he needed me alive to wear the jacket for killing Marilyn. He'd found my name in her apartment and saw how I could be a fall guy. He remembered Bohler and contacted her, waving money. She went along.'

Jenny touched my hand. Mrs Galecki, who'd just set down four pitchers of beer for the cousins, charged up quick as a bullet, scribbling my check. She slapped it down onto the table, face up, and hovered close, waiting for me to look at it. I looked. She'd charged $112 for eleven drinks, $81 for four pitchers of beer, $52 for stuffed cabbages, $15 and change for tax, and $71 for her own tip.

It broke the moment. I started to laugh. Mrs Galecki dropped one hand to the handle of the meat cleaver in her apron, daring me to dispute the charge.

Jenny looked at the tab and then up at her mother's steely glare. And then she started laughing, too.

'It's the Chicago way,' I managed.

We stood up. I set down six fifties, two twenties, two singles, thirty-five cents and the last of the lint I had in my pocket. It was all that remained of Marilyn Paul's money and all that remained of my own. Mrs Galecki nodded, satisfied that I'd been plucked clean.

We headed toward the cousins. They raised their beer glasses, toasting my largesse. Jenny stopped and put a hand on Bernie's shoulder, or perhaps it was Stanley's, or Frank's. I couldn't tell.

I touched her arm lightly. And then I went out alone, into the night.

SEVENTY-EIGHT

I switched off the television in Amanda's living room at six minutes past eight o'clock the next morning and went to the window to look out over the beach along Lake Michigan. I was warmed by the same blue-and-red striped terry robe I'd worn during our marriage – which, touchingly, she'd kept – and by the coffee I'd just made in the same Mr Coffee we'd bought as newlyweds. Which, touchingly, she'd also kept.

I took no comfort in the breaking news bulletin that had just aired on Channel 8. Jenny had been circumspect in reporting that senator-elect Timothy Wade was set to announce his resignation at a noon press conference. She'd reported the rumor that he was stepping away to care for his ailing sister, but then she pointedly mentioned that there were other rumors swirling around about him as well. She left no doubt that she wasn't done with the story.

Amanda came out of the bedroom dressed in a dark suit, pressing a last earring into place. 'I caught Jennifer Gale's report in the bedroom. She did a nice job.'

'So did you, with your friends.'

'I told them you do not yield once your mind is made up.'

'The pundits are going to rip apart Wade's announcement, looking for the truth.'

'He'll be brief and he'll take no questions,' she said.

'Perhaps someone will learn something in a month or a year that will force a re-examination of the Marilyn Paul case.'

'Jennifer Gale?'

'She'll never quit.'

'Fair enough. For us, there will be a newly appointed senator by the end of the month. A Democrat, as was agreed, until a special election is held. The committee is meeting next week.'

'Wade's Committee of Twenty-Four?'

'It's no longer Wade's.' She picked up her purse. 'What's up with you today?'

'A drive to the south side to pick up a new thermostat, then out west, for a humidifier, and then home to resume working on heat.'

'That reminds me,' she said and headed back into the bedroom. She returned with a small box wrapped in brightly colored paper and tied with a red bow. 'A little something I picked up for you.'

I opened it. It was a box of Band-Aids, plain ones.

'I'm to give up the Flintstones? No more Fred, Wilma and Barney flapping around on my hands?'

She touched the sleeve of my old robe. 'Get your furnace finished. I'll be looking for heat at your place, too.'

I gave her one of my finest leers.

It wasn't until two o'clock that I rolled up to the turret but someone had rolled up before me, quite literally. A bronze-colored Lexus sedan had run up and over the shallow curb in front of the turret and rested diagonally across the narrow ribbon of grass I pass off as a front lawn. I was not alarmed. The jolt of smacking the curb must have killed the motor before the car could slam into the turret. Only the wipers still arcing across the windshield, switched on by a driver hoping to see through a blur, signaled that the ignition was still on. It had not rained for days.

The purple Northwestern University decal in the rear window betrayed the identity of the woman whose frosted blonde head was leaned back on the front seat, slack-jawed, sound asleep.

I tapped on the side glass. Nothing. I tapped harder. Still nothing.

I beat it with my fist. The woman jerked forward, wild-eyed.

'Bipsie?' I shouted to the glass.

She powered down the window. 'You Dek?'

I opened the door and she pushed herself toward the opening. I caught her before she tumbled to the dirt and helped her out.

'We thought we'd stop by after luncheon,' she said with remarkable clarity, steadying herself against the side of the car until it and the ground stopped moving. 'Long time no hear.'

I bent to look inside the car. It was empty.

'You came with someone?' I asked.

She bent to look in the front and the back. 'Well, I can't imagine . . .'

I had the queasiest of flashbacks, an unreasoning and irrational remembrance, of a Bipsie who'd plucked my name from a sorority newsletter, a Bipsie more sober, more officious. A Bipsie more dead.

I ran, afraid and unthinking, around the turret and down to the happily bobbing plastic debris in the Willahock.

This Bipsie lay on her back on the bench, like something tossed up by the roil of the river. One of her feet pointed more or less toward the dam; the other had dropped to the ground. Her eyes were closed, in peace, but her mink coat was open, as was her mouth. She snored mightily.

I laughed in relief.

I'd been restored to my more rightful matters.

Lightning Source UK Ltd.
Milton Keynes UK
UKOW04f2351071217
314069UK00001B/3/P

9 781847 517678